COCKY CAPTAIN

ELLIE MASTERS

COCKY CAPTAIN is a standalone story inspired by Vi Keeland and Penelope Ward's Mister Moneybags. It's published as part of the Cocky Hero Club world, a series of original works written by various authors, and inspired by Keeland and Ward's *New York Times* bestselling series.

Visit Ellie's Website (elliemasters.com) where you can view excerpts, teasers, and links to her other books.

Editor: Erin Toland

Interior Design/Formatting: Ellie Masters

Published in the United States of America

ISBN: 978-1-952625-00-8

DEDICATION

This book is dedicated to my one and only—my amazing and wonderful husband.

Without your care and support, my writing would not have made it this far. You make me whole every day. I love you "that much." For the rest of you, that means from the beginning to the end and every point in between. Thank you, my dearest love, my heart and soul, for putting up with me, for believing in me, and for loving me.

My husband deserves a special gold star for listening to me obsess over this book and for never once complaining while I brought these characters from my mind to the page.

You pushed me when I needed to be pushed. You supported me when I felt discouraged. You believed in me when I didn't believe in myself. If it weren't for you, this book never would have come to life.

ALSO BY ELLIE MASTERS

Sign up to Ellie's Newsletter and get a free gift. https://elliemasters.com/FreeBook

YOU CAN FIND ELLIE'S BOOKS HERE:

ELLIEMASTERS.COM/BOOKS

Contemporary Romance

Mistletoe Mischief

Cocky Captain

(VI KEELAND & PENELOPE WARD'S COCKY HERO WORLD)

Firestorm

(KRISTY BROMBERG'S EVERYDAY HEROES WORLD)

Romantic Suspense

EACH BOOK IS A STANDALONE NOVEL.

Twist of Fate

The Starling

Redemption

The One I Want Series

(Small Town, Military Heroes)

By Jet & Ellie Masters

EACH BOOK IN THIS SERIES CAN BE READ AS A STANDALONE AND IS ABOUT A DIFFERENT COUPLE WITH AN HEA.

Aiden

Brent

Caleb

Dax

Light BDSM Romance

The Ties that Bind

EACH BOOK IN THIS SERIES CAN BE READ AS A STANDALONE AND IS ABOUT A DIFFERENT COUPLE WITH AN HEA.

Alexa

Penny

Michelle

Ivy

Rockstar Romance

The Angel Fire Rock Romance Series

EACH BOOK IN THIS SERIES CAN BE READ AS A STANDALONE AND IS

ABOUT A DIFFERENT COUPLE WITH AN HEA. IT IS RECOMMENDED
THEY ARE READ IN ORDER.

Ashes to New (prequel)

Heart's Insanity (book 1)

Heart's Desire (book 2)

Heart's Collide (book 3)

Hearts Divided (book 4)

Dark Romance

Captive Hearts Series

EACH BOOK IN THIS SERIES CAN BE READ AS A STANDALONE AND IS
ABOUT A DIFFERENT COUPLE WITH AN HEA. IT IS RECOMMENDED
THEY ARE READ IN ORDER.

She's MINE

Embracing FATE

Forest's FALL

Romantic Suspense

Changing Roles Series:

THIS SERIES IS ABOUT ONE COUPLE AND MUST BE READ IN ORDER.

Book 1: Command

Book 2: Control

Book 3: Collar

HOT READS

EACH BOOK IS A STANDALONE NOVEL.

Off Duty

Nondisclosure

Down the Rabbit Hole

HOT READS

Becoming His Series

THIS SERIES IS ABOUT ONE COUPLE AND MUST BE READ IN ORDER.

Book 1: The Ballet

Book 2: Learning to Breathe

Book 3: Becoming His

Sweet Contemporary Romance

Finding Peace

~AND~

Science Fiction

Ellie Masters writing as L.A. Warren

Vendel Rising: a Science Fiction Serialized Novel

1

ANGEL

It figures the cocksure captain would be late.

Less than half an hour until takeoff and Captain Logan Reid was nowhere to be seen.

Not surprising.

The ex-Blue-Angel's legendary exploits preceded him. He could drink every man under the table and drop the panties off every woman within a hundred-foot radius with nothing more than his devastating smile. He probably fucked like a stallion too, making his conquests scream and walk bowlegged for weeks.

But he couldn't make it to work on time?

Just perfect.

I had a thing for fighter pilots, not in a good way.

It wasn't animosity exactly, but rather a deep-seated dislike. Maybe it bordered on hatred. They got all the glory while the rest of us sat at the butt end of their jokes and withered beneath their ridicule.

I hated fighter pilots. There, I said it. I hated the arrogant pricks with a passion.

Since this was our first time flying together, you'd think the asshole would deign to be on time. *Or, here's a thought, Captain Logan Reid why don't you try showing up early to meet your co-pilot?*

I bet he was nursing a hangover or trying to untangle himself from some leggy blonde while the sheets twisted around her freshly fucked perfect body.

Standing at the top of the airstairs, I watched as my good friend, Bianca Truitt, walked across the tarmac from the private terminal. Her rescued Greyhound, Bandit, slunk a step behind her, looking as if he was being tortured and taking his last steps.

A smile lit my face. Despite the issues with my captain, the Truitt's were a pleasure to fly with. If I could spend all my flights with just them this would be the perfect job. Unfortunately, they only occasionally chartered a jet from our company, JetAire.

As CEO of Montague Enterprises, Mr. Truitt had a fleet of company jets to choose from. I'd heard their jet had been grounded for maintenance, which was my gain. Not to mention we were flying them to the Caymans for the weekend.

They requested we stay down there in case Mr. Truitt needed to fly home urgently for business, which meant I was looking at a few days in paradise with nothing but down time.

"Angel!" Bianca Truitt's infectious smile and perpetual positivity never failed to lift my spirits. "Are you flying us today?" She practically squealed with excitement.

They were easy clients, respectful, thoughtful, gracious and thankful. Suffice it to say that I loved when their names showed up on my manifest.

"I hope so. Still waiting on our captain." *Logan, where are you?*

"When are they going to promote you to captain?" She stopped at the bottom of the airstairs and looked to Bandit. "Come on boy."

Bandit looked as if she couldn't be more wrong. I held back a chuckle, loving the wealth of expressions on the poor dog's face.

"Not yet, but soon." Or so I hoped.

I hadn't worked up the ranks in my civilian job to the coveted first seat. Maybe in another year, I could shed the 'co' in co-pilot and finally be the *wo*-man in charge again.

Bandit balked at the foot of the stairs. Tail tucked between his legs, ears pressed low, he didn't want to budge.

Bianca gave him a gentle nudge and he painfully took each step up the stairs as if he was in great agony. The dog really played it up, acting as if this was the worst indignation he had ever faced in his life. He gave me the side-eyes as Bianca cajoled him to take another step and board the airplane.

"Come on Bandit, it's not that bad." She glanced at me and shook her head. "You'd think he would be used to this by now."

"Some pets just don't like flying." I was ready with a secret weapon which would take Bandit's mind off the fact he had to endure yet another flight.

"Well, it's not his first time." With an exasperated sigh, she gave the slightest tug on Bandit's leash, trying to urge him to take another step.

"Jets smell funny. They're loud. The engines whine. With their sensitive noses drying out at altitude, it can be uncomfortable as well."

Bandit made it to the top of the stairs.

"You're going to be okay, buddy." I scratched between his ears.

Bandit rolled soulful eyes at me and glanced back the way he'd come. It didn't look like he agreed, clearly not a fan of flying.

I reached into the pocket of my flight suit and pulled out a Bully-stick. His ears perked up and his nose twitched. I may even have seen his tail wag. He nosed the chew stick with interest, but didn't snatch it from my hand. The dog had the best manners.

"Go ahead." I offered it to him to get him interested, but didn't let him take it from my hand. "It's for you." With a flick, I flung it down the aisle.

Bandit bounded after it, prancing like a puppy when he got it in his mouth, and just like that, he forgot all about being on a plane. He trotted to the back of the private jet where I'd set up a dog bed and plopped down with his treat.

I glanced back toward the private terminal.

"Is Mr. Truitt on his way?" Punctual to a fault, it was unusual for Dexter Truitt not to be on time. I wish I could have said the same for the captain.

"He's with Georgina Bina." Bianca hooked a thumb back at the terminal. "One last pit stop before the flight."

"Ah, gotcha."

Their little daughter wasn't a fan of the lavatories on planes. A private jet, the facilities on board were pretty fancy, but the little girl didn't like the cramped space, and there wasn't a lot of room for her parents to help her out.

While Bianca got settled, I returned to the cockpit. If Logan didn't show in another five-minutes, I was calling back to base. Meanwhile, I prayed he showed up. I'd hate to explain to the CEO of Montague Enterprises why we delayed his family's vacation.

With nothing better to do, I began pre-flight checks and turned my attention to that important task. A few minutes later, a little girl's voice sounded from outside.

"I'm flying!" she giggled. "Higher! Fly me higher!" Her excited squeals drew me from my seat where I looked out on the tarmac.

"You like circles?" A deep voice rumbled and a gorgeous man ran in a big circle with a little girl in his arms, lifting her up and down as she stretched out her arms.

"And dips. I love the dips."

Georgina *flew* in a strange man's arms while her father walked beside them.

Dexter Truitt carried a pink Hello Kittie bag over his shoulder, a pink Hello Kittie purse was clutched in his arm, and he carried an overly large stuffed Hello Kittie in his other hand.

Beside him, the man swung the powerful CEO's daughter in an arc. Seriously? That was Logan Reid?

Of course it was. Not only was he a hotshot fighter pilot, the man was freakin' hot, like jaw-dropping gorgeous. He glanced up at me, flashed a set of perfect pearly whites, blew me a kiss, and lowered his mirrored sunglasses to give a devastating wink.

My knees turned to jelly and I gripped the wall. *Oh God! Was that a damn superpower?*

Tall, the man filled out his brown flight jacket with broad shoulders and muscular arms. His bright blue eyes gave a second panty-melting wink as he spun Georgina in another circle.

My stomach did a little flippy thing. He had a chiseled jaw and dark hair which looked like it had been mauled during sex by a well-satisfied lover. If fuck-me hair was a thing, this man had it.

Longer than military regulations allowed, he had let it grow to the perfect length to drag my fingers through during sex.

Whoa! Where the hell did that come from?

Six hours was going to feel like six years. I needed some

fresh air. Only he was out there with all the fresh air, and in another few seconds he would be in here, with me, sharing any air that was left inside.

God, I hated fighter pilots.

Logan plopped Georgina on her feet at the foot of the airstairs and the little girl ran up the steps. Her father followed with his menagerie of Hello Kittie paraphernalia while Logan stayed down below.

His gaze flicked to mine and our eyes locked for the briefest second. I didn't know if my jaw was gaping, stunned by his looks, or if my eyes were pinched tight with disgust.

Arrogant, cocky bastards were definitely not my type.

Instead of coming up the stairs, Logan took a walk around the plane.

I'd done the same when I arrived. Just an exterior inspection, I always liked to check and make sure there wasn't anything obviously wrong. Our company jets had impeccable mechanical records. There wouldn't be a problem with the engines, or any other part of the plane, but taking a walk around the plane was a hard habit to break.

"Hello." Georgina gave a flap of her hand as she ran past me. "Mommy, daddy almost forgot Kittie."

"Oh no!" Bianca made a show of putting her hands to her cheeks. "Good thing he didn't."

"He had to call the driver back. Kittie would've been looooost." Georgina drew out the last word, as if that was the worst possible thing in the universe.

Mr. Truitt gave a soft laugh and gestured to his burdens. "Good morning, Angel. I was really pleased when they said you'd be one of the pilots for our flight to the Caymans."

"It's nice to see you again, Mr. Truitt."

"Please, how many times do I need to tell you to call me Dex?"

"About a thousand more."

Calling Bianca by her first name was one thing, but the CEO of Montague Enterprises? That felt like crossing a line. I gave a smile as I took the large stuffed Hello Kittie off his hands, then headed down the aisle ahead of him.

He gave a soft laugh, but didn't force the issue.

"Miss Georgina, which seat are you going to be in?" I asked. "We need to make sure Kittie's seatbelt fits."

"Right there!" Her gorgeous eyes lit up, excited with the prospect of flying. She pointed to the set of chairs closest to Bandit's bed.

Bandit was going to town on his treat, completely recovered from the indignation of having to board the plane.

"Do you want me to tuck Kittie in, or will you be doing that?" I winked at Bianca who sat quietly in her seat as her precocious daughter took care of her stuffed Kittie.

"You can," Georgina patted Bandit's head and played with his ears.

As intent as he was on gnawing the Bully-stick, I was a little concerned he might bite her, but Bianca didn't seem worried and neither did Mr. Truitt.

"Okay. Do you think Kittie wants the aisle seat or the window?"

Georgina twisted her lips and pinched her eyes as she considered the very important question.

"Kittie gets sick if she looks outside the window." She pointed to the aisle seat and gave a sharp nod with her decision.

"Gotcha!" I placed Kittie in the aisle seat and made a show of buckling the stuffed animal in while telling Georgina how important it was to be safe in the plane, where the exits were, and how the oxygen masks would drop down from overhead if there was an emergency.

We operated without support staff in this plane, which meant passenger safety fell to me as the co-pilot. With Kittie taken care of, I went over emergency procedures with her parents. Georgina sat beside Bandit and whispered into his ear about all the fun things they were going to do in the Caymans.

Still waiting for Logan Reid to board, I headed to the cockpit and wedged myself into the snug co-pilot's chair. On a jet this size, space came at an economy and very little was spared for the comfort of the pilots. Which meant me and smoldering hot Logan were going to be sitting shoulder to shoulder for the duration.

A presence loomed behind me.

"When they said I would be flying with an angel, I didn't think they meant it literally. You're breathtaking." Low and throaty, with a little bit of a rasp, that voice sent a shiver fluttering over my skin.

I turned around, checklist in hand, and glanced into magnetic blue eyes which stared a little too intently at me. With a gulp, I thrust my hand out, a little too awkwardly, as I tried to rein in the strange flash of heat which followed the path of that shiver.

2

ANGEL

DAMN, HE'S GORGEOUS. PANTY-MELTING HOT. TOP GUN material with leather fight jacket, aviator sunglasses, and requisite smirk, Logan Reid was exactly the kind of man I *didn't* want to spend the next six hours trapped with inside a cockpit at thirty-five thousand feet.

There would be no escape.

"In the flesh." I flashed a smile I didn't feel and prayed that heat hadn't travelled to my cheeks. There was absolutely no need for him to know any of the hundred inappropriate thoughts swirling in my head. The cockpit was too small, or I would have stood and greeted him properly.

His gaze slanted down to regard my hand, then he slowly extended his to complete the greeting. The moment our hands connected that shiver returned, followed by another blistering wave of heat.

Large, broad, and calloused, his hand engulfed mine, and my mind headed into no-man's land with thoughts of what it might feel to have the rest of him wrapped around me.

Get your head out of the gutter.

Instead of shaking my hand and letting it go, he brushed the pad of his thumb over my skin.

I gave a slight tug, feeling entirely too self-conscious, but he didn't release me. Instead, his grip tightened.

"The Angel of the Skies…" He shook his head. "Are the stories true?"

"Excuse me?" How did he know that? The intensity of his stare had me sucking in a breath and I yanked my hand out of his grip.

"Are you an angel?" His gaze swept me from head to toe, lingering on the soft hollow of my neck before dipping to my chest. There was little to see, not with my flight suit on, except I suddenly realized I'd failed to pull the zipper back to my neck and had my cleavage on display.

I yanked the zipper to my throat and crossed my arms defensively across my chest.

He gave a low laugh.

Nothing should sound that sexy, but by the way his lips turned up at the corners, and how his eyes smoldered, I couldn't help but lean in to that sound. It was like I couldn't get close enough, and that was very unlike me. I wasn't the kind of woman who lost her shit around a sexy man.

Get it together, Angel!

Harder than it should have been, I leaned back and turned my attention to the checklist.

"Well?" He placed his hand on the back of my chair. "Are they true?"

"I guess that depends on what stories you're referring to."

Do not look at him!

It took every ounce of my willpower to keep my eyes focused on the checklist. I should be halfway through the long list, but for the life of me I couldn't read the words.

"The stories about you being a guardian angel?" He gave a shrug. "I checked you out." His tone sounded as if checking me out was standard procedure.

The problem was I didn't know if that meant professionally or...more intimately. This was exactly the kind of distraction I didn't need.

"You did what?"

"I checked you out," he said with a rasp.

Okay, now it sounded very unprofessional and I was acutely aware of the cleavage I had inadvertently flashed.

"You know, looked into who I would be flying with? I do that." He drew his hand along the back of my chair and his long fingers pressed into the cushion. That made me think about what it might feel like to have those fingers massaging my neck, or other places.

Stop it!

Okay! I snapped back at my inner voice. *But it's not easy.*

"Do you check out all the pilots you fly with?" I asked.

"Nope." He popped the 'p' and when I turned around he was most definitely staring at my tits.

At least they were covered up now.

"No?" I spun around and the bastard didn't bother to hide the direction of his gaze.

The corner of his lip lifted in a smirk. Leaning forward, he lowered his voice to a whisper. "Just the chicks."

He crossed his arms over his chest and waited. Almost like he was testing the waters. Maybe he wondered which direction I would jump. He would be upset with my reaction. I didn't date people I worked with and I never dated a pilot who I flew with.

Distraction in the sky came with a death wish.

I don't think he's interested in dating you.

No. A man like him didn't date. He fucked.

A steady throb built between my legs. At thirty, I'd never been properly fucked. Of course, I've had sex. I dated. I loved and I'd had my heart broken. But I'd never encountered anything like what was promised in those devilishly sinful eyes.

The man practically eye-fucked me just standing there, and I may have been doing exactly the same right back at him. But I wasn't in a place where I could indulge in such a fantasy. I guess I never had been.

You should loosen up.

Someday, but not today.

I couldn't.

But I did look. My entire focus took in his poor tee-shirt

and the struggle it waged to contain the impressive breadth of his chest. I dropped my gaze.

Wrong move.

Now I was checking out his abs and, from the look of it, they were exactly as I'd imagined. Stacked, ripped, and ready to fulfill endless female fantasies.

"I guess I'm not the only one who likes checking out their coworker." He dropped his arms and that low, rumbly laugh filled the cockpit laced with sin, seduction, and an unspoken promise.

Spinning around, I clamped my jaw shut. *Way to make a first impression.*

"I wasn't checking you out. That's not what I was doing. You really are full of yourself, flyboy."

"Flyboy?" That low chuckle returned and he climbed in beside me, taking the captain's chair. "It's no biggie if you were. You're easy on the eye as well, something I'll appreciate for the next six hours as I wonder whether it's a matching set. And for the record, my call sign is Stallion, not flyboy."

"I wasn't checking you out."

Stallion? I would love to hear the story behind how he got his call sign.

"Pretty sure you were," he insisted.

"Well, get over yourself. I was simply sizing up the competition."

"Competition? Hun, we're not in competition, and for what it's worth, you're scorching hot. It's going to be a *very* long, and uncomfortable, flight." The bastard didn't even hide when he adjusted his trousers. "So, do they match?"

Do not look!

I looked and immediately regretted it. From the bulge behind that zipper, my thoughts launched deep into inappropriate territory. I'd never been this horny. Long flight indeed.

"Excuse me?" My embarrassment at getting caught doing exactly what he accused me of quickly morphed to anger. That was an emotion I had much more experience with and it was far easier to handle than this weird chemistry turning the air into a buzz of static electricity.

"You say that a lot," he said with a snicker.

"Say what?"

"And you repeat things." Amusement rounded out his tone and spurred my anger.

"I do not." I hated how petulant and defensive I sounded.

"Well, like I said, it's no biggie. I'm used to it."

"Used to what?"

"See," he said with a smirk, "you're doing it again."

"Doing what?"

"You repeat things when you're nervous."

"I'm not nervous."

"That's a lie."

"Excuse me!" Heat filled my cheeks, but not from embarrassment. *How dare he?*

He cleared his throat. "It's okay to be nervous, Angel,

the sexual tension in this cockpit is through the roof. Sadly, we'll have to wait to indulge our mutual fantasies. There's work to do."

"I don't know who the hell you think you are, but we're not indulging in anything, and there are no *mutual* fantasies going on here."

He took the preflight checklist from my hand and placed his finger over the first line item. "If that's what you need to think, hun, that's okay. Meanwhile, how about we get this show on the road?"

"How about you stop calling me hun? I'm not your honey."

He gave a wink. "No, but you're definitely an angel. Now tell me, are the stories true?"

The stories? Was it weird that I didn't like thinking about the stories which earned me my call sign?

Most people got cool call signs like Hotshot or Ace. Others got more ignominious names.

One of my favorites was DASH which was given to one of my buddies in flight school. Larry was a kickass pilot, but dumb as shit when it came to anything else in life. It became a joke in the squadron until eventually someone said we should call him DASH for dumb as shit. Names like that tended to stick for life, unfortunately for Larry.

"You shouldn't believe the stories people tell." Deflecting came naturally, unfortunately I didn't think Logan would allow it. He seemed to be a man used to getting what he wanted. Right now, he seemed intent on rifling through my past.

"I find there is truth in stories, secrets we don't want others to know."

"Is that so?"

"You leading off with another question?"

"Are we back to that?"

"It depends on whether the next thing out of your mouth is a question or an answer." He progressed through the checklist with an economy of effort while I confirmed each line on the list.

"I don't like talking about it. How about that?"

"Hmm, I'm going to let that one slide; seeing how the question came at the end."

"Questions are a normal part of conversation."

"I suppose…" His words trailed off, leaving me to wonder whether there might be more to that thought.

Briefly, I considered asking, but decided against it. In fact, I resolved not to ask another damn question if I could help it.

"Tell me what you've heard and I'll tell you whether it's true or not."

"That's fair," he said.

We prepped for flight while we talked.

"My buddy said you landed your Stratotanker with only one engine."

"True."

"What, no details?"

"There's not much to tell, lightning struck the starboard wing, one of the engines caught fire. I landed, although technically I still had engines 1 and 2 on the portside wing."

"You received a medal for it. No souls lost." He sounded genuinely impressed.

"I got a medal for doing what anyone would have done. We trained for shit like that."

"What about when the landing gear went out?"

Did he research my entire career?

"It didn't go out, just failed to deploy. I landed that one too."

"With no loss of life and minimal damage to the fuselage."

"They didn't give me a medal for that one."

"But they did the next one."

"I don't really like talking about it."

"Why not? They call you the Angel of the Skies for a reason. I thought it was just a piss-poor nickname at first. Angel for Angelica. Cool name by the way, but it looks like you earned Angel because you have the divine touch."

"I guess it depends on your perspective."

"How's that?"

"Either I'm the Angel of the Skies or incredibly cursed."

"I don't believe in curses."

"You should." I mumbled under my breath with no intention of him ever hearing me.

My record might reflect superior performance under stress, but accidents seemed to find me. I didn't believe in curses either, but I'd been involved in three major mechanical failures. It didn't matter that I landed each and every one without losing a life. I was the Angel of the Skies with the Devil on her tail.

"Ready for sterile cockpit?"

"Ready."

The sterile cockpit rule came into effect after several accidents revealed pilots had been distracted during crucial moments during flight. It applied during taxi, take-off, and landing through ten-thousand feet. It was meant to increase pilots' attention to essential operational activities and reduce accidents.

From the moment we began our taxi to the runway, until we passed through ten-thousand feet, Logan and I would cut the chit chat and focus on flying the jet.

Logan toggled Air Traffic Control requesting clearance to push off from the gate. The radio squawked and Air Traffic Control responded.

ATC: 452 cleared to Grand Caymans. Depart Bravo-1.

We taxied to the designated runway and pulled up short to await final clearance to take off. Logan called in, informing Air Traffic Control that we were in position, waiting short of the Bravo-1 runway.

Logan: 452, hold short at Bravo-1.

ATC: 452 clear to takeoff runway Bravo-1, contact departure 1-2-8 decimal 8 in the air.

Logan: 452 clear to go.

We pulled onto the runway. This was my favorite part of

flying. The way the thrust of the engines launched me into the air never ceased to take my breath away.

Only, this time it wasn't the takeoff which took my breath away. It was a pair of sinful magnetic blue eyes and the wink which promised far too much.

3

LOGAN

Sitting beside Angel felt surreal. The chick was a legend within the flying community.

When I found out I would be working with what amounted to a living hero, nervous didn't begin to describe how I felt, which was odd considering my background.

Very little unnerved me.

I'd never been fond of the sterile cockpit rule, but I gave thanks to it as I guided the plane through the first ten-thousand feet. It gave me time to get my shit together and not act like an idiot around the stunning Angelique Mars.

The woman looked nothing like the photo in her bio. I'd stared at her severe expression for the past week, wondering how I would endure this job beside what for all intents and purposes appeared to be a woman who was all business and no thrills.

Hell, I'd flown with other female pilots in the past, but there was something about Angel's expression in her profile photo, a hardness which bristled with *the humor stops here.*

In the photo, her midnight black hair had been tied back in a severe bun. I preferred it loose and flowing like it was now. The slightest curl gave it a sensual bounce and her long layers would be fun to thread through my fingers.

Her long, flowing hair softened her features and revealed her true beauty. Which was strange, because I preferred blondes with blue eyes, not raven-haired sirens with dark eyes hiding secrets I yearned to uncover.

A treasure awaited a man persistent enough to chip away at her defenses and peel away the protective layers. Not really sure why, but in that moment, I determined to be that man.

"Passing ten-thousand feet," she called out beside me.

"Roger." I could talk freely now, but held my tongue. There was simply too much to process with the woman sitting beside me.

I had been one of the elite of the elite and earned the swagger which came with being a hot shot, Blue Angel fighter pilot. Despite my prowess, however, I had never saved lives.

I flew crazy precise formations and insane aerobatics for the crowd, a public relations machine which showcased the best the Navy had to offer, but I didn't bring broken planes safely out of the sky.

My job had been to look pretty and sell the sexy Navy fighter pilot image.

I didn't save the day.

She had.

Not once. Not twice. Three fucking times.

We continued to climb and Angel called out our altitude. Neither one of use broke the tense silence with small talk. We were all business.

Nerves explained why I'd been late this morning, something I wasn't proud to admit, but I needed to bring my A-game to this job, because no man flew with the Angel of the Skies without bringing his best.

It had taken over half an hour to find where I'd buried my flight jacket. In this new, civilian job, my flight suit had been traded in for khaki pants and a polo shirt proudly sporting the company logo, but I felt a need for the gravitas only my flight jacket could bring. I needed the armor of my former glory.

Another glance brought her back to the center of my attention. No khaki pants. No polo shirt. She wore a flight suit. Not the one from her Air Force days. This was blue instead of olive green and the company logo had been embroidered over the front left pocket.

With my favorite pair of khaki jeans, a comfortable tee-shirt, my aviator sunglasses, and my trusty flight jacket—which, let's face it was a veritable chick magnet—my confident swagger returned.

Not that I'd lost it. That's not what this was about. This was about meeting Angel on an equal footing.

"You're not what I expected." I broke the silence and ditched the sterile cockpit rule. I could finally admit what had been keeping me occupied during our ascent. Sterile might mean cutting the chit-chat, but that didn't mean my brain cut off. This was one woman I needed to figure out. Before we landed, I'd already decided her secrets would be mine.

"I'm not what most expect." Her reply was soft, hesitant, and sexy as fuck, but also sounded like it had been said dozens of times.

I flashed one of my panty-melting smiles, but she didn't dissolve into a quivering mess. Instead, she regarded me with clinical interest, sizing me up. Not the reaction I had hoped for. This chick was going to be a tough nut to crack.

"Smart girl."

"Not a girl." She gestured to her body. "Grown ass woman, flyboy."

"A fact I'm acutely aware of." I shifted and tried to relieve the discomfort from the tightening in my pants.

My dick was getting a workout, and not the good kind, because there was no easy relief in sight. One look at this beauty and my body had a mind of its own. Or rather, my dick had a mind of its own. It was on the prowl and it wanted her.

She ignored my brash comment. "In my experience, I receive one of two reactions in this job. Either the men I work with expect me to be incompetent because I'm a woman and underestimate me, or they know about my past and overcompensate. Which one are you?"

She sounded as if she was tired of dealing with assholes who didn't extend her the respect she'd earned.

Shit, is that what she thinks of me? We were headed in the wrong direction and needed a course correction STAT. How could I respond and not sound exactly like either of those two options?

Try telling her the truth, jackass.

Fine, it couldn't hurt.

"I could respond to that a few ways," I began, "but I'm going for option three."

"And what is option three?"

"Well, first of all, let's address options one and two."

Angel had it nailed down. It was entirely too common for men to look down on female pilots. Like many women, she'd spent her career fighting unfair stereotypes.

Aviation was a career filled with egotistical bastards who perpetuated the male dominated group-think that women couldn't do this job with the same skill as a man. Most men were also chauvinistic assholes who gave women shit. I wasn't one of them, but from the look on her face and the fatigue in her voice, that's exactly what she expected.

"First of all," I said, "I've worked with many kickass women. The last year I was with the Blue Angels we inducted our first female pilot. As far as underestimating you because you're a woman, I've flown with the best of the best. Lisette

James was one of them and it didn't matter one bit that she was female. I don't doubt your credentials or capabilities."

"That's good to know seeing as how we're stuck with each other for the next few days, and thank you." Her eyes softened with the curve of her smile.

Did I just sense a thaw in her icy exterior?

I swear that was the first genuine smile she had graced me with since first setting eyes on each other. Everything before now had a guarded edge to it, but that seemed real.

And it felt fucking amazing. I needed more of those.

"I don't mind being stuck on you." Time to test the waters. How much flirtation would she allow?

"Excuse me?"

I flashed another grin. Respecting women in my chosen career didn't mean I didn't go after what I wanted, and from the reaction of my body, I most definitely wanted this one.

"As for the second," I continued, "I've never had a need to overcompensate for anything. I'm pretty confident about my skills. I'm the whole package."

"You seriously didn't just say that?" Her brow arched as she gave me another look. "The whole package?" She gave a snort. "You're a pretty ballsy bastard. Are you going to ask me if I want to ride you? That's usually what comes next."

Well, shit. This wasn't going the way I hoped.

"I'm a confident bastard with some pretty big balls. So, I guess I agree with that statement. And for the record, my package is impressive. And since you're wondering, it's well worth the ride." I shifted in my seat. "And speaking of my balls…I think they're going to be blue and aching by the time we get to the Caymans."

"Sounds rough," she teased. "I feel for you, but I'm good."

"Good?"

"Yeah, no need to ride anything. You're getting ahead of yourself."

I couldn't get out of my own way fast enough. She didn't flirt like most women. Challenge laced each word.

"You can feel them if you want."

"Feel them?"

"My balls. You said you wanted to feel them."

Her cheeks pinked and she cleared her throat. "That is not what I said."

"Oh, I must have misunderstood." But I wish she had. "You're cute when you snort."

I couldn't help but poke fun at her and I couldn't keep myself from staring. From her pert nose, to her kissable lips, and to the tiny point of her chin, it was impossible not to look. I had to remind myself I was still cruising to altitude and check the instrument cluster to make sure I didn't overshoot.

"You're not supposed to bring attention to that," she said.

"What?"

"When a woman snorts."

"Why not? It's sexy as fuck. Not to mention genuine. Too many chicks are fake."

"I'm sorry they fake it with you." Her eyes twinkled with mischief. "With your *impressive package* and all."

I couldn't help the grin spreading across my face. My girl teased back. Victory would soon be mine, but I couldn't let that comment stand.

"It's all real beneath the sheets, against the wall, on the floor, and as they ride their way to heaven, but we're not supposed to be talking about sex."

"I'm going out on a limb here, but I assume you have difficulties with boundaries." Her tone bristled with a warning that I was crossing a line. "With all these women falling at your feet, it must be hard when one doesn't."

"They usually fall to their knees." I waited to see how she would react. When her pupils dilated, I knew I'd scored a hit. She was now thinking about what came after going to her knees.

My pants felt painfully tight and my dick throbbed with need. I couldn't wait to feel those pert lips wrap around my cock.

Although, it was time to ease back a bit. The direct approach wasn't going to work with this one. I needed something much more subtle. Damn if my dick wasn't standing loud and proud. It loved a challenge too.

When was the last time I had to work to get a girl?

Never.

"I go after what I want," I said. "Nothing wrong with that."

"It is when you work with the other person." Tension stiffened her spine and her shoulders rolled back.

"I'm not suggesting we strip and go to town here and now." I waved toward the instrument cluster. "We're technically on the clock and that is one of my hard limits. No fucking and flying."

"Well, I'm glad to hear that. Since, you know…safety first. Good to know you have limits."

"Everyone has limits and it's just a little innocent flirting between coworkers." My tone was entirely too defensive. "It doesn't mean anything."

"That's what they all say."

It sounded like she'd been on the receiving end of overly aggressive advances in the past. Not one to have a sexual harassment complaint filed against me, I eased back.

"You can relax, Angel. I'm a pretty decent guy, a perfect gentleman."

I wasn't.

I was as far from it as possible, but I would be whatever it took to get this girl. "And I'm sorry if anyone has crossed a line with you in the past. I don't mean to make you feel uncomfortable."

"Thanks. I guess it comes with the territory. Sorry if I'm coming across as bitchy. It's just that I find it easier if I'm clear from the start."

"Me too." I hoped she understood being a gentleman

didn't mean I wouldn't pursue her once we weren't on the clock.

Our attraction wasn't a force that could be stopped. It was a runaway freight train, inevitable and unstoppable. This was happening.

She blew out a breath. "Well, great. Now that we've settled that, how about a movie?"

4

LOGAN

We had a long flight ahead of us and the plane did most of the flying. Except for takeoff, landing, and the occasional navigational correction, there was very little to do unless we encountered an inflight emergency.

I usually brought a good book, but I wasn't against watching a movie.

"You have no idea how much more charming I can be when on my best behavior." I put my hands behind my head and threaded my fingers together. "What do you have in mind? Porn?"

"Porn!" She rolled her eyes. "I see being a gentleman doesn't come with good behavior. You know, I can head back to the Truitt's and give you some privacy to take care of that woody you're sporting."

"For the love of God, don't call it a woody?"

She giggled. "Not when it makes you squirm."

"For the record, I'm not squirming." But I shifted in my seat because my erection was practically drilling a hole through the fabric of my pants. For a split second, I seriously considered her offer to give me a little privacy to take the edge off.

I might be concerned about crossing *boundaries*, but the tension eased between her shoulder blades and she rewarded me with a smile. This might be the only opportunity to push things a little further and test the waters to see what might be possible.

"I'm guessing you're a rule follower?" I turned my attention forward and adjusted the controls.

"Rules are good." She spoke with absolute conviction, but I knew better.

"Bullshit. Rules are meant to be broken." And I intended to break her no sleeping with coworkers rule as soon as possible. "I know of one rule you should consider breaking."

"You barely know me and you're already trying to get into my pants. Not sure if I should be offended or flattered."

"I've never had a complaint. Consider it flattery. What do you say? How about we twist the sheets together in the Caymans?"

Her lower lip curled between her teeth and it was all I could do to hold back a groan. When I thought I couldn't take any more, the pink tip of her tongue peeked out to wet her upper lip.

This was going to be one damn long flight.

"You're killing me, Smalls. Killing me."

"How? I'm not doing anything."

"You're a knockout and if you keep sucking at your lower lip like that I'm not going to be held responsible for what comes next."

She regarded me for a long-assed second, a moment of eternal time, as those dark eyes of hers weighed and measured me.

"I'm curious," she said, "have you ever had a woman tell you no before?"

"What do you think?" I didn't mean for it to come out sounding cocky as shit, but from the expression on her face that's exactly how it sounded. "Sorry, didn't mean it like that."

"No need to apologize, and I'm pretty sure you meant it exactly like that. You're a man who's used to getting what he wants."

That was true, but I would be a fool to admit it to her. Instead, I kept silent and flashed a cocky grin. Let her decide where the truth might lie.

"We can save you a lot of trouble, because it's a hard no with me."

"How's that?"

"I don't sleep with coworkers. So, you can save all the bullshit sexy talk for someone else. It won't work on me."

The hell it wouldn't. This woman ate up my sexy talk.

Or tried to. I hadn't put my finger on it yet, but her hesitation came from someplace deep within her.

Some place dark.

It made me wonder if someone had hurt her in the past. And that thought stirred an immediate anger to punch whatever asshole wounded her so much that she felt a need to be defensive.

I may flirt. It may be over the top. But, I knew when to pull back. Putting a woman on edge was a new thing for me, and while we weren't there yet, I was dangerously close to pushing too hard.

"Darlin' don't get ahead of yourself. I haven't asked you to sleep with me, but when we do fuck, you can be damn well sure there won't be any sleeping going on."

"A bit cocksure, are we?" Her challenge wasn't lost on me. "You're going to be disappointed, flyboy. I suggest you find some pretty blonde in the Caymans to take the edge off that woody."

"I prefer brunettes, not blondes..." That was a total lie. I'd never been interested in a brunette until my eyes landed on Angelica Mars. It was as if lightning struck, and I found myself powerless in her presence. I needed her to want me.

And that made no sense at all. What the hell was happening to me?

"Funny, I took you for the perfect ten, blonde Barbie kind of guy."

"I like blondes, but there's just something about

brunettes. They're mysterious and I'm betting a lot more fun. Definitely worth the chase."

"Uh-huh, how many brunettes have you dated? I'm guessing not many."

"I'm not dating anyone right now, blonde or brunette, although I hope that changes soon."

What the hell was I doing? This wasn't the kind of shit a guy admitted to a potential conquest. It made me seem needy and that most definitely was not me.

The thing was, Angel was right about one thing. Within an hour of landing, if I wanted it, I could find some willing blonde to take care of this erection which didn't seem to want to go away.

"Don't look here," she said. "My rule stands."

"Are you sure about that? What if I enjoy a challenge?"

She didn't bristle at my comment. I was a little concerned this whole conversation headed in the wrong direction, but the air buzzed and static electricity crackled all around us.

She may not realize it, but she gave herself away with the way she licked her lips when she didn't think I was look-ing. And of course, I could see her pulse hammering away in her neck. Not to mention the rise and fall of her breasts increased when we talked about sex.

I wasn't the only one who was hot and bothered. She wanted me. She just wasn't ready to accept it yet. That was okay. I would wait until she was ready.

Time to regroup and take things slow.

Actually, that kind of appealed to me. I couldn't remember the last time when I'd gone for the slow burn. I'd always been about chasing tail and getting laid. It never mattered to me to actually take the time to get to know my bed partner. With great difficulty, I resisted the urge to rub my hands together in anticipation.

It was rare when I had to chase a woman. I hadn't been exaggerating, or overcompensating. A blink, a smile, or the simple crook of my index finger, was often all the effort required on my part to get a woman to drop her panties and let me do whatever I pleased. It was going to be fun to work for it.

"Erection," I suddenly blurted.

"Excuse me?"

"You called it a woody, which sounds very junior high. I'm aroused and have an erection. E-R-E-C-tion! We're adults and should use adult words."

"You're not shy about sharing that with the world, are you? I might take offense to that kind of comment, but it's probably best to remind yourself there's a little girl in the cabin behind us who probably shouldn't hear you say that word."

"I'm not ashamed of it, and she can't hear me. You're an attractive woman and I can't help the way my body responds. It's a natural reaction, like a sneeze, and I'm not in control of it."

"Did you just compare your erection to a sneeze?" Her soft laughter fluttered through the cabin, but it quickly morphed into another snort. She held her hand to her mouth and laughed.

"From the way you've been checking out my crotch, there's no way to hide it, and I'm not the kind of guy who's embarrassed when a beautiful woman stirs a very natural reaction."

"Well, keep that thing in your pants, flyboy, and let's find something else to talk about other than your little woody."

"My woody is far from little, and I can't wait to show you."

"Oh, I bet."

"Absolutely, but I'm not going to..." I flashed an evil grin, "until you beg for it."

"Well, you might just want to settle in, because I'm not doing that."

"Never say never, Angel."

We had far too many hours left in the cramped quarters of this cockpit. Damn but she smelled like heaven. I hadn't figured out the scent, something floral and light which drove me insane. I wanted to lick her neck and see if I could figure it out from the taste of her. I bet she tasted like sin.

"I think we're done talking about...that."

"What do you want to talk about?" This was a good place to step back. From the way her pupils had dilated, the flushing of her cheeks, and from the rapid rise and fall of her glorious tits, I'd struck a nerve. All I had to do was sit back and wait for the perfect opportunity to present itself.

"Well, you know how I got my call sign," she said. "How about you tell me how you got yours?"

"Sweetie, you don't want to talk about that."

"Why not?"

"My call sign is Stallion and I'll give you a moment to think about how that name may have come about. Since we're not supposed to be talking about sex anymore, it would be highly inappropriate for me to mention how women love riding the stallion."

Her eyes widened once it clicked. "You've got to be kidding me."

"You want to hear the story?"

"I think I'll pass."

"Fine by me, but it's not going to be my fault when you can't fall asleep tonight because you're wondering about *it*." I made a vague gesture towards my groin.

"I'm certain I won't be thinking about *that* when I go to bed."

"You sure? Because I'm pretty certain it's going to bug you. I can tell you…"

She held up a hand. "Nope, we're keeping the rest of this flight professional. You're incorrigible, you know that?"

"That's an awfully big word, incorrigible. I prefer irresistible."

"You may be irresistible to the ladies, but not to me."

"You saying you're not a lady? Considering the red lace of your bra, I'm pretty certain you're most definitely a lady."

"You peeked at my bra?"

"I didn't peek. You flashed me. I was an innocent bystander. Which, by the way, you never answered my question."

"What question was that?"

"Do they match?"

"Does what match?"

"Your panties. It's all I've been able to think about." I'd been thinking about a lot of very inappropriate things. That was merely one of them. "I've been wondering if you're wearing matching panties, or maybe a thong?"

"We're not talking about what I may, or may not, be wearing. How about we talk movies?" She turned away as her cheeks turned bright pink. "What's your favorite?"

"Panties? I actually prefer thongs or the ones where the ass cheeks hang out."

"No! Movie, what's your favorite movie?" She shook her head and the pink in her cheeks turned beet red.

"Top Gun. I especially loved the hot tub scene." My gaze dropped to her chest and I wondered about the red lace of her bra hidden behind that zipper.

"You're staring at my boobs."

"Am I?"

"Yes. My eyes are up here." She gave a low chuckle. "Look who's answering with questions now."

"And you're staring at my crotch. Do you want to see what's behind the zipper?"

"No!" She thrust out her hand as I reached for the zipper.

I was only teasing. She had her rules about fucking coworkers, which I would respect—at least until she changed her mind. But I had mine as well and I didn't fuck around on the job. I could be a rule follower too.

"Well, what are we watching? You up for a little Top Gun?" That movie was riddled with errors when it came to flying, but had sexy as fuck scenes. If I could get Angel all hot and bothered by the time we landed in the Caymans, then maybe she'd turn that *No* into a definite *Yes*.

"No Top Gun. How about an action film?"

"As long as it has sexy scenes," I teased.

Mischief danced in her eyes. "You want hot?"

"Yeah, the hotter the better." I wracked my brain for movies with the best sex scenes but came up totally blank.

"Ah, I think you're in luck. I happen to know Georgina brought her favorite movie. She's over the moon in love with *Frozen*."

My jaw dropped. "*Frozen*! No way in hell are we watching that. What happened to hot?"

"What happened to boundaries?"

"Watching sexy movies is not pushing boundaries."

"You're telling me you can watch a sexy movie with me and not turn it into something sexual?"

"If the movie has sex in it, that's not me turning it into something sexual."

"I meant the comments and sexual innuendoes."

"You're going to be the death of me, Angel. You're making this incredibly hard. And, if you're wondering, I'm talking about my dick."

"I'm taking that as a no." Her lips twisted as she thought. "How about we watch one of those movies about a dog finding its way home?"

"Snooze-a-thon, how about we not. *Fast and Furious* is good. We can watch that. It's got sexy cars."

"And hot sex." She winked at me and my jaw about dropped.

"Hey, you said it not me. *Fast and Furious* it is. But I get to pick the next movie."

"Sounds fair." She gave a shrug as if it didn't matter, but I had a plan.

Something devious was at work in my head. This woman's tough exterior would crack and I'd worm my way into her heart.

I didn't give up easily.

5

ANGEL

IN-BETWEEN WATCHING THE HIGHLY UNREALISTIC *FAST AND Furious* and zooming toward our destination at thirty-five-thousand feet, I got to know Logan Reid a little better. Not quite as abrasive as I initially thought, he kept me laughing from one car chase to another with his over the top narrative.

"You really aren't a fan," I said after a particularly derisive comment about the franchise.

He glanced at me. "Who is?"

"Every man on the planet? Come on, sexy cars, leggy women dressed in postage-stamp sized dresses, car crashes and explosions? That's every man's wet dream."

Why I brought up sex was beyond me. I didn't want to discuss wet dreams and encourage Logan with more talk about sex.

"It's all crap." He pointed to the tablet between us. "I mean, worth an evening's entertainment, but at the expense of losing brain cells. I'm the more sophisticated type."

"That crap has made billions. You're probably one of a handful of men with a pulse who doesn't love that *crap*."

"That's true, but there's too much smashing of cars and over the top stunts for me. I'm more of a slow burn kind of guy. Where was the heat and the passion?"

"The heat was in the ten-thousand explosions we just saw, and there was plenty of passion in the sex scenes."

He gave a wave of his hand. "That was gratuitous sex for the sake of audience titillation."

"Funny, I thought that would be right up your alley."

"You'd think and you'd be wrong. I can't wait to show you how wrong."

The wink he gave wasn't nearly as devastating as the previous ones, but it still brought a strange fluttering sensation to my belly. The thing was, if I was being completely honest, I wanted a little bit of what he promised. Unbridled sex for the pure enjoyment of it had never been something I'd experienced.

There was one problem.

Too uptight to ever let myself go with someone, I couldn't get out of my own way and indulge my fantasies. Most definitely, I couldn't do that with someone I worked with, although why I was thinking of doing anything with Logan was beyond me. Nevertheless, I wished I had half the passion of the man sitting beside me.

"We have another hour before descent." He picked up the tablet. "Not enough for a full movie, but we can start one and finish it at the hotel."

His words sounded innocent enough, but there was no way I would be spending any time with him on the ground. The man was simply too dangerous, too tempting, and too much of everything.

"Let's pass." I unbuckled from my seat. "I'm going to check on our passengers. Can I bring you anything?"

"I'm good." With his head dipped toward the tablet, he pulled up a list of books. "But I'll take a little break when you get back."

Funny how I didn't want to leave. A few hours ago, I might have said I couldn't get out of that cramped space with him fast enough, but he was growing on me. Easy with his smiles, funny with his movie narratives, and much easier to be around after he stopped with all the innuendoes, I found myself relaxing and letting down my guard…with him.

My focus turned to the fullness of his lips and my mind imagined what those might feel like brushing against mine.

"I'll be right back." I couldn't get out of there fast enough. Where had that sudden heat come from? I squeezed my thighs together in an attempt to ease some of the insistent throbbing between them.

Exiting the cockpit, I took in our passengers as I tried to take my mind off the sexy man I'd left behind.

Little Georgina curled around her stuffed Hello Kittie

and appeared to be asleep. Bianca glanced up and pressed her finger to her lips telling me to be quiet. I gave a nod and tiptoed down the aisle toward the lavatory.

Even Bandit seemed to have quieted down. The dog was in his bed, rolled over on his back with his rear legs splayed and front paws crossed on top of one another. Bandit followed my progress through the cabin with a lazy roll of his eyes, but otherwise didn't stir. Bianca sat with her husband, hands clasped, as they watched a movie on the main cabin screen with earbuds in place.

I closed the door to the lavatory and took a moment for myself. I loved flying with a passion bordering on insanity, but sometimes the lack of privacy bugged me. A quick check in the mirror, after I washed my hands, revealed pretty much what I expected, a plain Jane stared back at me with dark lackluster hair and nondescript muddy-brown eyes.

What little makeup I had on was practically nonexistent and I hadn't brought anything for a touch up. Obsessing over makeup wasn't really my thing, except I had a sudden urge to add some blush to my cheeks and line my eyes in the deepest kohl black.

Outside the lavatory, I grabbed four waters from the tiny galley kitchen.

"Here you go." I gave Bianca and Mr. Truitt a bottle each. "Make sure you hydrate."

"Thank you." Bianca took the water with a smile and twisted off the cap.

With nothing further to keep me, I headed back to my

mobile office, the best place in the world. When I opened the cockpit door, I took a moment to take in the blue skies and smattering of clouds outside the window.

Logan turned around. "How are our passengers?"

"Watching a movie. Georgina is asleep, so try not to wake her."

He gave a nod and unbuckled from his seat. "I'll be back in a minute. Try not to miss me too much."

"I'll try." A genuine smile slipped past my defenses.

My attention turned to his tablet and I picked it up, curious as to what kind of reading material interested him. No surprise. It was a CIA spy novel involving a race around the globe to stop terrorists from destroying the world.

Settling into my seat, I decided to be nosey and check out his library. Suspense thrillers scrolled past, but then something unexpected caught my eye.

"Whatcha doing?" His rumbly voice surprised me and I gave a little jerk, unaware that he had returned.

"Snooping at your literary choices." Lifting the tablet, I showed him exactly what I'd been doing.

He glanced over my shoulder and sucked in a breath. Holding back my laughter, I decided to have a little fun. "I'm a fan of Tom Clancy too, but the rest of your reading choices are not what I expected from a hotshot flight jock."

He ripped the tablet, with the cover of Fifty Shades of Gray prominently displayed on the screen, out of my hands.

"Nosey girls better watch out, or they won't like what comes next."

"Keep it in your pants, flyboy. I'm just teasing you. Not something I'd expect, that's all."

"It's my sister's. We share an account. All of our books are intermingled."

"Uh-huh, it's okay if you like reading that kind of stuff. No judgement." He riled me up too easily, it was nice to turn the tables on him for once.

"Have you read it?"

Shit. That was not the kind of book I wanted to have a conversation about.

"Maybe."

"There's no maybe about it. I'm guessing you devoured it, saw all the movies…twice, and then reread the juicy bits."

"You're making a lot of assumptions."

He was one-hundred percent correct. I'd done that and more. My reading choices were eclectic, spanning thrillers to romance to fantasy and science fiction, but I devoured that book and had been excited by the steamier scenes.

My romantic encounters had been extraordinarily vanilla, if that book was any judge. But then, I'd never been with a man with whom I would feel comfortable exploring anything like what happened in that book.

"It's been some time, but yeah, I read it." As much as it killed me to admit anything to this man, I was learning it was the safer path to fess up. If he didn't think something bothered me, he couldn't tease me about it. "Everybody with a pulse has read it."

"Really." He put his finger to his neck, making a show of

locating his pulse. "I've got a pulse and I've never read it." With a wink, he swiped the page. "But now I'm thinking I need to for research purposes. What are your favorite parts? I can skip to them and then ask you if I have any questions. Or need a demonstration? What do you think about that?"

Oh, hell no! Talk about flame and burn. That was exactly what I'd been trying to avoid. In for a penny, in for a pound, he had me. But that didn't mean I was done.

"As popular as those books are, I'm surprised you haven't read it…you know, for research?"

"Not my kind of reading material, and I don't really need help in that department. I'm pretty skilled as it is."

"Well, chicks seem to dig it. Although, if you're not the kind of man who keeps a woman around for more than one night, it probably doesn't matter if you knock her socks off or not. I'm sure you simply crook your finger and a new girl comes running."

Insulting his prowess wasn't what I'd intended. I rarely engaged in locker room talk with the guys, because I inevitably fucked it up and crossed lines I never saw coming.

A scowl filled his face and he pursed his lips.

"Sorry," I rushed to apologize, "that was a shit thing to say. I'm not good at this."

His brows drew together. "Not good at what?"

"I didn't mean for that to come out sounding like shit, or insulting your…"

"My ability to leave my sexual partners so thoroughly satisfied that I've ruined them for all men who followed?"

"Wow, that's a bit cocky, but yeah…that."

"I've never left my partners wanting. I please them first, several times if I can, before seeing to myself."

"Okay, it was a shitty thing to say. I'm sorry."

"It was kind of shitty, but what is it that you're not good at?"

"Banter." I gave a shrug. "You know, lobbying insults back and forth? I suck at it."

"You can be a bit bristly," he admitted, although he didn't look upset.

Ouch, that hurt, not that I was surprised. He spoke the truth.

"Well, I was trying to tease."

"I don't think that's what you were doing." A spark of interest flashed in his eyes.

"Can we pretend that didn't just happen?"

"Which part? The part where you insulted my ability to please a woman or the fact you were flirting with me?"

"I wasn't flirting with you."

A huge grin split his face. "You're right. You weren't flirting. You were bombing in your attempt to flirt with me." He winked. "Fortunately for you, I'm willing to let you practice until you perfect your craft."

"Excuse me?"

"Practice." He slid into his seat and gave a chuckle as he buckled in. "On me. We'll call it Flirting 101 with the Man of Your Dreams."

"You are full of yourself. Man of My Dreams?" I

reached out and punched him in the shoulder. "And I was *not* flirting with you. It's called locker room humor, which I suck at considering I've never been in a male locker room."

"Call it what you need to, luv. I'm just thrilled you think I'm hot and that you're interested. It makes things easier." He flashed another devastating wink and followed it with his mesmerizing smile. "I'll play hard to get, though. I don't want to make things too easy on you."

"You're having fun with this, aren't you?"

"Oh, I haven't even begun to have fun." He lifted his tablet and opened up to the first page in Fifty Shades. "And I have research to do." He tapped the screen. "What women like and how to get them coming back for more."

"Obviously, you're not letting me live that down."

"Sweetie, I'm going to milk this for all I can get." He flipped through the first pages. "I heard there was something about a special room…"

"Before you get ahead of yourself, I may have read the books, but don't waste your time researching too much. There's a difference between reading something for pleasure and…"

"Oh, I've got that covered, luv. I'm going to learn all about this pleasuring thing…especially since you think I need help in that department. But we'll work on your flirting deficiency first. Right now, we have to figure out how to land this thing."

Saved by the bell! I'd never been happier to hear the radio squawk.

Logan communicated with Air Traffic Control as we entered the airspace approaching the Grand Caymans. While he confirmed our altitude and flight path, I began our descent following the directions provided by Air Traffic Control. We were still some distance out as I nosed us from our cruising altitude through twenty-seven thousand feet.

"You want to take point on the landing?" He glanced at me.

"If that's okay."

As the captain, and pilot in charge of the aircraft, he decided who took the controls. It wasn't unusual for the captain to have the copilot land. Next to takeoffs, landings were my favorite part of flying.

"Bring us in, Angel. It's been a long, *hard* flight. It's probably time for you to take over. I'm definitely in need of a feminine touch."

"What makes you think I'll be delicate?"

"Ah, now that is better. You get an A+ for that one. For our first time together, let's not get too *experimental*. Just take it slow and steady. We'll save the hard stuff for later. Now, don't forget the thrust."

I would have to increase the thrust of the engines as we chipped away at our altitude, but he clearly meant something else.

I shook my head. "I'm so going to regret insulting you, aren't I?"

"Yes, and it's going to be so much fun to make you pay.

You owe me a drink for that and I'll be cashing that in at the hotel bar."

"What if I don't have plans to drink at the hotel bar?"

"It's up to you, luv. It's one drink. How much trouble do you think that can be?"

I had a feeling it was going to be far more trouble than I wanted, but I couldn't help but want to find out.

6

LOGAN

SITTING BACK WHILE ANGEL FLEW ALLOWED ME TO ENJOY
the simple act of watching the most gorgeous woman alive
handle the power of a jet like it was as natural as breathing.

Her long, silky, black hair flowed down her back, making
me want to run my fingers through the gentle waves. She
gripped the flight controls with delicate fingers that were
both confident and feminine. It made me wonder what
those fingers might feel like stroking up and down my cock.

My mind clearly was in the gutter and there was no
hope. As long as I was around her, that's where my thoughts
would land.

Considering we were co-workers, this intense attraction
was problematic, but I couldn't help any number of wildly
inappropriate fantasies flying around in my head. I wanted

her. Plain and simple, I wanted Angel in my arms, in my bed, and in my life.

This wasn't something I understood, this raging need within me. I'd always been in control, but with her I lost it. All I could think about was staking my claim. She was mine.

Staking my claim?

Where did that thought come from?

I didn't lay claim to women. I used them to satisfy mutual pleasure, but never really kept one around. There'd been no reason to bother, honestly. And some of what Angel said was embarrassingly true. All it took was a crook of my finger and I could fill my bed with a nameless chick.

I had an urge right now, but this felt different because I wanted conversations over dinner, drinks at the bar, and I hoped I could convince her to spend some of her free time with me in a bed.

We would get there. It was an eventuality, but I wanted to get to know her better before jumping into bed. I'd never wanted to do that with any woman.

So, why now?

Angel eased us below the ten-thousand foot ceiling and the sterile cockpit rule once again took effect. I settled into the rhythms of flying, but other than read out the altimeter and double check our heading, there wasn't much for me to do. It was all in Angel's capable hands.

This was the first time, since transitioning to civilian life and flying with a co-pilot, that I had ever surrendered the controls during landing. Control wasn't something I gave away, and considering most accidents happened during takeoff and landing, I felt better being in command during those parts of flight.

However, this was freakin' Angelica Mars, Angel of the Skies. She'd landed planes with broken landing gear, engines on fire, and that last mission. If she'd been a dude, I never would've handed over control during landing, but she rocked a quiet confidence I found sexy as hell.

Angel communicated with Air Traffic Control as they talked us down to the ground. With a perfect flair on the landing, we touched down like a feather. Normally, there's always a little bounce, but she had the touch of a pro. We taxied to the private terminal and pulled up outside our designated gate. Once there, I was finally able to speak freely.

"That was some damn spectacular flying, Angel."

"Thanks." Her kohl-brown eyes smiled back at me with true warmth. "I don't always get to land. Some people have problems handing over control, so thanks. It's my favorite part of flying."

I'd never been so happy to let go of my strangle hold for control. The joy in her eyes made my heart swell. And there was no way I was going to tell her that I was exactly like all the other pilots she'd flown with before.

"How long have you been with the company? I'd think you'd be up for captain soon."

"Maybe another year or two. You know how it goes? Gotta put your time in and start from scratch."

"I'm sure you have far more flying hours than I do."

She gave a shrug. "Probably, but flying a tanker doesn't come with the same fanfare as a jet."

"Does that ever piss you off?"

"Not really. I mean it would if it was any different for my male counterparts, but even they have to put the time in."

"I meant that fighter pilots get preferential treatment." I wanted to know if she felt I hadn't earned my status as captain.

"I guess that depends." She placed her hand on my forearm and I nearly jumped out of my skin.

I hadn't been expecting it and freaked out that she felt comfortable enough to touch me. I also got hard again. This woman's touch electrified me.

"I'm not one to stand around measuring dick sizes, so it's a little different for me. There's more than enough jealousy and competition floating around. Flying jets takes a certain skill set. You need to be cocky, ballsy, and top of your game. There's a gravitas that comes with that. I think civilian employers put more weight in that. I find if I focus on my own path, I generally get to where I want to go."

Her outlook floored me. Most men would be stirring up shit, jockeying for promotion, stepping on toes and making enemies. Not my Angel. She'd get there because it was what she'd earned.

We powered down the engines. I opened the exterior

door and lowered the airstairs while Angel finished locking down the jet.

"Awesome flight." Dex thrust his hand out. "Softest touchdown I've ever had."

I hooked a thumb over my shoulder. "Angel gave us that sweet landing."

Dex stepped around me and poked his head into the cockpit. "Perfect landing."

"Thank you, Mr. Truitt. I hope you have a great weekend. Take Georgina to the turtle conservatory. It's tons of fun. She'll get to hold baby turtles and they have a little cove if she's brave enough to snorkel with them."

"Thanks. That sounds like a lot of fun, and it's Dex, Angel."

"I know, *Mr. Truitt.*"

He gave a low laugh. "One day, Angel. One day."

"Have fun, Bianca!" Angel called out behind me.

Bianca Truitt held her daughter's hand and I bent down to say goodbye to the little girl.

"Did you enjoy the flight?"

"Oh, it was the bestest! Miss Kittie slept the whole way."

I ruffled the top of her head and leaned in to whisper in her ears. "Miss Angel just told your daddy about a place where you can hold turtles, but I happen to know you can ride dolphins right across the street. You should see if he'll take you there."

"Thanks, Logan." Bianca shook her head. "She doesn't need any encouragement." Bianca lifted on tiptoe to speak to Angel. "See you in a few days, Angel. Don't do anything I wouldn't!"

"Bye, Bianca. Have fun! Georgina, don't let Kittie get sunburned. You need to take care of her."

"I won't, Miss Angel." Georgina hopped down the steps as Bianca hurried after her.

"Time to go, Bandit." Dex went to collect Georgina's Hello Kittie backpack.

Their retired Greyhound stretched and eyed the open door. He sniffed the air and then cautiously walked to the front of the plane. Once he saw the outside, he raced down the stairs and danced around Bianca and Georgina who were waiting outside as a white SUV drove up.

"I'll get your bags." I headed down the stairs with a lightness in my step. For the next three days, I literally had nothing to do. Angel and I had to close up the jet, but then we'd be on our way to our hotel.

Our hotel.

The Truitt's were headed to a friend's house they were using for the weekend, but Angel and I were headed to a luxury resort. Typically, we stayed in cheaper hotels when clients required us to stay overnight, but Dex arranged for us to spend our time in the Caymans in style.

The least I could do was load their luggage into the back of their car. With a wave, and two blown kisses—one to Georgina and the other to her stuffed Hello Kittie—I sent them on their way.

"You're pretty good with kids."

I gave a start, because I hadn't heard Angel come down from the plane.

"I like kids." I wasn't ready to settle down and have any of my own, but I came from a big family and had helped to raise my younger sisters.

"That's sweet, but I think Georgina just found her first crush. She couldn't keep her eyes off of you."

"Georgina is sweet. She's going to give her father grief once she hits thirteen."

"Not many single guys are good with kids."

"I'm the middle child of nine. My four brothers are much older than me. Dylan is the closest in age, but he's six years older and I have four little sisters I got to spoil. Angie, next youngest, is six years younger than me. So, I was kind of in no-man's land growing up. Tons of siblings, but basically an only child because none of them were really close enough in age to be in my peer group."

"That's a lot of kids. Your poor mother…"

"Is a saint," I finished her sentence. "I have the best mother in the world."

"That sounds wonderful." There was a smile on her face, but it got lost in her words.

I had a sense that would be a question for later.

"How do we look?" I glanced back at the jet. There wasn't much we needed to do. The ground crew secured it as we spoke and we wouldn't refuel until just prior to departure. Mechanics would take a look at it later today.

"Ready to go. Just need to get our bags."

"I'll grab them."

She packed light for a girl. When I retrieved the Truitt's bags, I set hers on the ground beneath the fuselage. I carried an over the shoulder bag, but she had one of those small rolling bags.

"I'm assuming we're sharing a ride?"

There was no reason to take two taxis to the hotel.

"Yeah, I'm ready to unwind."

"Me too." It was late afternoon, perfect timing to head to the hotel, have a drink, grab a bite to eat, and spend the rest of the night with an angel.

We walked through the private terminal and I called us a cab. In less than an hour, mostly due to traffic, we were pulling up to the hotel.

"Wow," she said, "Mr. Truitt went all out."

"Yeah, better than a roach coach. On the beach and everything." I pointed through the breezeway of the hotel lobby. "And I see a beach bar. What do you say? Ready to buy me that drink you owe me?"

She glanced at the bar, her gaze lingered for a moment before her brows drew together.

"I think I'll take a rain check. I'm going to head upstairs, take a shower, and chill."

At the mention of her stripping out of her clothes for a shower, my dick took notice. But I wasn't letting her get away that easily.

"You owe me a drink. Don't think you're getting out of it."

"Insistent, aren't you?"

"Well, it's not often a woman buys me a drink."

"I bet." She headed to reception. "How about we check in and deal with the drink later."

I felt her slipping away. If I didn't get her to commit, the next time I'd see her was on takeoff. How was I going to get her to lower some of those shields?

"How about we make a deal?"

Her left eyebrow lifted with interest. "A deal?"

"If I promise to keep my junk in my jeans and be the perfect gentlemen, will you agree to have a drink with me?"

"Your junk in your jeans?" She gave one of those adorable little snorts I was quickly falling in love with.

"Prick in my pants?"

"That's worse!" She slapped my arm.

"Contain my cock?"

We were drawing stares, but I wasn't backing down. There was only one acceptable outcome to this exchange.

"Stop it!" Her laughter intensified and it only made her more beautiful.

"Stable the Stallion?"

"Oh my God, stop!"

"Good," I said with a laugh. "I was running out of things to say."

"All right, flyboy." She lifted her index finger. "One drink, but that's it."

"Nope. The deal was for a drink and dinner."

"I don't remember dinner being mentioned. You get one drink then I'm calling it a night."

Deflated that she didn't warm up to my dinner suggestion, I decided to take the win.

"Meet me in the bar in ten?"

"Make it an hour. I still want that shower."

"Fine. One hour. I need a shower too. Might as well beat the meat and relieve some of this tension."

"You're incorrigible!"

"Hey, I try."

The receptionist, who had been quiet during our exchange, couldn't resist a smirk. Pretty and blonde, she was exactly the kind of woman I would normally entice into my bed. She slid Angel's card key over then turned to check me into my room.

Angel didn't bother waiting and headed upstairs.

"If you need any help…" The receptionist made an exaggerated show of checking me out, allowing her gaze to linger on the prominent bulge in my pants. "I can take a break."

Normally, I would have taken her up on the offer, headed upstairs and done a number of dirty things with her, but my dick deflated thinking about doing any of those things with her.

Was it broken?

I'd never had that reaction before. Always, when faced with a surefire lay, I rose to the opportunity. I glanced over my shoulder to the elevator doors which opened and took

Angel from my view.

What had this woman done to me?

Up in my room, I placed my bag on the counter and took a look at what I'd brought. Knowing I was going to spend three days in the Caymans, my overnight bag held shorts, swim trunks, an assortment of tee-shirts and nothing suitable for a first date.

Not that this was a date.

I practically strong-armed Angel into one drink, but if I could get through one drink, it could turn to two. Two drinks could turn into dinner and after that?

Shit, I wasn't going to make it through the next hour without relieving the tension wound up in my body and centered in my cock. If Angel was taking a shower, I would too, and I would pretend she was in there with me.

Shedding my clothes, I turned on the shower and waited for the water to get warm. My hand cupped my balls and a groan escaped my lips. This wouldn't take long. Jerking off to thoughts of sharing a shower with Angel would have me blowing a load before I could blink.

Easy boy.

I had to slow this down. The bathroom quickly filled with steam and I entered the glass shower. Using the hotel's ample supply of shampoo, I wrapped my fist around my cock and uttered the first of many moans as my heart hammered beneath my breastbone.

Dark eyes. Raven-black hair. Lips I couldn't wait to taste. My thoughts spiraled into oblivion as my hand ran up and down my shaft. Leaning against the shower wall, my right hand slowly stroked up and down.

The speed of my pumping slowly increased and the intensity of my strokes nearly sent me over the edge. My breathing became labored as I tightened my grip and closed my eyes. My chest heaved and her name burst past my lips on hoarse gasps of air.

"Angel. Fuck. Angel."

Furiously, my hand accelerated, stroking blindly as images of Angel flew through my head. I imagined fucking her against the wall, sending her to her knees, taking her against the counter, and saying hell to it all and laying her out on the floor.

"So close."

I reached down to cup my balls as everything in the world faded away. Pumping faster, my breathing became even more ragged as I murmured her name over and over again.

My orgasm slammed into me and spurts of cum shot into the air. My knees nearly buckled, my legs were shaking hard and I slid down to the floor as I braced my elbows on my knees. Placing my head in my hands, my entire body trembled, because I had to face a very sobering truth.

Angel had gotten under my skin.

7

ANGEL

A PERSISTENT BASTARD, IT DIDN'T SEEM LIKE I WOULD BE getting rid of Logan anytime soon. Hopes for *not* seeing him during our downtime went right out the window when he insisted I buy him that damn drink.

What exactly had I said?

I couldn't remember exactly.

Regardless, we had three days stretching out before us while the Truitt's enjoyed their mini-family vacation. The hotel upgrade was pretty slick and I'd have to remember to thank Mr. Truitt when I saw him again.

Meanwhile, what was I going to do with the next three days? More importantly, how was I going to minimize interactions with Logan? The man was getting under my skin.

Quick with the innuendos, he kept a smile on my face and a steady throb between my legs.

Which, when I really thought about it, was unusual in and of itself.

I chose a male-dominated career, but never let my male coworkers get to me. During my time in the Air Force, I'd been subjected to numerous unwanted sexual advances. Fortunately, the Air Force had strict regulations about fraternization. It kept most men on their toes.

Not that some didn't try. Those assholes, and their flirtatious conversation, felt more like fingernails scratching against a chalkboard and they soon learned to leave me alone.

But Logan?

He was different. Probably because he was the first man with whom I considered giving in to the flirtation to see where it might lead.

His voice, liquid smooth, and his eyes, full of mischief and fun, combined with the genuineness in his smile to make me feel as if I was the only woman in the world.

He's a player.

I know.

Hell I knew, and therein lay the problem, because I should walk away.

Did I want to be just another one of his nameless one-night stands? If I did anything now, it would be one night followed by two agonizing days and then another six-hour flight home. I'd have to sit beside him the whole flight and pretend he hadn't used me to get his rocks off.

But you'd be using him too.

That little voice in my head didn't seem to want to shut up and I really needed it to be quiet because I was beginning to think it might be right.

What would be wrong if I indulged in an evening of gratuitous sex with Logan? What harm could come from that?

Tons.

I shook my head thinking about all those old cartoons where there was an angel and a devil sitting on the character's shoulders. I seemed to have picked up a pair of conflicting voices. One wanted me to go for it and the other said *Hell-to-the-No!*

One hour.

Time was ticking down until I had to face the man I couldn't seem to stop obsessing over.

One drink.

I only owed him one drink. That's right, it came back to me, I'd been bitchy and insulted him. No insults tonight. I would be professional, personable—without leading him on —and we would separate for the duration and go our own ways.

I took a long shower and washed my hair. The hotel had the most amazing shampoo and conditioner. It smelled of lilac and rose; invigorating and I felt a need for the touch of something feminine.

Out of the shower, I took a look at what I'd packed. Knowing I was headed to the Caymans, I had packed light. Shorts, tank tops, a bikini, and one black dress. Not the most inspired wardrobe, and the dress may have been a little slinkier than I would have liked, but my mother had always told me to never travel without a little black dress.

Versatile and multifunctional, it could go from the beach to a five-star restaurant with nothing but a change of footwear. Which was a problem. I had my sandals, and I wore my boots, but I'd forgotten to take my heels.

Well shit.

But maybe this was good? If I showed up at the bar in a little black dress and three inch heels, that would definitely give Logan the wrong idea. Slipping on the sandals, I took a moment to check myself out in the mirror.

If I was going for the plain Jane look, this was it, but I kind of wanted to put a little more effort into this very odd date.

It's not a date!

I know!

Digging back through my bag, I retrieved my minimalistic makeup and spent a few minutes lining my eyes and putting on eye shadow. That's all I was going to do, but then I decided on a little blush. Since I was doing that, I might as well go for lipstick. Just enough.

When I stood back from the mirror, I couldn't help but smile. I looked hot. What would Logan think?

You're not supposed to care what he thinks.

Except I did.

A glance at the clock and I was twenty minutes late for

our rendezvous. My lips curved into a grin and I took one last look in the mirror.

It was good to make him wait.

With a flutter in my belly, I headed downstairs and followed the sound of people laughing. There was a crowd at the bar and music pumped through the speakers. People were smiling and having a good time, but a quick glance around and I saw no sign of Logan.

Odd.

There was an open space at the bar, a row of three empty barstools, and I headed to the one in the middle. My antisocial tendencies were in full force, but I wasn't here to meet people.

Yes, you are.

Logan is not people.

"Can I get you something?" The bartender placed a coaster in front of me.

I wasn't ready to order, but he stood there with an expectant expression. If I had this drink, would that count as the one I shared with Logan? Was it wise to get ahead of him in alcohol consumption? Good question, and I already knew the answer to that.

"What's your special?" I asked.

He wiped the counter. "Mango margarita is our special for the night, or I can whip you up a Mai Tai."

A man slipped into the stool beside me. Clean shaven, average height and build, he wore a suit despite the humidity. He was so pedestrian as to be unremarkable, except his presence buzzed all around me like a fly I couldn't swat.

That seat was for Logan, not a stranger.

He checked me out, eyes traveling from my face to my cleavage, where they stopped and lingered. It made me uncomfortable and I lifted my hand to fiddle with my necklace.

He lifted a finger to get the bartender's attention, but his eyes are all on me. "Corona and whatever the lady is having."

I turned to the suit. "Oh, that's sweet, but…"

"Hun, you look like you need a drink and a pretty lady like you should never drink alone." He extended his hand. "Clive Lowens at your service."

"Angelique." I didn't feel like giving him my full name.

His clammy hand engulfed mine and I shifted a little away. Instead of discouraging him, he leaned into the gap and swept a lock of my hair off my shoulder. A shudder rippled down my spine.

"I'm meeting someone." Maybe that would get him off my back.

"No problem, until they arrive, allow me to buy you a drink and keep you company."

It felt rude to refuse. "I'll have that mango margarita."

The bartender went to fix our drinks. I turned around to see if Logan had arrived, but there was no sign of the cocky pilot.

Clive leaned forward again, invading my personal space.

His breaths puffed out with the scent of whiskey flooding my senses. How many drinks had he had? Evidently, enough to think he had a chance with me.

To his credit, he was a charmer. He had that twinkle in his eyes and a voice smooth as silk, husky even, and he talked as if we were already in bed rather than sitting at a bar. He had confidence and an air of power, maybe too much power, because he hit on me as if it was already a done deal.

If he touched my bare shoulder again, I was going to pop him in the chin.

His finger lifted to do just that when the bartender returned. I took my drink and sipped at the straw. By the way Clive watched my lips wrap around the straw, that was a bad idea. I picked up the straw and laid it down on the counter.

Pegging the creep meter pretty hard, he had me weighing exit strategies, but because I'd allowed him to buy me a drink, I didn't think I could leave. I should, but I'd been raised to play nice.

The way he stared at me, hungry and on the prowl with his false smile and oily eyes, made me feel uncomfortable. He watched me like a wolf might observe its prey, with a smile which didn't quite reach his eyes, and he was doing more than just taking me in like a normal person.

I looked for reasons to leave. Any excuse would do, and since Logan seemed to have stood me up, I was even more eager to spend the rest of the night alone in my room away from predators in a bar.

Clive reached out, taking my hand in his, but when I tried to yank free, he tightened his grip. "How about we get out of here, hun, I've got a suite with a bed, and all night to—"

"Honey!" A loud voice called out from behind me, cutting Clive off. "Forgive me, I got hung up."

Clive scowled at the newcomer and I turned to see Logan striding toward me. I'd never been so happy to see one of my coworkers. He took one look at Clive and his brows drew together.

Shifting his attention to me, his left eyebrow hooked up, as if asking if I was okay. I gave a tiny shake of my head.

Clive puffed out his chest as Logan approached. "The lady has a date." His grip around my wrist tightened and he tried to pull me to my feet.

Darkness loomed in Logan's eyes and he stepped in front of Clive. Logan hooked his arm around my waist and swept me off the barstool. He deposited me on my feet as my entire world shifted.

"Is this guy bothering you?"

Yes!

"We were just sharing a drink while waiting for you." Logan needed to know I didn't appreciate him leaving me hanging.

"Hey man, I was here first." Clive tapped Logan on the shoulder, asserting his claim.

"Let's see what the lady thinks about that."

Logan grabbed me by the waist and pulled me tight against his chest. His hand gripped my hair and he looked at me in a way which melted me from the inside out.

A small, but teasing smile, crept across his face as goosebumps lined my skin. Not the kind I got when I was cold but the other kind, the kind one gets when nothing else matters except what happens next.

And I had every expectation Logan had something up his sleeve. He cupped my face and tightened his grip on my hair. My heart-rate accelerated and it had nothing to do with fear, but rather from the sudden rush of electricity racing through my body.

Logan reoriented my face, putting it exactly where he wanted. The smile disappeared, his signature smirk was gone, leaving only the intensity of his gaze and the promise of an inferno to come.

If I'd been smart, I would have pulled back.

Poor Clive certainly seemed to be pushing away from the bar. Only I wasn't smart. It was impossible to think with the frenzy of sparks going off in my head. The feel of Logan's hands upon me rocked my world and before I realized it, my head tilted back and my lips parted.

Thoughts of right and wrong melted away as his lips crashed down upon mine with a kiss steeped in passion and primed to ignite a firestorm.

I gripped his arm, not sure if I really wanted this kiss. I

certainly didn't understand it, except Logan swept in out of nowhere to save me from one royal creep of a man.

My heart skipped a beat as his lips slid against mine in a full-on, open-mouthed kiss. There was no teasing licks, no hesitation. In fact, Logan appeared starved for the taste of me.

And I loved it.

I loved everything about it, how my small body pressed against his hard physique, how our lips fit together, how his dark and sultry taste overwhelmed my senses, and how he played with my hair, holding it tighter and tighter as he deepened the kiss.

When we broke away, he looked at me with a smoldering gaze.

"Now that was worth it." Logan turned to Clive Nobody. "She's taken. Shove off."

Clive retreated in a huff as I sat frozen in Logan's embrace.

Did that really happen?

From the bruising of my lips to the taste of him which still lingered on my lips, it had. Logan leaned in until our foreheads touched. He closed his eyes and his breaths shook.

"Damn, Angel, but you taste like heaven."

"Why did you do that?" My voice broke barely above a whisper.

"Kiss you?" His voice was low and husky, hungry too.

"Yes." My voice wavered.

"To get Mr. No Personality to leave you alone. It looked

like you needed a savior. Besides, I didn't like the way he was touching you." He ran a finger up my arm, swept it along my collar bone, and swirled it in the hollow of my throat. I shivered beneath the sensual touch. "I don't regret it either."

We pulled apart, each taking shaky, shallow breaths.

"You shouldn't have."

"But I did, and you liked it. Don't pretend you didn't feel that too."

"It can't happen again." I tried to make my voice sound firm and strong, but it cracked and shook as my gaze lingered on his lips. Lips which had kissed me. Lips that I wanted to taste again.

I pushed my barely touched drink over to him.

"One drink, as promised." Then I shoved against his chest and took a step back. I followed that with another and then another, slowly regaining my balance as the entire world tilted around me. Damn, the man could kiss.

Leaving Logan at the bar, I made my exit and practically ran to the elevators. A quick glance over my shoulder revealed no pursuit. I wasn't sure why that bothered me as much as it did, but I knew one thing.

Logan Reid was a very dangerous man.

8

LOGAN

Gobsmacked.

Kissing Angel had not been what I planned and yet it completely rocked my world. My plan for a slow, relentless attack failed miserably.

Hell, I marched in there and lit an inferno.

But what was I expected to do?

That asshole in a suit had his hands on Angel and, from her stiff body language, she wasn't pleased.

I didn't know for certain, but it wasn't hard to read the signs.

So, I did what any man would do. I marched in there and laid claim to what was mine, leaving no doubt in that asshole's mind that Angel belonged to me.

I kissed her.

I fucking kissed her, and it wasn't a light and tender kiss.

The moment I had her in my arms, I was a goner because the sweetness of her lips flooded my senses. There was no going back. As soon as her body yielded, and pressed against mine, I lost my fucking mind.

Sweet? That was an understatement.

She tasted like heaven.

So why the hell was I standing at the bar with my dick hard and my girl gone?

Good fucking question.

She shoved her drink at me and ran away. I should have gone after her. I should go after her now, but I sensed that would be the worst possible thing I could do. Instead, I stood at the bar with her drink freezing my hand and sipped a syrupy-sweet mango-fucking-rita like an idiot.

If only I had been on time.

Fucking Gabriel and his phone call.

My eldest brother had to brag about his good news. Baby number four was on the way. I think he and his wife, Veronica, were trying to outdo our parents and crank out kids as fast as possible. The baby was due around Thanksgiving and he asked me to be its godfather.

Gabriel and Veronica were working down the sibling list, assigning us as godparents to each child as their family grew. Two of my sisters were married, one was engaged, and Lizzy was fresh out of high school. She had some time before the family pressured her to get hitched. Except for Gabriel, none of my brothers seemed interested in getting hitched.

Gabriel remained tactful, but he clearly felt a little uncomfortable entrusting the life of his child to a brother who had never had a steady girlfriend and had failed time and again to bring a girl home to meet the family.

I might be a success in my career, but in my family's eyes I fell short in one major category. I suppose that made me unstable, which made the whole godfather thing a touchy subject.

"Can I get you something?" The bartender removed Angel's drink leaving me to stare. When had I sucked down all that frozen mess?

"Yes, give me a crown and coke." I needed a real drink. "And make it a double."

That conversation with Gabriel screwed up my evening with Angel, because he talked my ear off. I swore he couldn't get to the point if it killed him. There was always a story, and that story needed a story to set it up.

If I'd been on time, the asshole in the suit would have never moved in on my girl.

So, what do I do now?

We had three days in the Caymans and I'd lost my opportunity to corral Angel into spending more time with me. Or had I?

My thoughts churned while I sipped at my drink.

Twice, young women approached the bar, sliding into the seat next to me. Twice they tried to get me to buy them drinks. Normally, one or both of them would have wound up in my bed, but I wasn't feeling it. And I didn't buy them any drinks.

Instead, I headed upstairs alone and set an early alarm.

Not knowing Angel's morning routine, I set my alarm ridiculously early. Up, shaved, and dressed for pretty much anything, I waited in the lobby with a direct view of the elevators. When Angel came down, I would see her. And I made good use of my time, talking to the concierge to set up a couple activities. If we didn't do them, no sweat off my back, but I wanted to have something in reserve.

The breakfast hour came and went with no Angel in sight. I squirmed on the couch, wondering if I should go to her room. One problem with that, she'd headed upstairs last night before I could get her room number and I hadn't been on top of my game to peek at it when the receptionist handed over the keycard.

I tried.

I tried to get them to tell me what room Angel was in, but I wasn't able to charm the burly clerk who manned the desk this morning.

Getting frustrated, I took a walk around the lobby and found myself wandering out toward the beach. The warmth of the sun kissed my face and the gentle breeze blowing off the ocean lifted my hair and ruffled the fabric of my shirt.

Bright and piercing, I covered my eyes with my hand to shield them against the sun and peered out at the waves slowly rolling in. It really was a picture-perfect day.

With the beach relatively protected by an outer barrier

reef, the waves hitting the shore were tiny things, but exciting enough for the kids who jumped through them and tried to bodysurf what amounted to little more than a ripple. A few adults swam further out, stretching graceful arms overhead as they traversed the shoreline with long, fluid strokes and powerful kicks

Patient mothers and fathers huddled beneath the protective shade of their rented umbrellas while snapping pictures of their kids having fun.

For the first time ever, I felt like maybe Gabriel might be right. Was I missing out on an important piece of life? But I had never felt that urge to settle down.

Then I saw my angel rising out of the waves. She'd been one of the swimmers cutting through the crystal-clear waters.

Had she been out here all this time?

What a vision.

A bikini stretched across her hips. The tiny triangle of red seemed to reveal more than it hid, but all the fun parts remained covered, much to my chagrin. And the bikini top cupped breasts I couldn't wait to explore. They were the perfect size to fit in my hands, not too big, nor too small.

She wiped the water from her face with her eyes closed as she stood in thigh-deep water, then she ran her fingers over her head, wringing out the water from her hair.

My jaw dropped and my heart-rate accelerated. I placed my hands over my crotch to hide the sudden tightening in my pants. Perpetually hard seemed to be my curse when around her.

When her eyes opened, our gazes collided across the beach. Her mouth dropped into an 'O' of surprise and then she hesitated.

No. No. No. We couldn't have that. I didn't want her overthinking our kiss last night. Well, that wasn't true. I wanted her to think about nothing but our kiss.

Hell, I hadn't stopped thinking about it, and I'd jacked off to fantasies of what should have come next several times before finally falling asleep.

I raised my arm overhead, although there was no need, and waved at her. She lifted her hand and gave a much more reserved finger wave back. With nowhere to go, she glanced over her shoulder before heading out of the water.

Not knowing which of the empty chairs with beach towels belonged to her, I shoved my hands into my pockets and slowly approached. She angled a little to the left where a lounge chair sat with a towel folded on top.

Bending over, I admired the gentle curves of her body, then gave a groan when she wrapped the towel around her waist. She glanced down as I drew near.

"Good morning, luv," I said.

"Good morning, Logan."

"I didn't realize you were already up and out. I was waiting for you."

From the way her eyes widened, it may have been a mistake to admit I'd been waiting on her, but I didn't care. It was too late to pretend there wasn't something between us. Although from the look on her face, she was ready to backpedal and pretend it didn't happen.

"I got up early for a run and morning swim. I've been up since six."

"Early riser."

"Old habits. When I was in the Air Force, we did PT at six. Never really got out of the habit."

I understood that. Squadron physical training was a mandatory event for most of the Air Force. After getting out of the Navy, however, I shifted my running and gym time to the evening.

"I never liked working out in the morning."

She took the towel to her hair, pressing the wet strands in the soft cotton. I took the opportunity to watch her tits sway back and forth and to admire the creamy expanse of her tight and toned stomach. I wanted to slip my finger beneath the edge of that bikini, but resisted that urge.

"I find it relaxes me. You know, gets rid of any tension I might be carrying from the previous day. Then I feel like I've accomplished something first thing in the morning."

"Speaking of morning, I had some ideas how we can spend ours."

"Logan..."

I lifted a hand, palm out. "I'm talking about things we can do around town, although if you're offering to head back upstairs..." I left the rest unsaid and studied her reaction.

She curled her lower lip between her teeth and glanced at her toes as she dug them into the sand. "About that, I just don't think it's a good idea for us to socialize outside of work."

"Fuck that, you're not going to brush me off like that, not after that kiss."

"A kiss you stole."

"A kiss which saved you from an asshole."

"I was handling that situation."

"Oh, I'm sure that's exactly what that asshole was hoping for…for you to *handle* him."

"Your mind is perpetually in the gutter."

"With no hope of getting out while I'm with you."

"Which is exactly why we shouldn't hang out."

"I'm not talking about hanging out." Shit, that's what college kids did. I intended to drown in her presence until I couldn't breathe anything but her. "I'm talking about spending the day together."

"Same thing."

"Totally different."

She nibbled at her lower lip and I held back a groan. Angel was a knockout in her baggy flight suit, but in that little red bikini, with a towel draped over her shoulder, I could barely breathe next to her stunning beauty.

"About last night…" she began.

"That kiss happened, Angel. I swooped in to save you, you're welcome by the way, and I take full responsibility for that kiss. You can't pretend it didn't happen, or that you didn't like it half as much as I did."

I fucking loved that kiss. I ached to kiss her again and kept my hands to myself only with great difficulty. "But that's not what I want right now."

"It's not?"

I rolled my shoulders back. "Okay, I'd fucking love to kiss you again, but that display might be a little too much P.D.A. for a beach like this."

"I haven't heard that in a while." Her cheeks flushed and she could barely look me in the eye. I bet she was thinking about that kiss.

"Come on." I stretched out my hand. "Same rules as before. I'll keep my—"

She held up a finger. "Oh no you don't. We're not talking about junk, pricks, cocks, or stallions or it's a no go."

"Well, that's no fun."

"Promise?"

"Well, since I'm not wearing jeans, pants, or have a stable nearby…"

She burst out in laughter. "I don't even know why I try."

"You try because you're secretly infatuated with me, and you're already wondering when I'm going to kiss you again."

"That's not what I'm thinking."

I lifted my brows. "I like where your mind is headed, but we have the whole day ahead of us. We can wait for the sexy-times later."

"Sexy-times? You do realize when you say it like that the sexiness factor turns into a negative number?"

"I'm not worried." I turned toward the hotel and gestured for her to head back. "Come on, let's get you dressed. I have a full day planned."

"You do?"

"Most definitely."

"Were you feeling a bit cocky? What if I had said no?"

"Technically, you haven't said yes yet, but I'm not worried. It's going to be a kickass day, and what else are you going to do? Sit under the sun and burn to a crisp?"

"I was thinking about reading a book."

"You can do that anywhere. This is the Grand Caymans! And we have shit to do."

She paused for a moment, as if considering whether to put her foot down and stick with the dumb book, but I knew I had her. She was dying to see what I had come up with. I just hoped it wasn't totally lame.

When we got to the lobby, I waited with her by the elevators. The chime dinged and she stepped on board. I did not.

"You're not coming up?"

"If that's an invitation to join you in your room, it's going to make it incredibly *hard* for me to keep my promise about…you know." I made a gesture toward my groin. "I'll wait for you here."

"Okay."

"And Angel…"

"Yeah?"

"Keep the suit on. I plan on getting you wet several times today."

Her eyes widened and her pert, luscious lips rounded into an 'O' of surprise. I gave a snicker as the elevator doors closed, then reached down to readjust my erection.

9

ANGEL

Logan was going to make me wet?

One look into his magnetic eyes and I was a goner.

He came looking for me on the beach and planned out a couple activities for us. My tummy did a little flip knowing he'd been thinking of me. Truthfully, I hadn't been able to stop thinking about him all night.

That kiss.

It did something to me, shifted the foundation of my world, and pierced the defenses I'd set in place. I felt like a school girl flirting with the new boy in town.

A tiny giggle escaped me as I practically pranced down the hall to my hotel room. It was everything I could do not to skip.

I hadn't felt like this since Danny Long asked me to the

prom. Giddy and light, I couldn't wait to see what Logan had planned.

But I wasn't wearing my tiny red bikini for our day out, not with the way he devoured my body and practically eye-fucked me on the beach. I couldn't, because my body heated under that gaze. It wanted something I wasn't ready to give.

That kiss.

I hadn't stopped thinking about it since last night. Really, the best thing right now would be to march downstairs and put my foot down. Tell Logan we couldn't socialize outside of work, sit my ass on the beach and read a trashy novel. The only problem was any trashy novel I read would have me thinking about that damn kiss.

Three days was a very long time to avoid someone. And really, I'd like to think I wasn't that immature. I could do this. I could spend the day with Logan and keep things professional.

You're not a very good liar.

That was true. But what I could do was be strategic about how this day panned out. He said he was going to make me wet. With all the innuendos he spouted, he clearly had something planned involving water. From the way he devoured me in my bikini, and the heat licking along my skin beneath that stare, I needed to be smart and I kind of felt like being a little bit of a pain in the ass.

Logan was always getting the upper hand with me, teasing me until my cheeks turned bright red. I could have fun too, and denying him something he obviously wanted seemed like exactly the right kind of payback.

Fortunately, I had the perfect solution. Digging through my bag, I pulled out a pair of neoprene swim shorts and a bright yellow tank top. Not a bikini top, but a modest swim tank. The neoprene shorts were comfortable enough to wear all day long and served the secondary role as a swimsuit.

I'd get wet, all right, but I'd be the one making Logan squirm.

Not needing much beyond an ID, some cash, and a credit card, it didn't take long to pack my fanny pack. It was far from sexy, but that was the point. Time to douse the inferno brewing between Logan and I.

When I returned downstairs, Logan turned and his jaw dropped when he took in my attire.

"What the fuck is this?"

I made a show of spinning in a circle. "What do you think? Practical and waterproof."

"I was expecting tiny short shorts, some barely-there top with that fabulous red bikini poking out, but what is this? You're wrapped in neoprene?"

"I thought this would be safer."

"Safer?"

"Yup," I gave a knowing look and meant to hold his gaze, but my eyes dipped down to take in the fullness of his lips. I squeezed my thighs together against the sudden ache. This was going to be a very long day.

"You're killing me, Smalls."

"Hey, you promised to keep it in your pants. I'm just trying to make things a little easier on you."

"That's…" He made a vague gesture toward my outfit, "not easier. It's a fucking disappointment."

"You say the sweetest things." I flashed him a smile. "Take it or leave it, but this is what you get."

"I *can* keep it in my pants," he said with a frown. "You didn't have to steal my eye candy for the day."

"Come on, flyboy, close that jaw and settle down. After that kiss, we can both use a breather."

"At least we sorted that out."

"What's that?"

"That kiss rocked both our worlds."

"We're going to pretend it never happened."

He shook his head. "Not going to happen. There's no way I'm forgetting how perfect you felt in my arms, how fucking amazing you tasted, or how your breathy little moans made my dick stand up and take notice."

"Breathy moans?" My voice rose with indignation. "I did not…"

He lifted his finger. "Yes, you did, and don't worry I'm satisfied doing the five-knuckle hustle thinking about those moans for now."

"The five-knuckle hustle?"

"You know the fist jam?"

"The what?" I knew what he meant, I'd just never heard it called that before. But he not only continued, he picked up steam.

"Jerkin the gherkin, slam the clam, slap the salami, spank the monkey, wax on whack off, adjust the antennae, badger the witness, beat the bishop, crank the shaft, flog the hog, slay the snake…"

"Oh, my God, stop!" I shoved him back and glanced around the hotel lobby, mortified if anyone listened in to our conversation about male masturbation.

"What?" He gave me an innocent look. "What's wrong?"

"You know exactly what's wrong. What if a kid hears you?"

"I love when you blush." He glanced around the relatively empty lobby then turned his attention to my chest. "Not a kid in sight, luv. We're safe."

"I'm not blushing." Heat filled my cheeks, and if heat filled my cheeks, it was a sure thing that blush extended down my neck to my chest. From the direction of Logan's rapt gaze, he was following the path of that blush with avid interest.

"This is going to be a very long day," I said with a sigh.

"Oh, I hope so. I mean, if you want to come back early for some aggressive cuddling and adult nap time we can, but I've got some pretty cool stuff planned."

"Aggressive cuddling?"

He pointed to a young couple who exited the elevators with their two boys. "Trying to keep my language clean, sweets. You know, so the wee-ones don't know we're talking about taking an afternoon delight."

"Afternoon delight? Where do you get this?"

"What about assault with a friendly weapon? Although, seeing how the stallion has been put in the stable, you'll have to wait if you want me to attack the pink fortress."

I pulled him toward the exit. "You have got to stop."

"Why? It's so much fun watching you blush."

"You're having too much fun, flyboy."

"And loving every minute of it."

"Is it a boy thing?"

"Wanting sex with a beautiful woman?" He scratched the back of his head. "Usually that's a man thing, and I score *big* in that department."

I rolled my eyes. "That's not what I meant."

He flashed a wicked grin. "What did you mean, then?"

"Do you guys go to a special school to learn all that shit?"

"You mean about making amorous congress, a bit of the old in-out, in-out, or the more popular bow-chick-a-wow-wow?"

"I'm sure you've got tons more, but how about less of the bedroom rodeo talk and more of the two adults going out on the town kind of stuff."

"I don't know, that's kind of fun stuff for two adults to do."

"Okay, how about what's first on your list for today?"

His eyes twinkled. "Oh, I'm making a list for sexy-time."

"I have no doubt, but if you don't have anything planned for today, there's a good book waiting for me."

No way was I picking up a romance novel. Not with thoughts of Logan swirling in my head.

He reached down and took my hand in his. Instant heat licked up my arm, and I should have pulled away, but it felt too damn good. The doorman called us a cab and Logan held the door to the car while I slipped inside, reluctantly releasing my hand to do so.

After buckling in, I turned to him. "Where are we headed?"

"Do you want it to be a surprise, or want me to tell you now?"

"I'm not really good with surprises."

"That's fair." He seemed to have sobered up, dropping the teasing with a thousand and one ways to say sex. "You mentioned to Georgina about the turtle conservatory. I've been to the Caymans a few times and always drove past it, but I've never been to it. They let you hold turtles and swim with them. I thought that would be kind of cool. It's also *very* public, which makes it safe for us to be together."

"Safe?"

"Yeah, no way am I behaving if we ever get to a place where we're alone. I can still taste you on my lips, luv. So fucking sweet."

"Public sounds just about right." I gripped his hand. "It would be really cool to see turtles. I've never been. I just read about it and thought it sounded neat."

"Great, something we get to experience together for the first time, you know…like two turtle virgins."

"Turtle virgins!" I burst out laughing.

Logan couldn't help himself. The man was sex walking on a stick with his mind perpetually in the gutter.

"You know what they say about virgins?" I said.

He glanced at me with an expectant expression, but didn't jump in with a sexual innuendo. When he didn't answer, I continued.

"The first time isn't usually that great. There's a lot of fumbling around looking for the right hole and it's usually over before it begins."

He lifted my hand to his mouth and feathered kisses along the back of my knuckles. "Hun, I'm going to blow your mind. I'm not a one pump and done kind of guy. The slow burn can be a bit frustrating, but sometimes the prize at the end is worth the wait. I'll tone it down for the day if that makes you more comfortable. I was just having fun back there. It's hard when I know what I want."

With his lips pressed against my knuckles, I momentarily lost the ability to think. Only after he lowered my hand and released it did I realize he'd said anything at all.

"Thanks." I cleared my throat, and wanted to tell him it was okay.

I enjoyed his banter, but that wasn't what I said. As a matter of fact, as the taxi wound through morning traffic, I said very little and picked at the hem of my neoprene shorts. I wished I'd worn my bikini instead. I was flustered, hot, and bothered.

We settled into a somewhat awkward silence. I could tell

Logan wanted to talk, but he pulled back and stared out the window. Every now and then, he pointed out something interesting, but for the most part we settled in for the duration of the ride.

We drove along the famous Seven Mile Beach and passed through the hotel zone. Tour buses parked outside the Governor's Residence unloaded eager tourists who stopped to snap photos.

Flashes of the beach peeked between the rows of hotels and we travelled through a residential area where narrow passages between properties provided public beach access.

The cab had no air conditioning, so we had the windows rolled down. The sounds of automobiles intermingled with the steady rush of wind blowing off the ocean.

It was a picture-perfect day; blue sky, brilliant sun, and a smattering of puffy clouds drifting lazily across the sky. While turtles sounded fun, I kind of wanted to spend a little more time on the beach. This place was a paradise meant to be ingested and appreciated.

Finally, our driver pulled up to the Cayman Island's Turtle Farm. Logan paid the fare while I stretched my legs.

"Hey, we're in luck." He came to my side and reached for my hand. "No cruise ships in town. Shouldn't be a crowd."

I squeezed his hand, marveling at how natural it felt to be holding hands. "Crowds don't really bother me."

"They don't?"

"Well, sometimes, I guess, but I enjoy watching other people having a great time. People watching can be fun."

"That's insanely odd. I prefer to avoid crowds. I guess that makes me a bit selfish?"

"I don't think so." I glanced toward the entrance. "Not everyone likes crowds."

"Have you read up on this place?" He shifted topics.

"A long time ago. All I really remember is that you get to touch turtles."

"And more. We're going to swim with them."

"Really?"

"Yes. It's the first time I'm getting you wet today."

It wouldn't be the first time, but there was no way I would share that with him.

He pulled me toward the ticket booth, and before I could protest and pay my own way, he bought two tickets for access to the entire park.

"They have a turtle lagoon where we can snorkel with the fully grown turtles and of course the touch pool where we get to hold the babies. There's also a pool with a water slide if you're interested."

His excitement was infectious and I couldn't wait to explore the park with him. It would mean so much more than coming here myself like I'd originally planned.

"A pool seems kind of *meh* compared to swimming with turtles."

"I know, but it has a water slide. I hear it's pretty *slick*."

"Slick?"

"Yeah, slippery wet, tons of fun to ride."

"It's impossible for you to stop, isn't it?"

"I'm really going to *blow* your mind later."

"Really?"

"Yes, but you have to wait for that one. We need an adequate buildup first. Come on Turtle Virgin, let's go."

We gathered with several other tourists as we waited for our guide. Our ticket included a brief tour until we were cut lose to explore at our leisure. The guide explained the purpose behind the turtle conservatory, how it was really a breeding and research center. All the other stuff was just a way to get tourists in to help pay the bills.

While our guide talked about turtle breeding programs, Logan and I watched a pair of iguanas sunning themselves. We took pictures, getting as close as the lizards would allow, and obediently followed our tour guide until we got to the coolest part.

"We ask that you wash your hands and feet before and after entering the holding tanks..." Our guide showed us where to wash and how to hold the baby turtles. "You must hold them over the water the entire time. Do not hold them over the concrete. Our staff will assist you."

I glanced at the hard concrete and had a morbid thought. I leaned over to Logan. "How many turtles do you think have accidentally been dropped?"

"God, I hope none." He pulled me to get in line and we waited patiently for our turn to hold yearling turtles. We took the obligatory tourist photos, which they tried selling to us for an arm and a leg.

Logan refused and somehow managed to talk them down from twenty dollars for one picture of us holding two yearling turtles over the wading pool to getting the entire series of twenty pictures for half the cost.

"Impressive," I said as he showed me the photos sent to his phone.

We had huge smiles as we leaned out over the hexagon wading pool with plate-sized baby turtles in our hands. The yearlings flapped their little flippers as they squirmed. We didn't keep them out of the water long.

"We make a good couple." He pointed to a particularly great shot where he had shoved his turtle near my face.

The smile on my face was free and unfettered, something I hadn't felt in a very long time. Logan made it easy to relax and I didn't feel as if I needed to hide who I was around him. I couldn't remember the last man I'd been with that I hadn't been guarded around.

"I think I'm going to send this one to Gabriel," he said.

"Who's Gabriel?"

"My oldest brother, and the reason I was late last night. I was a little pissed at him at the time, but seeing how the evening ended, I owe him a beer."

"How's that?"

"Well, if I'd been on time, the asshole in the suit wouldn't have moved in on my territory and I wouldn't have had to defend it."

"I'm not an *it*."

"No, but you're one hell of a kisser." He sent off the picture to his brother and tucked the cellphone in his back pocket. "You ready to swim with the turtles?"

"I'm all in," I said, not entirely sure if I meant the turtles or something else.

In addition to the turtle touch pool, the center had a turtle lagoon. Massive in scope it was a huge manmade lagoon-sized pool at least a couple acres in scope. We got our mask and snorkels at the shack by the makeshift beach and secured our valuables in the lockers provided. Then we donned our gear and waded into the water.

Before long, we were snorkeling over turtles. The manmade lagoon was a concrete construction with a beach entrance that quickly deepened to waist deep and then plunged to over twenty feet below us. In the lagoon, they had scores of turtles chilling at the bottom, swimming through the water with graceful sweeps of their flippers, and rising to the surface for a breath of air.

Warmed by the sun, the water was refreshing and surprisingly clear. With a slight greenish algae tint, we had no problems seeing the turtles below and far in the distance. Logan dove down to get as close as the turtles would allow.

They didn't mind us at all and soon Logan and I were diving down and making a contest of holding our breaths as long as we could. I tried to swim alongside a turtle, but there was no way my gangly human body could keep up with their streamlined shapes.

The outside world disappeared as Logan and I played with the turtles, but eventually my stomach began to rumble. I gestured for him to join me at the surface and spit out my snorkel.

"Hey, you hungry?" I'd skipped breakfast after my morning swim and regretted it now.

"Sure, I think I saw a place to eat in the park."

We swam back and handed in our gear then headed toward Schooner's Bar and Grill. Of course, we had to stop by Smiley's Saltwater Lagoon.

Smiley, their nine-foot saltwater crocodile was enjoying his lunch. He jumped out of the water to gobble up a dead chicken one of the employees dangled over the water on a long pole. Definitely not a lagoon I wanted to swim in.

Schooner's Bar and Grill had basic food, but it hit the spot. We continued exploring the park, checked out the butterfly exhibit where I stood as still as possible while a majestic blue butterfly landed on my shoulder. Larger than my hand, Logan was able to get a really great set of pictures.

We wanted to visit the hatchery, but there was a long line to get inside. It was kind of a shame because it was only open from May to October, and the chances of me getting back to the Caymans was pretty small.

After we explored the entire park, Logan took my hand in his.

"You ready for part two of our tour."

"Part two?"

"Yes luv, I'm going to get you wet again."

Intrigued, I let him practically pull me through the gift shop. We crossed the street and I clapped my hands.

"We're doing this? Seriously?"

"Have you ever swum with dolphins before?"

"No, have you?"

We entered Dolphin Discovery and Logan went to the front counter to check in. I tried to pay again, but he'd already purchased these tickets from the hotel.

"What do we do?" I hovered behind him as the attendant pulled out two clipboards for us to sign release forms. Once we did that, we were led back to the tanks and met our guide.

Our guide, Jacque, introduced us to Daisy and Pietro, two bottlenosed dolphins who were our ambassadors for our dolphin experience. We buckled up our life jackets then joined Jacque in the tank where we said hello to our new flippered friends.

"You want to go first?" Logan pulled me into a hug. The thick life jackets made it a bit awkward but I enjoyed the brief contact.

I glanced at Daisy and Pietro who were showing off their jumping abilities and decided I didn't need to blaze this trail.

"How about you go first?"

Our dolphin experience included a dolphin kiss and two opportunities to glide through the water with the dolphins.

One was a dorsal tow, which looked the easiest, and the other was the foot push.

Jacque brought Daisy and Pietro over for the kiss and hug and we petted their rubbery skins to let them get used to us. Then it was time.

Logan hopped in and swam to the far end of the tank, stopping short about twenty feet from the far wall. Then he waited for Jacque's signal.

Jacque's lifted his arm and then swept it down. Daisy and Pietro took off on their signal, diving deep and swimming around toward Logan.

Then he was moving through the water. The bottlenose dolphins put their noses on the bottom of his feet and propelled him through the water. There was water everywhere with Logan rising above the surface with a huge grin on his face.

"See," Jacque said, "it's easy, just keep your knees locked and hands fisted by your side."

I didn't believe him, but if Logan could do it, I would too.

Daisy and Pietro set Logan down and he slowly sank until his lifejacket buoyed him at the top of the water. He turned toward the low platform where we waited and closed the distance in strong, steady strokes.

"That was awesome!" He sat on the edge of the swim platform. "You're going to squeal like a little girl, my angel. So fucking-fantastic!"

Before I lost my nerve, I took a step off the swim plat-form and swam to my designated spot. Heart pounding, pulse thumping, I watched Jacque raise his arm over his head. He commanded the full attention of the dolphins and when he lowered his arm, the dolphins dove under the water.

Trusting to the process, I stiffened my entire body. Knees locked. Arms pressed against the side of my body, I forced my fists tight against my outer thighs.

Suddenly two hard snouts pressed up against the arches of my feet and I was rising out of a plume of water as they propelled me across the tank. And I squealed. I squealed like a little girl, shouting at the top of my lungs as they pushed me through the water. Then I was dropping back down and floating on the surface.

Daisy and Pietro made it back to the swim platform in a blink of an eye while I slowly made my way back. Logan crouched beside the dolphins. I'm not sure if his hand was on Daisy or Pietro, but he patted the dolphin and watched me as I stroked my way back.

"That was intense," I said.

"No kidding, I love the way you squeal. Can't wait to hear more of it."

I gave a shake of my head as I pulled myself onto the swim platform.

"You two ready for the dorsal tow?"

"Heck yes!" Logan rubbed his hands together with anticipation.

"Back in, both of you. This one is easy. All you need to do is hold on. Daisy and Pietro will do all the rest."

We jumped in like two eager little kids and bobbed on the surface of the water while Jacque gave the dolphins treats. Then he blew his whistle and Logan and I braced to grab hold. Afraid I would be the one tourist too dumb to grab a hold and hang on, I was not going to miss this.

The dolphins drew close and slowed down. Okay, maybe they'd done this a time or two before. Once we both had a grip of our respective dolphin's dorsal fin, they took off.

Water filled my face, shot up my nose, and I think I swallowed about a gallon of tank water. I did not want to think about what went in my mouth, and truthfully I didn't care. I hadn't felt this free in years and yes, I did squeal.

We took photos with the dolphins, and unlike the turtles, Logan couldn't talk the price down. We left with amazing memories and indisputable photographic proof of the best day ever.

After we cleaned up, taking advantage of their showers to rinse, we headed outside dripping wet.

"See," he said with a smirk. "I told you I'd make you wet."

"Yes, you did." I grabbed his arm, pressed my body against his, and lifted on tiptoe to kiss the scruff of his jaw. "You certainly did, and I'm dripping wet with the biggest smile on my face I've ever had. This has been an amazing day. Thank you."

"It's mid-afternoon girl. Surely you don't think I've run out of stamina so soon?"

I cocked my head and smiled. "Ok, silly stallion. What's next?"

"Don't mock the stallion baby, not until you've given it a good hard ride."

My gaze dropped to his crotch and the noticeable bulge which appeared to be growing before my eyes.

"You might want to contain that cock, there are little kids here."

He covered himself with his towel and an evil glint gleamed in his eyes. "Brave words, my dearest angel. But let's see how brave you feel with your feet dangling in the air."

"Excuse me?"

"Oh, this is going to be a surprise, and you're going to love it."

10

LOGAN

LISTENING TO ANGEL SQUEAL OFFICIALLY BECAME MY NEW favorite pastime.

I loved seeing her loosen up and be free with her emotions. I had a suspicion she rarely let herself open up like this with anyone and I loved that I got to see such an intimate side of her.

I'd like to see another *intimate* side of her, but this would suffice for now.

I teased her relentlessly, it was too much fun to stop, and enjoyed each blush I brought to her cheeks. I especially loved how that rosy color spread down her neck and moved between her breasts. Staring at her cleavage, which had previously been my number one favorite pastime, and still came a very close second, made me want to lick all of that rosy glow.

We heard nothing but the whispering of wind as the aquamarine waters passed a hundred feet beneath our feet. That may be an exaggeration. I didn't actually know how high we flew in the tandem parasail, but damn did I love when the boat driver let us drop.

I paid extra for an extended ride and more to have him drop us until our toes brushed the water several times. Angel squealed and squeezed my hand each time.

"Do you love it?" We had splashed down for the third time and were now rising back into the air.

"It's nothing like what I thought it would be. It's eerily quiet and calm up here."

There was wind. It wasn't like there was no sound, but it ghosted past us, gentle and light. It grabbed her deliciously long hair and blew it out behind her. Strands freed from her ponytail licked along the side of her face, and made my fingers itchy to push them back behind her ear.

We had the best day possible, although I didn't know how many bad days the Caymans had. From our vantage point we marveled at the coral reefs below us. We saw, after a little debate, what we finally decided was a small pod of dolphins swimming beneath us. I said they were sharks. She insisted on dolphin.

We were being pulled through the air strapped to a parachute, but I had to agree with her about how amazing it was.

"It's pretty damn quiet." And we were very much alone.

"Is this your first time?" Her deliciously dark eyes lit with excitement.

We were both ex-military pilots. We'd had parachute training, but I had to admit I'd never done this.

"I'm a parasailing virgin. What about you?" I couldn't believe I hadn't asked.

"First time."

I took her hand in mine and brought it up to my lips. Gently, I fluttered kisses over her knuckles, then I freed her index finger and slowly sucked it into my mouth while watching her eyes widen.

Did I dare kiss her?

God, I wanted to lock lips with her and kiss her as we soared over the ocean.

I released her finger. "You're stunning, you know that."

"Please," she glanced down, "you don't have to always say that."

"Why not? It's true."

"No. It's not."

How could she not know? But it didn't surprise me. A woman like Angel spent her life competing against men. I doubted she spent very much time pampering herself and I bet her pool of female friends wasn't that deep.

I got an idea for what we would do tomorrow.

"I want to kiss you again." Maybe I should have just grabbed her and pulled her in for a kiss, but I wanted her to want me with as much passion as I had for her.

"I know."

"Way to leave a guy hanging, Angel." I couldn't believe that's all she said.

"I don't think it's such a great idea."

"Why not?"

"Because we work together for starters."

"So?" I really didn't see that as the massive roadblock she made it seem.

"So, it can get complicated." She looked into the sky. "When we're up there, sharing the cockpit, there's a very clear chain of command. For now, you're the captain. I'm the co-pilot."

"I don't get it."

"If we disagree up there, it's clear how we resolve our issues. Introduce feelings into that and things get complicated fast. Under stress, we don't need that confusion. Our passengers don't need it."

"For the record, I disagree with you. I'm perfectly capable of separating the two."

"Well, then I guess it's my fault, because I don't think I can separate it. I'm not interested in a one-night stand and I'm not really interested in a three-day fling in the Caymans. I don't want complications to turn into something which might jeopardize my career, or that I might regret later. I've worked too hard to get where I am."

Regret later?

But who was I kidding. I was suggesting exactly what she didn't want, a three-day fling, because I didn't do relationships. My brothers teased me relentlessly about the revolving door of women who graced my bed and filled up my social media feed. I think the longest relationship I'd ever had barely spanned the length of a month.

It gutted me realizing this, because it had always been how I managed my sex life. Find a chick who interested me. Enjoy her company and the sex. Move on before complications set in.

Complications.

I couldn't believe I just used the same word Angel had used.

"You know, there are ways to work things so that isn't a problem." What the hell was I thinking?

"Such as?"

"First off, when we get back, we tell corporate that we won't fly together. Second, we get you promoted to captain. That would make sure we don't work together. We can still be together and not fuck up your career."

We can still be together…

Together? For the first time, I envisioned an affair longer than a few weeks. Was I considering a relationship? With a woman I'd known for a little over a day?

I supposed I was.

"But we're working together now," she said. "You do see how it's complicated."

"The best things in life are complicated. You just need to decide what's worth fighting for and go after it with everything you have."

"We barely know each other."

"True, but there's a good way to fix that."

"How about we take a pause and just enjoy the day?"

A pause. I didn't want to take a fucking pause, but dammit. I would.

I would *pause* but hell if I was going to stop. There was something about this woman I couldn't get enough of.

When we finally came down for the last time, the sun dipped toward the horizon. I gave a fat tip to our boat captain and took Angel's hand in mine. Paused didn't mean I wasn't going to hold her hand.

"You hungry?" I turned to her.

"I'm still full from lunch and it's still kind of early."

"How about a drink?"

"I could do that."

"Great, I saw a cool place on the beach." And we would have a spectacular view of the sunset. Those were romantic and I planned on waging a devastating attack to convince her that *paused* was the wrong word to use when it came to us.

We wandered down the dock and stopped several times to look at the fish swimming along the pylons. Her enthusiasm was infectious and I found myself crouching down beside her to look at the tiny tropical fish who used the security of the marina as their nursery.

We took our shoes off when we hit the beach and let the sand massage our feet as we walked along the waterline. I wanted to throw her in the water. Hell, anything for an excuse to put my hands on her, but I was trying to be a damn gentleman.

When we finally arrived at the bar I'd spotted, we grabbed a table with prime seating and angled our chairs to look out over the beach.

"What can I get you?" The pretty waitress came to take our orders.

Blonde, blue-eyed, with a rack a man could get lost in, she was exactly my type, and yet I had zero reaction as I ordered two waters and some big fruity drink for two.

I was more of a scotch and whiskey man, but this was one of those big round bowls that came with two straws. Whatever I could do to increase the intimacy between Angel and myself, I was on it.

Angel leaned back and put her feet up on the low bannister separating our seats from the sand. "This has been a terrific day."

"Has been? We've got all night."

She stretched her arms overhead. "I'm not sure *all night* is the best idea."

"Why not?" *All night* sounded just about right for me. All night, into the morning and all the days and nights from there.

"Because you're a very dangerous man."

"I like the sound of that, and that definitely sounds like an *all night* kind of thing."

"I know. That's what scares me."

Scares her? I both loved and hated that she was scared.

As the sun dipped to the horizon, we sipped our mammoth drink and watched the sky as it lit on fire.

Deep crimson reds melted with bright yellows and sultry oranges as nature painted a canvas of beauty over our heads.

We spoke little, enjoying the moment, as the day faded and the sun set.

"It's beautiful," she said.

"Absolutely gorgeous." But I wasn't looking at the sunset.

She glanced at me and noticed my stare. "You really don't have to say that all the time."

What did she have against a man telling her she was beautiful? Honestly, I didn't think women heard it enough, and it's not like it wasn't true.

"Does it bother you?"

"It makes me feel uncomfortable."

I pointed to the fiery glow in the sky. "I wish I had a camera. I'd take a picture of you beneath that sunset and show you what I see."

"Logan…"

"You're stunning and that's not something I can keep quiet about."

She wrapped her lips around the straw and took a sip of our drink. Impossible to hold it in, I gave a groan of frustration.

"What's wrong?" She released the straw and lifted her head.

"Nothing." I lied.

Her gaze flicked to the straw and then back at me. "Your mind is perpetually in the gutter. You know that, don't you?"

"You love that about me," I said, countering. "Just wait until you really get to hear my dirty talk."

"I'll wait."

I crossed my arms over my chest and leaned back. "You do realize what you just said."

"I said I'll wait."

"Uh-huh."

Her brows pinched together. "I don't get it."

"You said you'll wait, which means it's going to happen. That's okay, sweets, I'll wait as long as you need. Now about tomorrow…" I leaned forward, crowding her space, and breathed in her light floral scent. "I have something you're going to love."

"You really don't have to. I'm perfectly capable of entertaining myself."

"I'm sure you are, but tomorrow you're going to do something I bet you've never done for yourself before."

"Really?"

"Definitely."

"What?"

"Since I know you don't like surprises, I'm most definitely going to make you wait for this one."

"You should just tell me. If I don't like it…"

"You're going to love this."

"How can you be so sure?"

"Because I'm peeling away the layers, baby. Peeling away the layers."

I would let her mull over that for a bit. Raising my hand, I got the waitress's attention and ordered us another drink.

"Can you bring some water?" Angel added to my order.

"Are you getting hungry yet?"

She nodded. "A little, are you up for bar food?"

"Depends on what else you packed in that bag of yours. If bar food means I don't get to look at you in another skimpy dress, then I'm okay to wait and head back to the hotel."

"Hm, I'm thinking it's probably safer if we don't head home too soon."

"Head home?"

"Sorry, I meant the hotel. My mother always said home was wherever you rested your head for the night. We moved around a lot and I think it was her way of helping me feel like I was always home."

Her expression pinched with what looked like painful memories. I wanted to erase the crease in her forehead, smooth out the tension around her lips with a kiss, but I held back.

We were breaking down walls, but I had a sense she wasn't ready to get that personal with a man she had just met.

For me, it felt like I'd known her for an eternity. We

seemed to click, but I was wise enough to know she needed more time to come to the same conclusion.

"Well, the hotel is not that far." It was less than two miles down the beach. "Are you up for a bar and beach crawl?"

"Sounds interesting."

"We'll finish our drinks here, then head down the beach until we find someplace that looks interesting. Have dinner, then head down to the next bar for drinks, then find someplace for dessert." I wanted her to be my dessert. "And then finish up the evening at the hotel bar. Maybe we can run into the asshole in the suit and I can steal another kiss?"

Her soft laughter made my heart swell. "I love your persistence."

"Is it working?"

Our waitress returned with our drinks. Once she left, I eagerly waited for Angel to answer my question, but she stared out at the sky as warm yellows deepened to deep, dark, umber reds and appeared lost in thought.

The sky was on fire and my heart swelled with something I'd never felt before. I joined Angel in a moment of quiet reflection as I tried to sort out what felt different about her compared to all the others.

11

ANGEL

A BEACH AND BAR CRAWL SOUNDED FANTASTIC. AFTER AN amazing day, I needed something to unwind. With the two drinks we shared at the first bar, I needed to stretch my legs and get some food in me before taking on any more alcohol.

The cool waters of the ocean tickled my toes as my feet sank in the sand. Logan walked beside me and neither of us cared if we got wet. I had my sexy-as-fuck fanny pack on, along with my neoprene shorts and tank top.

I wanted to go for an evening swim, but there was no place safe to leave our things. I ventured calf-deep in the water and took in the scents of salt and sand, the remnants of tourists' suntan lotion, and breathed all of it in.

Beaches were my happy place. I'd grown up near the ocean but had moved away from it after high school. I missed the easy living in touch with the rhythms of the ocean. Two more days and it would be back to reality.

I really needed to thank Bianca and her husband for this unexpected treat.

Logan and I walked for what felt like a mile on the beach, but was probably far less, when he pointed to a shack with mouthwatering smells coming from it.

"How does that look?"

"It looks like a dive but smells like heaven."

"Sounds like we found dinner."

He took my hand in his and a current of electricity shot up my arm. Every time he touched me I held back a tiny gasp. I wasn't a touchy-feely kind of person.

Generally, holding hands made me think of sweaty palms and I couldn't wait to yank my hand back, but with Logan it didn't feel that way. Warm, solid, and confident, he took hold of me as if was the most natural thing in the world.

"Mmm, I smell burgers." His low, raspy voice vibrated in the space between us.

Sexy as sin, all the man had to do was breathe. He turned heads too. With his deep-blue eyes, muscular physique, and a well-groomed beard, that I was finding sexier by the minute, I wasn't the only woman who couldn't keep her eyes off the cocky captain.

"Sounds perfect."

Our luck at getting the perfect table continued as we were seated yet again right along the beach. He ordered a beer while I settled for a soda. Too much alcohol thrummed through my system and I didn't trust myself to get drunk around Logan Reid.

That was a place full of bad decisions, choices I wanted to make, but knew I should stay far away from.

We ordered and sat back to watch the few beachgoers pack up their things. As the beach emptied and darkness fell, I realized our walk back on the beach would be interesting.

"Hey look," he pointed to the eastern horizon, "a full moon."

Great, just what I needed. Sexy as fuck man. Moonlit beach. Fresh ocean breeze. Gentle waves. The perfect night.

The universe conspired against me.

We laughed over dinner, talking about everything and nothing. He told stories about his childhood and growing up as the middle sibling with older brothers and younger sisters. I had much less to share, but it didn't matter. He had enough stories for us both.

I learned about his first day in kindergarten when his four older brothers walked him to school, making sure no one bullied their youngest brother. His four older brothers were all within a year or two of each other. Dylan, the one closest in age, and starting sixth grade at the time, had been assigned protective detail over their little brother.

He told me how he repeated the same scene when his next younger sister, Angie had her first day in kindergarten. He was starting sixth grade and had been ordered to look after her.

They had a tight knit family, something I never had. Logan told me stories about his childhood.

"So, you can imagine Angie's poor date when he came to pick her up for prom."

"You didn't terrorize the poor guy, did you?"

"All five of us waited for him to show up. Gabriel put the dude in the middle of the couch, while Dylan and Colt sat beside him. I've never seen a kid more terrified."

"No kidding. How old were you?"

"Angie was fifteen. I'd just turned twenty-one, so Dylan was twenty-seven..." He rattled off the ages of his older brothers while I imagined a poor fifteen-year-old boy getting grilled while waiting for his prom date to come downstairs.

"That poor boy."

"Oh, don't worry. We made it a tradition. It gave us a reason to come home and mom loves a family gathering."

"I'm sure your sisters *loved* it. Did you do that to all their dates?" I laced my words heavily with sarcasm.

"Oh, definitely. Lizzy, the youngest, tried sneaking out of the house to avoid it."

"She did?"

"She tried, but we intercepted her. Took her back into the house, called her date and told him we were not pleased he was trying to take our baby sister without meeting the family."

"What did your dad think of all of that?"

His expression darkened. "We lost our father a few years after Lizzy was born."

"Oh, I'm sorry." It looked like we had more in common than I thought.

"It's okay. It was a long time ago. My mother had my brothers to help out. How about you? Any crazy sibling stories?"

"Not really. It's just me."

"An only child then? That means you were spoiled rotten, right?" From the glimmer in his eye, I didn't want to ruin the mood. Instead, I smiled.

"My mother did an amazing job raising me. I wanted for little." I had learned how to want very little and found joy in what she could provide. My mother and I had been close and that was enough for me.

A yawn escaped my mouth, cutting through the conversation at a perfect moment. I didn't want to talk about my family, or lack thereof.

"Oh no you don't. No yawning allowed. The evening is still young, my sweet angel."

"That may be, but this has been an eventful day and I didn't sleep well last night. We may need to skip the bar and just head back."

His eyes pinched but he gave a grudging nod.

"We can do that on one condition?"

"What's that?"

As long as it wasn't another bid to get me in bed I was up for almost anything. The truth was I had very little resolve left. If he asked, I would likely say yes.

"I want you to promise to have breakfast with me tomorrow and clear your schedule between nine and two."

"Because my schedule is so incredibly full?"

"Well, I know you want to read your book. I've got some *stiff* competition with Mr. Fifty Shades. I really need to do my homework so I'll be ready for all your dirty fantasies."

I had wanted to lay on the beach and read my book—not that book—at least until I realized how fun Logan could be. I didn't want to spend any time away from him. It was precisely because of that kind of intensity, I knew I needed space. Spending the rest of the night in a bar was far too dangerous and my self-control slipped by the minute.

"Okay, breakfast and I'm yours from nine until two."

"Hmm…all mine? To do with as I please?"

"That is not what I said."

"Hey, they were your words, not mine, but I like the sound of it. I really need to get on my research: do you like metal cuffs, leather, or just old fashioned rope, and silk? Silk tie? Or will one of my shirts do?"

"One of your shirts?"

"For the blindfold, silly. I need to get my shit together to rock your world."

"Oh my God. Just because I read it doesn't mean I want to live it."

"Never say never."

"Be careful or you'll get none of me, flyboy. That cracking sound is the thin ice you're stepping on getting really thin."

"You've already promised me your undivided attention."

"I can say no."

"Can't go back on a promise. It's a rule. Oh, and I'll need your undivided attention from six until midnight."

"That's incredibly specific."

"I know."

"Care to tell me what you have planned?"

"It's going to be a surprise."

"You know I don't like surprises."

"That's what makes this so much fun. The tease and anticipation is going to keep your dirty little mind going nonstop." He leaned close and took my hands in his. "Do you trust me?"

The funny thing was that I did.

"I guess I do." I hated to admit it, but I trusted him implicitly. If he came up with anything half as amazing as the day he planned today, it was going to be exciting.

"Great, but there's one more thing." He leaned in close and lowered his voice to a whisper.

"Really?"

"We'll forgo the next bar on our beach and bar crawl and skip dessert, but we're stopping in at the hotel bar."

"Why's that?"

"Because if the asshole in a suit is there, you're going to let me kiss you."

That was a very bad idea, but the fluttering in my belly said I very much hoped Clive was at that bar.

"I don't think that's a very good idea."

"It's a horrible idea. After I kiss you, it's going to be very hard to let you go. And I'll have a very long night thinking about you. But bad ideas are often the start to great beginnings. What do you say? You willing to take a chance? If he's not there, we'll end the evening with a handshake."

"A handshake?"

"Yes, as boring as that sounds."

"Well, it's a deal then. Your goodnight kiss is now up to the fates."

"Wait, are you saying I was going to get one anyway?"

"Maybe."

"No maybe. Were you, or were you not, going to blow my mind with a goodnight kiss?"

"I don't know about blow your mind, but it was on the table."

It was totally not on the table.

There was no way I could kiss him and not spend the rest of the night doing all the deliciously naughty things I knew he'd already fantasized about. I had no strength left to resist his charms, but he didn't need to know that.

"I know something else you can blow."

"You mean blow you a kiss?" I pretended innocence, but from the hard bulge tenting the fabric of his swim shorts there was no denying what he meant. "That sounds safe."

His rumbly voice deepened with disappointment and the husky rasp sent shivers racing across my skin.

"Not a kiss. I can't wait to feel your lips wrap around my cock. It's going to be divine."

"Ah, what a shame. That's not what I was offering."

"But you were going to give me a goodnight kiss tonight, weren't you?"

"I guess you'll never know now. Kiss or no kiss, it's now all in the hands of your buddy Clive."

"Clive? Who the fuck is Clive?"

"The asshole in a suit."

"Oh, well that makes sense. Clive is a dick name. It fits him."

"What do you say we catch a cab and head back now?"

My chances of surviving a mile-long walk on a moonlit beach in paradise with Logan Reid was a definite zero. I knew sex on the beach sounded way sexier than it was. All that sand getting places it shouldn't. I didn't want that, but I might just consider it if it meant finally being able to feel his mouth on me.

"Let's do it, and let's hope Clive is in that bar."

I said nothing to encourage Logan as he paid the bill, called a cab, and helped me out of it at the hotel. We walked into the hotel bar and scanned the room.

No Clive.

"Sorry, flyboy, looks like you're out of luck."

His brows pinched. "I'll take the loss, but since we're here, how about one last drink?"

He guided me up to the bar. I unbuckled my fanny pack and placed it on the stool beside me while I settled myself on the barstool.

We had the same bartender from the night before. He placed two coasters on the counter. "What'll it be?"

"The lady wants a frozen mango-rita and I'll have crown and coke."

"Aw, you remembered," I said.

"How could I forget? You left me to finish that sweet disaster of a drink."

"You didn't have to drink it. You could've left it on the bar."

"How could I not? Knowing your lips had graced the rim of that glass?"

"You're weird. You know that."

"I also have to take a piss."

"And smooth. That was real smooth," I teased. "Next time, just say 'excuse me for a second.' No need to announce it."

"I'll be right back." He flashed a grin and hopped off the stool. "Don't do anything I wouldn't do."

He disappeared and I turned around to watch the bartender mix our drinks. He slid over my frozen mango-rita, with two straws and a wink, then put Logan's drink in front of his stool. A presence loomed over my right shoulder, and thinking it was Logan, I spun around.

"You still want that kiss?" My eyes widened as a slimy smile spread across Clive's face.

"Well, since you're offering." He leaned into my personal space but I put out my hand and pressed it against his crisp, but damp, button-down shirt.

"I'm sorry. I thought you were someone else."

"The guy from last night? He's a loser."

The hairs at the back of my neck bristled. "He's a pretty decent guy actually. I'm sorry, but I thought you were him." I turned my back, but Clive slid onto the stool beside me.

"How about that drink?"

"Um, I'm with Logan."

"He seems to like stranding you at the bar. How about we take a bottle of wine back to my room and get to know each other better?"

"That's my girl." Logan's shout cut through the noisy bar.

Clive rolled his eyes. "Your loss sweetheart, but if you change your mind, I'm in room 619."

His room was two doors down from mine? A tingling sensation swept down my spine and I gave a little shudder. Would the hotel think it weird if I wanted to change rooms?

"I think you should go."

Clive gave an indignant snort and pushed away from the bar. "When he leaves you again, the offer stands." He placed my fanny pack on the counter and shoved it toward me.

His wink made me want to barf, but I managed to keep everything down.

"You okay?" Logan wrapped an arm around me and kissed the crown of my head as Clive stormed out.

"That guy is a grade A jerk." I grabbed Logan's arm,

knowing exactly what he intended. "Don't go after him. He's not worth the wasted breath."

"He shouldn't have approached you like that, or said those things."

"He smelled like whiskey and is probably drunk." I pointed to Clive as he left the bar. "Look, he's probably going upstairs to lick his wounds."

"I want to throat punch the guy."

"Not worth it," I said. "How about we just forget about Clive and finish our drinks?"

Logan didn't look like he agreed with me, but he took his seat. I owed him a kiss, but after running into Clive, and sharing the same air, it kind of ruined any heat that had been brewing with Logan.

I think Logan sensed it, because he didn't push for the kiss. We finished our drinks and he paid the tab. Another yawn escaped me.

"Are you ready to head upstairs?" He rubbed my back, a soothing gesture, I could definitely get used to it.

"Yeah, I think I'm beat." That last bit of alcohol did me in. I couldn't keep the yawns from coming.

We headed to the elevators and punched the button to head up.

"What room are you in, luv?" Logan's sultry voice promised more than I was ready to handle, but everything I wanted.

"623…hmm."

"What's up?"

"I can't find my room key. I wonder if it fell out earlier today?" Although with Logan paying for the entire day, I couldn't remember if I'd opened the fanny pack at all.

The elevator dinged behind us and the doors opened.

"I need to go to reception and get another key."

"I'll come with you," he said.

"It's okay. It might be best if we went up separately. If you walk me to my room, that might lead to coming inside, and that might lead to—"

"I get it. Look, no pressure, right? This is supposed to be fun."

"Right." Relieved that he understood, I blew out a breath. "What time do you want to meet for breakfast?"

"How about eight? That gives us an hour before…" He lifted a finger and gave me a wink. "I almost spilled the beans there. Meet me at eight. They have an amazing buffet. I'm dying to try it."

"Any special way I should dress for tomorrow?"

"Something comfortable. You could put on those tiny shorts you denied me today."

"How do you know I have a pair of tiny shorts?"

"Just a guess." Another couple approached and he stepped to the side to let them in. "I'll take a raincheck on that kiss, but only tonight. Tomorrow is a new day."

With those words, he let the doors to the elevator close. The last thing I saw was his smirk and the wink which buckled my knees.

I headed to reception and explained about my card key.

Within minutes, I had a replacement and headed up to my room.

Lost in thought about the wonderful day Logan and I had shared, I exited the elevator and headed down the long hall to my room, passing past the teens to 621 and then my room 623.

A door opened behind me and I pulled up short as Clive stepped out.

"Clive?"

"I see you got rid of that jerk from the bar, not that I blame you."

"I didn't get rid of him."

I edged to my room and pressed the keycard against the electronic lock. The lock turned. I opened the door and dashed inside.

Closing it firmly behind me, I breathed hard. There was something wrong about that guy.

It may have been a good idea to call down to security, but what was I going to say? One of your hotel guests stepped out of his room and into the hall? He had the nerve to speak to me? Yeah, that wasn't going to fly.

I turned at a strange sound, the low click of the electronic lock of my door disengaged. The door swung inward. My eyes widened when Clive stepped inside.

"What the hell? How did you…"

He held a keycard. One which looked like all the other keycards of the hotel, but opened my door.

"How did you get a key to my room?"

He stepped inside and the door slowly closed. He lifted a bottle of wine. "How about that drink? And I'm thinking I'll take that kiss you offered."

My pulse skyrocketed and my mind churned trying to figure out how I was going to get around him. He blocked my exit and had me trapped. This was not happening.

He took a step toward me. "Now that we're alone, you can drop the act. Let's party."

"I'm not partying with you." I pointed to the door. "You need to leave right now before I call security."

His attention shifted to the phone on the table beside the bed the same time I took a step toward it. In the blink of an eye, he pushed me on top of the bed. His bodyweight crushed me and a strangled scream erupted from my throat. His sweaty palm covered my mouth as he leaned down to lick along my neck.

"Don't fight it. You know you want it." Ragged breaths pulsed out of him. He palmed my breast and squeezed.

"Get off of me." I tried to push him off, but he was too big.

Freakishly strong, he kept my mouth covered with one hand while he pulled at the tie around his neck. While I squirmed, he rolled the tie and shoved it in my mouth, stretching my jaw painfully as I gagged against the silk. Then he removed his belt and unbuckled his pants.

"You like it rough, don't you? You fucking slut. Teasing me from the moment you walked into the bar. Playing hard to get, but I know you want me. That skimpy black dress, with your perky tits were asking for this. You've been begging for me from the moment we met."

I thrashed beneath him as he pushed his pants down. With my eyes bugging out of my head, he straddled me and pinned my wrists beneath his knees. I couldn't move.

He dug beneath the waistband of his boxers and freed his erection. Gripping it with one hand he wrapped his other hand around my neck, cutting off my air. He leaned over me and with low grunts, jerked himself off while I struggled to breathe.

My heart beat beneath my breastbone and my pulse hammered in my ears. My vision grew black as my sight narrowed to a pinprick.

A low pounding reached my ears, but it was hard to hear over Clive's animalistic grunts.

I was going to die.

With this beast on top of me, I was going to suffocate and die.

12

LOGAN

HEADING TO ANGEL'S HOTEL ROOM HAD BAD IDEA WRITTEN all over it, but my feet had a mind of their own.

Before I really understood what I was doing, and before I could talk myself out of it, I headed up from my room on the fifth floor to hers on the sixth.

When I exited the elevator, I turned left and watched as asshole Clive stumbled against the wall. He pressed his keycard to the door of his room and disappeared inside.

Good riddance.

The bastard could lick his wounds all by himself.

Dismissing Clive from my thoughts, I headed down the hall, watching out for the room numbers. I was looking for 623 and passed the teens then slowed down. Clive had entered one of the rooms around here.

But which one?

I pressed my ear to the door of 619, but heard nothing. At 621, silence once again greeted my astute hearing. With my pulse accelerating and my gut clenching, I approached Angel's room.

The door was closed, and I don't know what possessed me, but I pressed my ear to her door rather than knock. At first I heard nothing, but then sounds of a struggle reached my ears.

It couldn't be, but what else explained it?

I pounded on the door.

No response.

I pounded louder.

Nothing.

I kicked the door and slammed my shoulder into it. If Angel wasn't answering something had to be horribly wrong. A woman poked her head out from the room across the hall, then ducked back inside with wide, terrified eyes.

I continued my assault on the door, kicking and body slamming it. These doors were built to withstand an attack because it didn't budge.

Not getting anywhere, I turned and pounded on the door of the terrified woman. She didn't answer. Not that I blamed her.

"Call hotel security!" I screamed through the door, hoping the woman heard me.

If she didn't call security because I asked, I prayed she called because there was a crazy man outside trying to knock down the door to room 623.

And I was shit out of my mind with worry over what was going on in Angel's room.

I became a frenzied animal, kicking and cursing, shouting and slamming my body against the door.

Finally, the elevator dinged and four men rushed out. I pointed to Angel's door.

"My girlfriend is in there. She's not answering. I saw a man enter and I can hear a struggle."

The four men rushed me. Two of them body-slammed me against the wall as I repeated. "My girlfriend isn't answering."

"Sir, you need to calm down." One of the men pressed his hand to my chest, keeping me against the wall.

"You're not listening. She's in danger."

If they didn't do something soon I was going to go ballistic.

"Sir, you need to calm down."

"Look, just open the fucking door. If she's not in trouble, you can arrest me, but if you don't open that fucking door, there will be hell to pay."

Two of them looked to the one holding me and he gave a nod.

"Do it."

One of them turned and unlocked the door. They rushed in while the asshole continued to hold me.

There was a commotion inside.

Clive shouted.

I heard a grunt.

"If you don't get your hands off me right now, I'm going to take you apart." I growled at the guy holding me, but he seemed to get the message. I looked inside Angel's room as it took three men to peel Clive off my girl.

Butt-naked, Clive's swollen dick swung between his legs and a rush of bile rose in my throat.

The man holding me back released me and I barreled past him, oblivious to the men tackling Clive to the ground.

Angel was on the bed and pulled out what looked to be a rolled up tie out of her mouth. When she saw me, she practically leapt off the bed and into my arms.

"Logan!"

I caught her and held her tight to my chest.

"He was…he was going to…"

I ran my hand over her hair. "Shh, it's okay. You're safe now. It's going to be okay. Did he…"

Thoughts of what could have happened rushed through my mind, and I gave thanks to my wandering legs. A quick inspection eased my mind.

Clive had been up to no good, but it didn't look as if he'd raped my girl. Her clothing was a mess, but she was still dressed. He hadn't ripped her clothes off which meant she hadn't been violated.

Violated?

Hell, that wasn't true. She'd been violated in the worst possible way and attacked in her hotel room where she was defenseless against a would-be rapist.

She shook her head. "He gagged me and pinned me down, then leaned over me while he jerked off."

I pulled back, needing to see her face. That's when I noticed the bruises all along her neck.

"What the fuck did he do?"

Her hand lifted to her neck. "He tried to strangle me."

Security had Clive under control. His hands were cuffed behind his back and one of the men reached down to yank up his pants.

"What are you doing?" He cried out. "The fucking slut begged me."

"Hang on." I didn't want to let Angel go, but my rage couldn't be contained.

While security held Clive, I stepped up to him, clocked him in the jaw, kneed him in the groin, then finished with an uppercut to his gut.

He wheezed beneath my fists, and one of the men pulled on my arm.

"Sir, you need to step back."

I noticed how they didn't hold my punches until I got three good hits in and gave the guy a nod. He understood.

From the way Clive wheezed, I hoped that knee to his groin broke his fucking penis. If I had a knife, I'd chop it off right then and there.

They had every right to detain me for getting my shots in on Clive, but they didn't. While three of them escorted Clive out of the room, the one who held me against the wall pulled out a notebook.

"Ma'am," he said, "are you injured?"

Angel shook her head.

I gestured to her throat, my voice rising. "He fucking choked her. Look at the bruises."

"Logan, I'm okay." Her soft, delicate voice trembled.

She was far from okay, but strong as shit. I could see she was barely holding it together though. Tears shimmered in her eyes and her entire body shook like a leaf.

"Okay, my ass. That asshole deserves to die for what he did."

"Please…" She pleaded with me with her doe-eyes and that's when I noticed that tears had breached her defenses and tumbled down her cheek.

Dammit. I didn't want to be the source of her tears. She didn't need me going off and making things worse. What she needed was something much different.

"Shit, Angel. I'm so sorry." I pulled her to me, tucking her head beneath my chin. I ran my fingers through her hair, straightening the tangles and erasing the signs of her struggle.

"It's not your fault." Her shoulders hunched. "But, if you hadn't come…"

"Thank fuck I did come. Fuck, I had to see you. I didn't want to leave you alone and I couldn't imagine spending the night without you. I was going to make you head downstairs and stare at the stars all night if that's what it took."

She brushed the tears from her cheeks. "Is that true?"

Not really.

I'd hoped to get her to let me into her room where'd I'd planned something else entirely, but after what happened with Clive, there was no way I was mentioning anything remotely associated with sex.

"Yes." I lied. "I can't seem to get enough of you."

A throat cleared behind us. "It's a good thing you came up here, Sir." The guy tapped his pencil over his notebook. "My name is Juan, and I'm sorry for what happened in the hall, but we thought you were the threat."

"Well, thanks for finally listening to me."

The man turned his attention to Angel. "Do you want us to take you to a hospital?"

"No, he didn't rape me. I don't think that's what he wanted. My neck hurts, but I don't think he did any damage."

"I need to take your statement." He looked apologetic as he flipped the notebook open and held the pencil over the paper.

"I know." She turned to me. "Can you get me some water please?"

"Of course." But damn if I hated leaving her for a second.

I quickly went into the bathroom and filled a glass from the tap. Returning I held it out for her and cringed at the way her hand shook.

I walked her over to the couch. No way was she sitting on that bed. Hell, there was no fucking way she was sleeping in this room.

I helped her to sit and then sat right beside her, keeping one arm draped over her shoulder the entire time. I wouldn't touch her at all, especially after what happened, except she appeared to take comfort in my touch.

Angel leaned against me and snuggled into my embrace. I was simply glad she found comfort in my presence and would do what I could to lend her my strength.

When I thought of what Clive had done to her, what he'd been about to do, thoughts of murder filled my mind. It was a good thing they removed him from the room. If I knew where they'd taken him, asshole Clive wouldn't survive the night.

Juan asked Angel a series of questions, forcing her to relive the attack, while my blood boiled with anger. I was pissed this happened to her, angry that I hadn't been there to prevent it, and terrified by what could have happened.

To my girl.

My Angel.

After Juan finished, he stood and looked around the room. "Ma'am, we will help you pack your things and relocate you to a different room. Will that be okay?"

"Yes." She gave a shaky nod.

"She's staying with me." I tugged her tight with the announcement. "I'm not leaving you alone."

"You don't have to do that."

"Yes, I do. There's no fucking way I'm leaving you alone tonight." I turned to Juan. "I'll pack her things."

"What room are you in Sir?"

"514."

"Of course." He tucked his notepad into his back pocket. "There may be more questions, Miss Mars. I'm sure the police will need to make their own report, but I'll hold them off until the morning."

"Angel..." I leaned down to whisper in her ear, "can you give me a second? I want to speak with Juan."

Her shaky nod gutted me. My girl was going into shock, but this would only take a minute.

Gesturing to Juan, I had him join me in the hall. "We're pressing charges, but she doesn't need to be put through that again."

"The police will need their report."

"Can't they use what you have?"

"Unfortunately, no."

"Look, I've booked a spa day for her tomorrow. She needs to get her mind off this horrible mess. I don't want the police interfering with that."

"When are you scheduled to leave?"

"Two days."

"Okay, I'll see what I can do."

"Thank you."

Juan excused himself and I went inside to catch Angel packing her things.

"Can I help?"

Tears flowed down her cheeks. "I was so scared. His hand...I couldn't breathe, and the expression on his face. I don't think I'll ever get it out of my head."

"That man was a monster and a predator, but he can't hurt you anymore."

"I know." She rolled her shoulders back and straightened her spine. "It may not look like it right now, but I'm good. I'll get through this."

It sounded more like she needed to say that to herself, and while I believed she could get through it, there was no way I was not going to be by her side. However she needed me, I would support her through this.

"I know, luv. I'm not leaving your side."

Within a few minutes we had everything packed. She had a small bag, so it didn't take that long. While she stood in the hall, I made a final pass in the room, making sure we hadn't forgotten anything. I grabbed her cellphone charger from a plug near the bed and met her in the hall.

"Come." I took her hand in mine and dragged her bag behind me.

When we got to my room, I put her bag on top of the dresser.

"What can I do for you?"

She stood in the middle of the room and ran her hands up and down her arms, looking as if something bothered her.

Of course something bothers her, asshole. She was assaulted.

Shit, I knew that, but I didn't know what she needed from me. Did I hold her? Give her space?

There really was no way for me to give her any privacy. It was a modest hotel room with two king-sized beds, a loveseat, a single chair, and a desk with a chair pulled up to it.

"I don't know." Her voice sounded tiny and weak. I could see a cageyness creep over her as her body began to twitch.

"Hey, how about you take a nice long shower, or a bath. I'll be right here. I won't leave you."

It was clear she didn't want to be alone, but also that she needed a moment to regroup. Angel was a strong, independent woman. I could tell she wasn't used to being seen as weak and needy. There wasn't anything I could do about that right now, but I could give her a moment to regroup.

"Yeah, that sounds good. I feel...dirty."

I gripped her arms and stared deep into her eyes. "You're not responsible for what happened. You know that, right?"

"I do, but it still feels wrong."

"Let me get the water running for you."

Dex Truitt had gone above and beyond getting us this hotel during our downtime in the Caymans, but we were booked in a standard room without a ton of amenities. Once Angel was in the shower, I intended to fix that. Top of my list would be one of those fluffy robes she could get lost in.

"Thanks."

"Bath or shower?"

"I prefer showers."

"On it."

She went to her bag and unzipped it while I went into the bathroom and did a quick sweep to tidy up my mess. I put a towel on the bathroom floor for her, closed the lid to the toilet, and placed two towels on top of it. Then I stepped outside and saw Angel holding clothes to her chest, hunched over, and sobbing.

I rushed to her and wrapped my arms around her from behind.

"What can I do?" I wanted to erase the memories and ease her pain.

"You're already doing it. Thank you. It's just going to take a moment."

"The shower is ready. I'm going to call and see about getting us upgraded to a suite. You're not leaving my sight."

"You don't have to do that."

"I know, but I'm doing it."

Tonight, we would share a room, but over the next couple of days, as she recovered, I didn't want to make things uncomfortable for her by forcing her into close quarters with me. And I sure as shit couldn't do all the things I wanted to do to her. Not after Cunt-faced Clive ruined everything.

I ushered Angel into the bathroom and gently closed the door. She would have the privacy she needed to come apart, and put herself back together again, before having to face me.

All the sexual tension from before had evaporated, but that didn't mean some indescribable force wasn't pulling us together. I felt it wrapping around my heart, relentless and irresistible, and knew she felt the same thing.

But what do we do now?

You take it slow.

Right, because that's what Logan Reid did.

I practically laughed out loud. I'd never been known to take things slow. There's a reason I'd earned my nickname.

But for Angel, I'd do anything.

13

ANGEL

WARM WATER SLUICED DOWN MY BODY AS I WASHED ANY trace of Clive off my body. The bathroom filled with steam and the mirror fogged over.

Which was good.

The brief look I had of my reflection wasn't something I wanted to repeat.

Logan.

What the hell was I going to do with Logan?

In protector mode, he hovered over me, suffocating me, when all I needed was to curl in on myself, have a good cry, and then pick up the pieces.

As pieces went there were only a few. I wasn't raped. I don't think Clive intended to defile me in that way. He seemed more interested in jerking off while choking me.

I think he intended to kill me.

Now, that was a sobering thought. There was a real chance I could have died.

Well, shit. That only made things worse.

I took my time in the shower and washed all trace of Clive from my skin, then I huddled on the floor and drew my knees up tight to my chest.

With my chin propped on my knees, I cried. I let it all out. This was the only time I would allow myself to break down.

I cried until my cheeks burned and my sobs stopped. I have no idea how long I stayed in the shower, except my fingers turned to prunes and the wrinkles had wrinkles. Thankfully, the water was still warm.

The bathroom had been turned into a sauna and I breathed in the heavy air, letting it restore me from the inside out. The mirror was completely fogged over and I was grateful for that.

Knowing my skin would be overly dried out after that shower, I took advantage of the lotion provided and lathered my skin.

There was a knock at the door.

"Hey Angel, I have a fluffy robe for you if you're interested."

A fluffy robe sounded divine. My skin glistened with a light sheen of perspiration. It was too hot and steamy in the bathroom to dry off properly.

"Thank you." I cracked open the door and my gaze collided with liquid pools of the deepest blue. His expression softened and a smile bowed his lips upward.

He handed me the robe and I shut the door to put it on. Then I took a deep breath and fortified myself against his incessant kindness. I didn't need kind right now.

I needed normal.

But when I walked out of the bathroom, he patted the bed beside him. I laughed when I saw the movie he had on the television.

"*Frozen*? You're watching *Frozen*?"

"*We're* watching *Frozen*. But since you hogged my bathroom like *forever* I went ahead and started without you. It's not that bad."

"That's great. You can sing the songs with Georgina on the flight home."

"I don't know about that." He pointed to his Adam's Apple. "Not much for singing."

"I don't think Georgina will mind."

"I suppose not." He glanced at the bathroom. "Are you done in there, because I kind of have to take a piss."

"Again with the bodily functions. You don't have to announce it to the world."

His banter eased my fears about being treated with kid gloves. Things felt natural between us again, and I gave a silent word of thanks as he hopped off the bed and went to use the restroom.

While waiting, I curled up on the bed and noticed the bottle of wine and several desserts. He must have ordered room service while I took my shower.

I settled in, loving the plush feel of the robe as it wrapped around my body, and plumped up the pillows.

Logan returned. "I didn't know what you wanted to do, but I figured we could watch a movie, share a bottle of wine, and enjoy something tasty. Something to kind of get your mind off…"

"It's perfect, but looks expensive."

"Oh, don't worry about that. It's all comp'd by the hotel, and best news is they're upgrading us to a suite tomorrow."

"Us?"

"Yeah, I'm not leaving you alone, or did you miss that part."

"That's not necessary."

"I know, it's also non-negotiable. I asked them to give us two rooms. You don't have to worry—gentleman here." He made a point of reminding me of his earlier promise. "Tonight, you have to share a room with me, but at least there are two beds. If you try any funny business with me in the middle of the night, however, I may or may not put up a fight."

I punched him in the arm and smiled.

"Thank you for that."

"For what?"

"For simply being the pervert you are."

"Hey, I was just doing the sexy-talk. We haven't begun to explore the kinky-fuckery pillow talk. I still have my research to finish in your favorite book."

"It's not my favorite book." But it was.

"And yet you've read it several times and watched the movie."

"I never admitted to that."

Okay, I was quickly losing this conversation and it headed into territory I wasn't yet ready to explore.

"You didn't have to, and for the record, you just did. I have my work cut out for me. So, if you don't mind waiting until tomorrow night to jump my bones…" He let his words trail away, leaving me to determine what he might have said.

"How about we finish watching *Frozen*? I can't wait to tell Georgina how much you loved it."

Our flight home was going to be torture for him. I would make sure of it. Georgina had a crush on the cocky captain. Watching an entire movie with him would make her day.

If I knew anything about Logan, and I was learning more by the hour, he would never let a little girl down.

We watched the rest of the movie and I rose my voice in song with each number, tickling him when he refused to sing the chorus with me.

Despite what he said, his husky voice sounded like sin when he sang. However, it soon became apparent I couldn't keep the yawns from coming or my eyes open.

"Come on, buttercup." He stood and went to the other bed where he turned down the covers. "Let's get you in bed."

I needed sleep. There was no denying that, but the thought of sleeping on my own twisted my insides into knots.

"Um…" I glanced at the bed. "Would it be too weird if we shared the bed?"

"You *want* to sleep with me?"

"Yes, the operative word being fall asleep in bed with you. I'm just still feeling a little off and I think I'd sleep better if I wasn't alone."

"You're not alone, luv." He gave me a wink. "But if you're going to sleep in my bed, you need something other than that robe. I'd suggest a bra, panties, hell you should put on those horrendous neoprene shorts, and a shirt. Do you have anything long sleeve? Hell, you should sleep in your flight suit."

"My flight suit is with the hotel dry cleaners getting cleaned for our trip back and other than shorts and tank tops, I packed light for a reason."

"Then it's ugly neoprene and you can wear one of my tee-shirts."

"I can sleep in one of my tops, and I'm not wearing those shorts to bed. They're way to hot, not to mention will reek by morning." Neoprene wasn't the most breathable fabric in the world. Hello, it was neoprene.

I said nothing about the fact I had just watched an entire movie sitting beside him wrapped in nothing but a robe.

"Fine. You put some clothes on, but you're wearing one of my shirts."

"I have shirts."

"Doesn't matter. These are the rules."

"The rules?" I said with a snort.

"Yes, the rules for sleeping in my bed."

"Oh, that's interesting. And these rules are for all women who sleep in your bed?"

"Yeah, for those who *sleep.*" He winked at me. "If you want to do something other than sleep, I have other rules."

"Is that so?" I couldn't help it, but his talk about rules and sleeping in bed were kind of turning me on.

"Yes, but you won't get to hear them until we're doing the non-sleeping kind of activities in bed."

"The non-sleeping kind?"

"Yes, the sexy-times."

"You know I hate when you say it like that. It kills the mood."

"Oh, was I building up to a mood? I thought we were supposed to be getting ready to sleep?"

"Oh, we are."

"Then don't worry about me killing the mood. God knows this is going to be torture on me. I need all the mood-killing I can get."

"Well then, non-sexy-times it is."

"Yup, now get out of bed and put some clothes on. Don't think I haven't been sitting here thinking about everything you *aren't* wearing under that robe. It's killing me that I can't touch you. That movie was dreadful."

"Fine, I'll put something on."

He went to his bag and pulled out a shirt. Tossing it at me, he lowered the register of his voice. "Now, put that on."

Damn but if that command didn't turn me into a quivering mess. Before things got too heated, I headed to the bathroom to put on panties, shorts, no bra, and his teeshirt.

When I exited, his jaw unhinged and dropped with admiration.

"Fuck, it's going to be a long night." He shook his head. "I'll be a gentleman but you need to promise you won't take advantage of me when—"

"When you sneeze?"

"Huh?"

"You know, a natural reaction?"

"Hah! Good one. Yeah, when my sneeze is poking you in the back, you better not tease me. Because it's going to happen."

"How about less talking and more sleeping?"

"I can't believe the first time I get you in bed, I don't get to touch you."

"Well, actually…do you think you could hold me?"

My nerves were frayed and I felt more vulnerable than I wanted to admit. Going to sleep in the arms of a strong man was exactly what I needed. I'd deal with the rest of it later.

With a little more grumbling, Logan finally crawled into bed with me. There was a little adjusting of positions before we settled. His large frame curved around me and his muscular arms wrapped me in a blanket of comfort.

Growing up, it had just been my mother and me. When I had a bad day, or needed a little more loving, she held me like this. Not that I was comparing Logan to my mother, because *Eww gross!* But it felt a little like coming home. In his arms, I felt complete.

I felt safe.

And I drifted off to sleep with my mind thinking about the man who held me in a loving embrace rather than about the man who had tried to strangle me.

When I woke, the long hard length of Logan's erection poked against my ass. I wanted to stretch, but if I did that I would rub up against him. And boy was there a lot to rub up against.

I'd seen his erection tenting the fabric of his pants. He packed something fierce, but feeling it pressing against the crack of my ass changed everything.

"If you wiggle your ass against my cock one more time, I swear I won't be held responsible for what comes next."

His low, husky voice flowed over my skin sending waves of electricity to light up every nerve in my body. And I do mean *every* nerve. I squeezed my thighs together and he groaned.

"I mean it, luv. Not responsible."

I scooted away from him. "I was not wiggling my ass against your dick."

"I prefer cock, but we can call it whatever you want." He turned over and stretched and my mouth dropped at the size of his erection as it pushed against the soft fabric of his boxers. "You might want to use the restroom while you have a chance." He made a vague gesture to his crotch. "Something tells me I'll be in there for longer than usual."

"You're certainly not shy."

"About my cock? Or that you filled my dreams all night long. Oh, the things I did to you…"

I wanted to ask about the things, but knew better to keep my mouth shut.

"I think I'll just pop into the bathroom."

After taking care of business and brushing my teeth, I let Logan know the bathroom was all his. He ran his fingers through his hair and scratched at his beard.

"Except for the erotic dreams, that's the best sleep I've had in years. Maybe I should keep you around as a sleep-buddy."

"A sleep-buddy?"

"Why not? If we're not fucking, might as well take advantage of good sleep." He pointed to my bag. "Don't forget to pack. We're moving into that suite after breakfast."

He disappeared behind the bathroom door. It didn't take long to pack what little I had, which left me to sit at the foot of the bed waiting for him. That's when I heard the low, throaty sounds coming from behind the bathroom door.

I should have stayed where I was. I probably should have moved to the tired looking loveseat on the opposite side of the room.

What did I do?

I tiptoed up to the bathroom door and pressed my ear to eavesdrop on Logan pleasuring himself.

My breathing quickened as his grunts intensified. My pussy throbbed each time he said my name. There was no question who took center stage in his fantasies.

"Fuck, Angel. Fuuuck." His groans turned to labored breathing as his orgasm barreled into him.

What the hell was I doing standing out here, being a voyeur, while a man fantasized about me? I should be in there...with Logan.

He moved around inside the bathroom, his heavy steps moved toward the door. Then there was a thud and the door shivered beneath my ear.

"Next time, hun, I want you in here with me."

I stifled a gasp. How long did he know I'd been standing here?

Shit. Shit. Shit.

His low laughter sent me scrambling to the loveseat I should have chosen over being a Peeping Tom. The shower turned on and the low warbling notes of him singing *Frozen* lifted to my ears. The shit-face was having fun with me.

That was okay. He may have caught me listening to him

masturbate, but I would get him later. He had no idea how fanatical little girls could be about their Disney movies, or how infatuated they were with their first crushes.

That's right Logan Reid. Make fun of me at your own expense.

14

LOGAN

HER SOFT FOOTSTEPS HAD ALERTED ME TO HER PRESENCE outside the bathroom. I'd been doing the five-knuckle hustle but couldn't complete the deed. Each time I got close to coming, I thought about what Clive tried to do to my Angel.

Talk about a mood-killer and dick-deflater.

My frustration level peaked at a solid ten out of ten.

Her soft tread, as she slowly approached, sounded from behind the door. There'd been silence, a long moment when I thought I imagined it, but the lightness of her breaths and a tiny gasp, told me everything I needed to know.

My girl was listening to me jack off.

Dirty girl.

Damn, I loved that. Knowing she listened, blood surged to my flagging cock. My erection returned and my balls drew tight with the promise of my release.

It didn't take long.

Having her close seemed to be the magic ticket. Even if we weren't fucking, knowing she was not only interested, but inquisitive enough to snoop, turned me the fuck on.

And I was going to have fun with her Peeping Tom tendencies.

First, I had an amazing day planned in the morning. It would be perfect to get her mind off what happened last night. Not that I planned it that way when I booked the spa. Sometimes, the universe delivers what we need when we need it most.

I came hard, beating the meat, and grunted through an epic orgasm. Then, I hurried through my shower so that I could join Angel in the room.

She glanced up and her cheeks turned a bright red. That rosy glow licked a path down her neck and angled toward her tits. My gaze followed that delicious path and I bit back a groan.

Someday.

Someday, she'd let me touch her the way I needed to touch her.

"I feel much better. Now to find my pants and put the—"

She held up her hand. "Please don't say it."

My grin stretched ear to ear. "After my hand solo, the Wookie is beat. Are you ready for breakfast? Have all your stuff packed?"

I had a towel wrapped around my waist and didn't miss

the way she checked me out. Making a show of tugging on the towel, I gyrated my hips.

"Wanna finish off your little peepshow with the real thing? Or, are we going to pretend you weren't listening in on my five-knuckle hustle?"

She vented a sigh and covered her eyes. "I won't peek."

"But sweets, I want you to peek. That's what makes it a peepshow."

"Can we not talk about…that?"

"Oh, I'm sure we're going to be talking about it all day long. I'm going to slip it in and out of conversation just to make you squirm. It may be hard, but I'm sure I'll find the right opening to slide it in."

She reached for a pillow and threw it at me. When I went to block, my towel came undone and dropped to the floor. I held the pillow to my chest while her eyes bugged out of her head as she took in my naked glory and fully erect penis.

Slowly, very slowly, I lowered the pillow to cover my engorged member.

"You going to cover those eyes or not?" My voice came out low, throaty, and very aroused.

"You, Logan Reid, are incorrigible." She pressed her palms against her eyes and leaned back on the couch. "Please, cover that beast up."

"Beast? You mean the stallion, don't you? We can let the stallion run. You can take it for a ride and…"

"Ugh!" Her frustrated snort brought laughter to my lips.

"If you say anything about putting it back wet, I'm going to kill you."

"No fun," I said teasingly.

Quickly, I dressed and drew the elastic waistband of my briefs over my jutting erection. To think I'd just rubbed one out a few minutes ago and was already hard? This woman kept me in a state of perpetual arousal.

I threw on a tee-shirt and pair of board shorts. I planned to spend time on the beach while she was in the spa. A quick call downstairs confirmed our accommodations were being upgraded. The new room wouldn't be ready until after lunch, but we could leave our things downstairs.

"You ready?"

She sat on the couch and bit at her nails, looking distracted.

"Angel?"

"Huh?"

"I asked if you were ready." I gestured to her bag. "Are you all packed? We're going to leave our things downstairs until the suite is ready."

"Yeah, sorry. I'm ready."

I grabbed my bag and slung it over my shoulder, then lifted her rolling suitcase to the floor. Pulling up the handle, I went to the door, opened it, and waited for Angel. When she passed me she looked troubled.

"Penny for your thoughts?"

"Clive." That's all she said, but I understood.

Memories of last night would linger for some time. My

job was to distract her as much as possible, but there would be no way to erase what happened.

I dropped our things off at reception and tipped the staff, then took Angel's hand in mine and headed to the hotel restaurant and the buffet I'd been reading about.

The hostess seated us looking out at the beach and we ordered Mimosa's before checking out the spread.

"It all looks amazing," she said. "I don't know where to start."

"I'm going to start there…" I pointed to the far left where the seafood sat and swung my arm in an arc. "And end there. You're going to have to roll me out of here when we're done."

"Hmm, I'm thinking pancakes to start."

"Go for it. I'm eyeing the raw oysters. You know, to help with my stamina."

"I doubt you need any help in that department."

"There's one way to find out, but if you're looking to jump my bones, you'll have to wait. You're booked from nine to two and then from six to midnight you're mine."

"When are you going to tell me what you have planned?"

"Nope, you're not getting me to spill the beans." I gave a playful slap to her ass. "Now, go get your pancakes while I load up on raw oysters."

She rewarded that tiny tap with a smile instead of a frown which excited me. It opened up possibilities and hinted at more than regular sex.

The pancake station was a bottleneck, which meant I made it back to our table before Angel. I popped out my phone and checked the group text all my siblings were on.

We had two family group chats; one with our mother and one without. Then the brothers had our secret box. I think the girls had one too, but no one ever fessed up to it.

I checked the one with mom first where I told everyone where I was and what I was doing. The standard strings of *Take care of yourself!* and *No way!* scrolled past.

Then the sibling chat popped up with a picture of Lizzy and what looked to be a ring on her finger.

Me: What the fuck is that?

Lizzy: What's it look like, Ace?

Me: Anyone vet this guy?

Angie: Chill. He's cool.

Colt: Gabriel and I are on it.

Me: Why is this the first I'm hearing of him? Does mom know?

Lizzy: Not yet! And shush! It's going to be a surprise.

We chatted about our baby sister's engagement for a bit while I picked at my plate and waited for Angel to make it back to her seat.

Lizzy was fresh out of high school. In a month, she'd be starting as a college freshman; far too young to be engaged. Not that I wanted my baby sister to play the field, but she needed to know what was out there before settling down. I opened up the brothers' only chat.

Me: WTF!

Colt: Chill. We've got this covered.

Me: Way to keep me in the dark.

Colt: No one is keeping you in the dark. It literally just happened.

Ryder: Hey Ace. How's paradise?

Me: Pretty damn hot.

Ryder: You live a tough life, dude. Any hot chicks?

Now, wasn't that a loaded question?

Colt: He's too silent. Dude? What's up?

Ryder: LOL. Slow on the trigger, Logan?

Me: It's complicated.

Gabriel: Yo! Leave Lizzy alone. And WTF does complicated mean?

I tried to switch the conversation back to our youngest sister and away from myself.

Me: Lizzy is too young to be getting hitched. I can't believe you're letting this happen.

Gabriel: She's not getting hitched anytime soon. If she does, we're not paying for college.

Our mother was amazing, raising nine kids, however, paying for college wasn't practical for a widow. Fortunately, the older brothers stepped in to fill the gap for their younger siblings.

Gabriel, Colt, and Ryder had college funds started by our father before he passed which paid for most of their school. Dylan had a football scholarship. I went to school on an ROTC scholarship.

When it was the girls' time to head to college, the brothers chipped in. We made it work.

Me: Does she know that?

Gabriel: We talked last night. Now, what's complicated in paradise?

Saved by the fucking bell, Angel finally returned to the table.

Me: Gotta go. My girl just got here.

I gave a snicker as I closed out of the chat and stood as Angel approached. The four of them would have to wonder what I might have said. It was going to piss them off, which was fine by me. I'd rather talk to Angel than my brothers any time, any day.

"Wow, he has manners." Her eyes softened with her smile.

"Is that a surprise?" I made a show of pulling out her chair and sliding it in as she sat.

"Unexpected, but actually not really. You're an interesting man, Logan Reid. Contradictions define you."

"Hmm, I like it when you say my name like that. It rolls off your tongue dripped in sin and seduction."

"You also have an overactive imagination."

"If you think my imagination is overactive, wait until you experience my sex drive."

"I thought we talked about not mixing work and pleasure?"

Shit, what a way to dampen the mood, but I was prepared.

"You can't resist the inevitable. We both know it's going to happen. Might as well give in."

"And there went the gentleman. Enter the overly-sexed scoundrel."

"You might like the scoundrel, but don't worry." I wanted to put her mind at ease. "It's all just words and sexy talk for now. Don't ruin all my fun and take that away."

"I wouldn't dream of it, and I don't think it would be possible." She pointed to my plate and the oysters I had yet to eat. "Not hungry?"

"I was waiting for you."

"You looked pretty intent there on your phone. Everything okay?"

"Oh, I was just talking to my siblings. We have a group chat. It's the only way to keep up with everyone."

"And you have how many siblings again?"

"Eight. Four older brothers and four younger sisters."

"That's insane."

"It's pretty cool."

"How do you keep them separate?"

That was an odd question. I may have a lot of siblings, but they were each incredibly unique. From Gabriel and his law firm, Colt with his medical practice, Ryder and his cars, to Dylan and his sports, we were an eclectic group.

The girls were no different. Angie was following in Gabriel's footsteps, pursuing her law degree. Christina was a school teacher. Delia was our resident genius, working on science I couldn't pronounce, and then there was Lizzy.

"I bet it's terrifying when you bring your dates home to meet the family."

"It might be, but I wouldn't know."

"How's that?"

"I've never brought a girl home."

"Never?"

"Well, I dated in high school, but all my brothers were already out of the house and I didn't really hang out with my sisters. Truthfully, I avoided them as much as possible. They were all little kids and annoying as hell. I quickly learned not to bring anyone home. And as for family reunions, there's just never been anyone worth bringing home."

"Have you ever been in a serious relationship?"

"Not yet, but I'm hoping that'll change." I picked up another oyster. "What about you? Any serious relationships?"

"One or two, but it didn't work out." She leaned back and regarded me for an uncomfortably long period of time. "He turned out to be a player and I don't do cheaters."

"Ah." I sensed her hesitation with me stemmed from whoever that jerk had been.

"Don't judge others by one bad apple."

"Right, says the guy who fucks instead of dates. Which is why, as much fun as the banter is, we should probably leave it there."

That was totally *not* what we needed to do, but how did I convince her to take a chance on a cocksure flyboy who played the field as if it was a real sport? Especially when all I'd done so far was brag about my conquests. I'd certainly screwed the pooch on that one. It was time for damage control.

"Perhaps, it's because the right girl never came along before. Maybe I've been searching all this time, but never found her until now?"

"The right girl?"

"Yeah." I picked up a raw oyster and slurped it down. "You."

She lifted two fingers. "You've known me for the span of two days. Two. You know nothing about me."

"I know you're insanely attracted to me."

She crossed her arms over her chest. "So?"

"You like listening to me jack off when I'm thinking of you."

She shifted in her seat and scanned the nearby tables, but there wasn't anyone close enough to hear our conversation.

"That was a momentary lapse in judgement."

"Did it make you wet?"

"Logan!"

"It's an honest question."

"One I'm not answering."

"You don't have to. I already know the answer. And as for getting to know you better, that's what tonight is for. It's a no-sex evening—even if you beg later—no sex. We're going to play twenty questions and you have to tell the truth."

"That sounds dangerous."

"Well, you can either agree to answer my questions

truthfully, or we can jump in bed and finally scratch this itch between us. I know what your mouth tastes like and I'm dying to find out if the rest of you tastes as sweet."

"Annnnddd… we're back to sex talk."

"You bet." I shoveled some egg into my mouth and watched her from across the table.

At any time, she could have shot me down. That she hadn't told me she loved the banter, but more importantly while she liked it, she couldn't appear to on the outside.

It was important for her to fight against this crazy pull between us. I was fine with that, because I had no problems taking the lead.

"What's happening between nine and two?" She countered with a deflection. "It's awfully specific."

"Between nine and two you will be treated in the fashion which you deserve." I rolled my wrist to glance at my watch. "Which is in less than thirty minutes. If you're going to waste any more time standing in line for pancakes, I suggest you do that now."

She wiped her mouth with her napkin. "Naw, I have something else in mind." Scooting out of her seat, she winked at me. "Be back in a second, flyboy."

While she was gone, I scanned my chat boxes. Mom's box had ten messages, about normal. The sibling box had over twenty. The girls were probably chatting about Lizzy's engagement. The Bro's box had over two hundred messages and I couldn't help but snicker.

My sex life was a constant source of amusement to my

brothers. We didn't share that shit with our sisters. And I had to admit some of my sexual exploits had been egged on by my brothers.

Ryder was the one who dared me into my first threesome. Dylan encouraged me to tie a girl up and do *some of that fifty shades shit.* Yeah, I may or may not know a thing or two about Angel's favorite book.

My brothers lived vicariously through me, but I'd never shared anything else with them about the actual girl.

A part of me wanted to tell them everything about Angel.

About the moment when our gazes collided on that tarmac and my heart skipped a beat. I ached to share all of that with them, but I also selfishly wanted to keep it all to myself.

The past two days felt like a dream. I couldn't shake the feeling I would ruin it if I dared admit any of it was real. For now, I would keep Angel all to myself.

Angel returned with a plate full of raw oysters and my mouth gaped.

"What the fuck? I don't need any more help. I swear my shorts have grown two sizes too short since we sat down."

She lifted an oyster and slurped it down. "Who said they were for you?"

Well, fuck me.

15

ANGEL

I DON'T KNOW WHAT THE HELL OVERCAME ME TO TEASE Logan like that, but I ate four slimy raw oysters in front of him. And I made a show of it, licking, slurping, and commenting on the texture and salty taste.

His eyes practically popped out of his head and I loved the way he squirmed in his seat.

"If you like that so much, I've got something to feed you." He practically growled at me.

"You do?"

"Yes, doll, I fucking do."

A young family had just been seated at the table next to us and the mother gave Logan a dirty look with his cussing. He tried to adjust his erection, but the little six-year-old girl stared at him.

It may have been more fun that it should have, but I really couldn't help myself.

He lowered his voice to a whisper. "And if you're not careful, I'll shove it down your mouth right here." He pretended to drop his napkin and adjusted what needed to be adjusted while he bent down to retrieve it.

"Really?"

"And smack your ass for teasing me, while I'm at it. You'd like that, wouldn't you?"

A needy throb settled between my legs and I pressed my thighs together trying to soothe the ache. It didn't work. I was hot, bothered, and my panties were wet.

The couple finally corralled their kids after ordering drinks and led them to the buffet while Logan's eyes narrowed.

"Teasing me is going to cost you."

"What?" I gave an exaggerated blink. "I have no idea what you're talking about."

"When you finally let me touch you, you're going to suffer, my sweet, not so innocent angel." His eyes narrowed with the intensity of his promise and it was my turn to squirm.

"What? It's just a little innocent flirting." I threw his words back at him and got his attention.

"Is that what this is about? Because I'm not going to stop. I'm a man on a mission and I won't stop until I'm balls deep inside of you."

"Didn't think you would, but I'm tired of blushing. You may not blush, but I know how to get a rise out of you."

"Ha-ha. Very funny." He shoved his index finger toward me. "Just remember that when my head is buried between your legs and you're begging me to let you come. It's a two-way street, baby. And if you want to make this a competition, I'm all on board."

Well, shit, that didn't work out how I planned.

"I take it all back." I glanced at a clock on the wall. "Actually, it's almost nine. Don't we have somewhere to be?"

"Ah, are you an eager beaver?"

My lips twisted. "You know that's one euphemism I've never really liked. Actually, I'm not sure it's a euphemism at all."

"Duly noted. I'll have to think on that, but if you're done with breakfast, we can begin part two of the day."

"Lead on, flyboy."

He jumped up and scooted around the table to help me out of my chair. I don't know why, but he seemed to have ratcheted up his gentleman's game.

I placed my hand in the crook of his arm when he offered it and bit at my lower lip. I didn't like surprises and it was time to put on my game face. Whatever he had planned, even if it sucked, there would be a smile plastered on my face.

We walked out into the lobby and turned around a corner down a long hall. That's when I saw the sign.

"A spa?" My steps slowed and he pulled to a stop.

"What's wrong?"

The smile I determined would be on my face slipped and failed me.

"It's just…I'm not really a spa kind of girl."

"I figured, which is exactly why I planned this."

"Um…" I was trying to parse what he said.

"I arranged for an entire day of pampering, something I'm one-hundred percent certain you would never do for yourself. And you have carte blanche."

"Really?"

"Yes, the only things you must do are the massage, the mani-pedi, facial, and the hair salon."

"Oh, is that all?"

"I left an option for waxing if you want to try that. Not that I'm saying you should, or that I have any particular preference. I just wanted to treat you like a queen for the day. Hair, nails, toes, face, and a massage to ease away any tension you might be carrying." His expression clouded.

"It's a wonderful gift and very thoughtful."

"So, am I right? Have you ever been to a spa?"

"Never, but five hours? That's a long time. Are you going to be with me?"

"Honestly, I thought about a couple's massage, but you need a day to yourself."

"That's probably the most genuine thing you've said since we met."

"How's that?"

"You're giving up time with me so that I can relax."

"Yeah, all fucking noble of me, isn't it?"

More than he knew. Clive had hit me like a ton of bricks, but in the hours afterward where I tried to keep my shit together and act normal, and in the nightmares which followed, stress built to an intolerable level.

I needed an outlet. Spending the day at the spa may not have been my choice. Sitting around doing nothing might make the obsessive thoughts worse. I was hoping for an aggressive hike or some other physical activity, but I'd do this. I was going to do it because Logan put in the time and effort trying to do something nice for me.

Besides, he was right about one thing. This was something I'd never do for myself. It was worth a little experimentation.

"What will you be doing?" I asked.

"I'm going to chill on the beach and read a certain book. Research a thing or two about…stuff?"

"Stuff?"

"Yeah, stuff."

"Don't get too far ahead of yourself, flyboy."

"Just hopeful. So, are you game?"

It wasn't clear if he was talking about the spa or the *stuff*. Not that it mattered. I was up for both.

"I have a choice?"

"Well, I can't force you to do anything you don't want to do."

Again, from his tone, he wasn't talking about spending the day in a spa.

A spa?

Of all the things I imagined, this hadn't made the list. The idea of sitting idle for five hours while other people pampered me felt a little uncomfortable. But how could I say no to those baby blues.

He dropped me off with a kiss to my cheek and promised to be back at two when my spa day ended.

My day began easily enough. I filled out a basic health questionnaire then changed into a robe and slid my feet into a pair of slippers. I had two massages planned for the day. The first was a ninety-minute deep tissue massage and I think I found heaven as my muscles were kneaded and forced to surrender.

My long locks were expertly assessed by the hair dresser. I didn't need much done except a cut and style. I did opt for a blow out and loved the silky texture of my hair. Deep ebony it shined like I'd never seen it before.

Mani-pedi was next. Not much a fan of the pedi, I endured that with a tight smile and gritted teeth. The mani was a struggle as well. There was just something about the nail file I couldn't get past. But, I had them do a French manicure and it was pretty fancy.

I ate lunch in the spa, enjoying a glass of champagne while deliberating a few options which had been left open. I had a facial and a rejuvenating fifty-minute massage to end my day. Which left me to debate the pros and cons of waxing.

I could get my eyebrows waxed or threaded. What was

threading? A quick google search revealed that answer and I quickly said no. Which left me to contemplate my bikini area.

Since I'd shaved my legs in the shower, getting my legs done didn't make sense, but what about *down there?* I'd never done that before, and the variety of options surrounding what was possible quickly became overwhelming.

"Have you decided?" My therapist, a petite beauty named Brittny—I think her parents forgot to buy a vowel when they named her—seemed to be the one responsible for guiding me from one station to the next.

"I don't really know what to do?"

"Have you ever had a bikini wax before?"

"No, and it seems a bit invasive."

Like how did that actually work? And who made it their life's passion to rip pubic hair off vaginas for a living?

"It's not, and our technicians are professional. People often think more of it than it really is. Are you interested in a standard bikini wax or a full Brazilian?"

"Explain that one to me? Why would anyone want that done?"

A serene smile ghosted across Brittny's face. "Some women simply love the feeling of being bare down there and many of their partners prefer it. For some, it enhances sexual pleasure. If you've never tried it, I'd recommend it at least once. It'll be a big surprise to your boyfriend and it could be fun later tonight."

"So, you've done it?"

"Not a hair down there and my boyfriend loves it. If I can be a bit forward…"

Forward, this girl had few filters, but I guess it was a part of her job; educating me.

"Please." I gestured for her to continue.

"Not only does it make cunnilingus more enjoyable for both parties, the smoothness of the skin heightens all sensation. I highly recommend it. And if you don't like it, just let everything grow back."

"But it hurts, right?"

"Beauty hurts, but trust me, it's worth it."

I bit at my lower lip. Doing this meant I was mentally making the decision to sleep with Logan. But who was I kidding? It was an eventuality determined only by how long I held out.

Not sleeping with my coworkers used to be a big deal with me when I was in the military. There had been one or two pilots where things got a little too friendly, but it had always been a line I never crossed.

I wasn't in the military anymore and those rules and regulations no longer applied. What was I afraid of?

You're afraid of being used and tossed aside.

That hit the nail on the head, but I sensed that wasn't the case with Logan. He could have sex with practically anyone he wanted. Sex on a stick, he was every woman's wet dream. If he was going to fuck and dump me, why waste this much effort on a woman playing hard to get?

The man was in paradise, the perfect place to find a

one-night fling. Yet, he stayed with me. He took me parasailing, rode dolphins with me, and snorkeled with turtles. He walked on the beach with me, doing nothing more than holding hands. And when he did kiss me, it had been to block asshole Clive.

That kiss. My eyes closed with the memory of that kiss. I wanted more of that.

"I'll try it." I handed the brochure back to Brittny.

"Great. I'll get it set up. Can I get you another glass of champagne?"

If they were going to be ripping out all my pubic hair, I'd need two more glasses of champagne.

"Please." I downed the last of the bubbly and handed the empty to her. Gathering my robe around me, I came to terms with my decision.

At two, I had been pampered to exhaustion. The yawns kept coming. When I left the spa, Logan waited in their tiny lounge. Toned and tanned, he looked amazing in his board shorts and a tee-shirt which struggled to contain his muscular bulk.

"How was it?" His charismatic smile took my breath away.

"It was incredible, actually."

That was the truth. My nether regions stung from the waxing, but I could already tell a difference. I didn't know if Brittny had been telling the truth or not, but I could *feel* my panties touching my tender bits. I never really thought about it, or felt that before.

It was a little erotic and I felt kind of naughty, like I had a secret I couldn't wait to share.

"What did you like best?"

Honestly, the waxing. Not because it felt good. It hurt like a mother-fucker, but because of what I hoped it would feel like later. No way in hell was I telling him about that.

"The massage was intense, but the facial kind of surprised me. Very relaxing. And I think I've decided to never do a mani-pedi again."

"Really?"

"Yeah, it was like dragging fingernails across a chalk-board. Not for me."

He lifted my hand and looked at my nails. "Pretty."

"Thanks."

"In fact, you look amazing. Gorgeous actually. I love what they did to your hair."

"Thanks. Did you have fun on the beach? Get all your research done?"

"I did, actually. Learned lots of interesting tidbits."

"Good." I yanked my hand from his and made a show of walking away from him. "I'll be interested in seeing how much you learned."

His lack of a comeback brought a grin to my face and I spun around to watch him stammer.

"Are you coming or not?"

"Well, damn woman. I practically just came in my shorts right then. I should book you more spa days."

"Don't get ahead of yourself. I'm exhausted from all that relaxing and didn't really sleep well last night."

Nightmares kept me up, but so too did the long hard length of him poking me all night long. Tonight, that wouldn't be a problem.

"I think I'm going to take a nap."

"A nap? Like a *nap* nap, or some aggressive cuddling? Because I can get on board with the cuddling."

"An actual nap. Let's save the aggressive cuddling for later tonight."

His eyes popped. "Later tonight?"

"Yes, flyboy. Later…"

"Well shit." He lowered his hands to cup his groin and I smiled at the prominent bulge he struggled to hide.

Leaving a frustrated Logan down in the lobby, I headed up to his room, then returned a few minutes later, chagrined. Apparently, I not only forgot we left our bags with the front desk but that we were also switching to a suite. I blamed Logan for my inability to think straight.

He stood by the receptionist's desk with a keycard in his hand.

"Missing something?"

I tried snatching it out of his hand, but he lifted his arm and took it out of my reach. I tried again, and we played a game of keep away which I lost.

Finally, I put my hands on my hips and blew out a frustrated breath.

"Give it to me." I nearly stamped my foot, but decided against it because of the smirk plastered all over his face.

"Oh, I'll give it to you."

"That's not what I mean."

"What do you mean, my naughty angel? I'm talking about a keycard. Are you talking about something else?" His eyes flicked down to his crotch.

My gaze followed. No bulge. He seemed to have tamed the beast lurking in his pants.

"I meant the keycard."

"Oh, it sounded like you meant something else."

"Well?"

"Well, what?"

"Are you going to give it to me?"

"I most definitely will, right after dessert."

My cheeks heated.

"But I need a little sample right now. I'll make you a deal."

"Something tells me I'm not going to like this." I blew out a breath, frustrated, but undeniably turned on and curious.

"Probably not, but then again, I think you're going to really enjoy it."

"What's your price?"

"A kiss for the keycard."

"A kiss?"

"Yup."

"Just a kiss?" I sensed mischief afoot.

"Yes, just a kiss."

"But…"

"Well yeah, there is a but. You, my darling angel, must kiss me. If you do a passing job, I'll give you the keycard."

"I could just have them make another."

"You could, but you and I both know there's no fun in that. And since the timeline of our evening activities has been set, you're safe from any inappropriate assault with a friendly weapon. On my honor."

"You don't say." I gave a soft laugh. "Passable? It only needs to be passable?"

"Yes. You can save the sexy stuff for later, when you kiss…something other than my lips."

"Hmm." I licked my lips thinking about what that would be like.

"Yeah, do that again."

"You're a pervert you know, and exchanging a kiss for what is rightfully mine is extortion."

"Of the best kind. What's it going to be? A kiss and a nap upstairs? Or, no kiss and no napping? Trust me when I say you really should be fully rested for tonight."

"That depends if I get to nap alone. I really am beat." More mentally than physically.

Physically, my body hummed. It wanted everything Logan promised and more. An ache built between my legs with the thought of it, and with my new bare skin down there, that ache took on a life of its own.

"As long as you're ready for dinner by six."

"Any specific dress code?"

"That slinky black dress is perfect."

It would be perfect because that's all I planned on wearing.

Without thinking about it too hard, I wrapped my arms around his neck and pulled him down until our lips hovered a kiss away. "Is this what you want?"

"You know what I want. I want your mouth on my lips, on my cock, I want them everywhere at once."

His words were magical things. I could feel my panties getting wetter and wetter with each ragged breath. I had him on edge and knew exactly what he fantasized about. But this was on me.

He wanted me to kiss him and he wasn't going to ask again. He stubbornly held that damn keycard above his head.

But I would drive him a little bit crazy first. Instead of kissing him, I lifted on my toes and sucked his earlobe into my mouth. He reached down and cupped my ass while a low groan escaped him.

He was rock hard and I could feel his erection pressing against me.

My body burned.

This was a really bad idea, but I couldn't turn my body off. I couldn't stop wondering what it was going to feel like when he finally slipped inside of me.

He was large enough I worried about the stretch I would

endure, the pain that would follow, and the pleasure which would ruin me forever.

I nibbled on his earlobe and teased him with light flicks of my tongue.

"While that is erotic as shit, my little vixen, that is not my mouth. Give me your fucking mouth before I turn you around and take you in front of all these people."

He wouldn't really do that, would he?

One look at the way his pupils had blown out with lust and I had my answer.

Logan moaned as I licked the seam of his lips, hovering mine a breath away.

"You have to promise to let me walk away when the kiss ends."

"I promise."

"When I say it ends."

"Fuck Angel, just fucking kiss me already. You're killing me here."

What if he didn't like the way I kissed? He had been the one who kissed me, controlling every aspect of that earth-shattering experience. I was more timid and unsure.

But this was my kiss.

Acutely aware we stood in a public place, I closed the distance and our lips touched with a burst of static electricity.

This was where good decisions went to die, because Logan Reid might very well be the worst decision in my life, not that I cared in the slightest.

I meant to keep it light and teasing. My goal had been to torture him. I failed miserably, because the moment our lips met, I needed more.

My arms wrapped around his neck and I pressed my body tight against his, rubbing shamelessly over his erection as I licked and nibbled and demanded entry into his mouth.

He let me in and lowered his arm to cup my ass cheek. Practically dragging me up his body, he rocked his groin against my pelvis as our lips tangled and danced. My fingers threaded through his hair, tugging on the strands, as I devoured his mouth with mine.

My eyes rolled back as he brought one hand up to grip my hair. Winding his fingers in my nape, he gave a sharp yank which broke our locked lips.

"Get your ass upstairs, now."

"Logan…" My voice was breathy and hot.

"I don't give a shit what you say, but I need to be inside you now. This is your one chance to say *No*. Speak now or forever hold your peace because we're going to fuck."

"What about tonight?"

"We'll fuck all through the night, but I'm not waiting any longer. Yes, or no, Angel? What's it going to be?"

I bit my lip and glanced toward the elevators.

"I'm taking your silence for the yes it is."

He pulled me through the lobby and stabbed at the button to the elevator. When the doors opened he released me and stepped inside, placing his back to the wall.

"Last chance, babe. You can stay if you want, but if you

step inside this elevator, this ends only one way, with me inside of you."

I took a step, and then another, until my tits brushed his chest. Each of my inhales rubbed my nipples against his chest, turning them into hard little pebbles.

He wrapped his arm around my waist and any space between us disappeared.

"You're fucking mine, my sweet, sweet angel, but I'm going to make you pay."

His words struck a match and a firestorm ignited between us. My arms wrapped around his neck and my lips lifted to meet his passion with my own.

I'm surprised we made it to the suite with our clothes intact.

16

LOGAN

So much for my grand dinner plans. I opened the door to the suite and yanked Angel inside. There would be nothing gentle about what happened next. I needed to be inside of her and it needed to happen now.

But I forced myself to take a breath and slow things down. Hard didn't have to mean fast, and I intended to savor our first time together.

My gaze dropped to take in her tight little body. The way her mouth moved as her tongue licked along her lower lip. She was watching me.

"I can't wait to feel your lips on me." Husky and low, I practically growled those words. With any other woman, I would have her on her knees sucking me off as I took my pleasure.

I'd dreamt about this moment too many times and fantasized about it with my hand wrapped around my cock.

I swallowed as she gave a slow blink and dropped her gaze to my shorts. The flimsy material did nothing to hide my raging hard on. Her eyes slowly returned to meet mine.

Off the charts, our chemistry electrified the air. The energy between us licked up and down my skin, firing all my nerves at once.

"Do you feel it? Can you feel the air sizzling?"

She gave a slow nod, and her pink tongue darted out to lick her lips again. I moved toward her, backing her up against the door until her back hit with a thud.

"I want to fuck you right against this door. I want to slide inside of you and feel what I've been dreaming about from the minute I laid my eyes on you. But I'm not going to do that. Do you know why?"

When she didn't answer, I placed my finger under her chin and forced her to lift her gaze and meet mine.

"Answer me."

"I want you to fuck me."

"Bad girls don't get what they want, and you've been teasing me nonstop. I told you I was going to make you suffer, and that begins now."

Her eyes widened.

Without a word, I pivoted and pointed to the couch. "Clothes off, and I want you sitting in the middle of that couch, legs spread, hands on your knees."

"Logan…"

"I mean it, Angel. You're mine. That means I get to do whatever I want, and I seem to remember promising to make you beg. Now strip and sit on that couch like a good girl."

To my utter amazement, and delight, she pushed off from the door and moved into the center of the room.

It was a fucking huge suite with a sitting room and two doors leading off either side, but damn if I cared anything about the decor. All I saw was my fucking angel as she reached down and grabbed the hem of her shirt.

Slowly, she lifted it over her head. I stood by the door, not trusting myself to move while my fists clenched and unclenched with my desire to rush over and rip the offensive piece of fabric from her body.

She tossed the tee-shirt to the ground, then reached behind her back to unhook her bra. The straps over her shoulders fell down her arms and she looked at me, almost as if asking for permission.

"Drop it." My growl rolled through the space between us and she dropped the lacy bra.

Her perfect tits with tight nipples begged me to go to them, kiss them, and knead them with my hands. Fuck, I would bury my face in them, kissing and licking her nipples. Hell, I wanted to slide my cock between her beautiful tits, moving ever so slowly until I couldn't stand it anymore.

"The shorts. Lose the shorts."

She seemed incredibly turned on by my commands, moving to follow each one. Her compliance sent blood racing to my dick. It was so fucking painful. I didn't know how my dick didn't explode.

Her shorts met the floor and I pointed to her panties.

"Everything. Strip for me."

Her fingers hooked under the top of her panties. When she slid her panties off, I let out a low groan.

Her hips shimmied while my mouth dried up from panting. Fuck that, I was struggling not to come in my pants.

"You're fucking bare. Is that for me?"

She gave a little nod.

Holy shit. She had the spa give her a Brazilian for me.

"That's so fucking hot." I pointed to the couch. "Sit in the middle and show me that fucking pussy. Are you wet for me?"

She gave another nod. Evidently, she had lost her voice. That was okay, and insanely hot. I loved her submission.

I had enough words for the both of us. As she took her seat, I stepped away from the door, freeing myself from the last anchor holding me back.

"Spread your legs."

Her knees knocked together, but then she took a deep breath. Her tits rose then fell and her knees slowly parted to reveal a glistening wetness I couldn't wait to taste.

Licking my lips, I pulled at the Velcro fastening of my shorts and reached in to free my engorged cock. With my hand on the shaft, I slowly drew upward until my palm covered the crown.

She was wet.

I was fucking wet.

Soon, we'd be wet together.

Fucking.

"Hands on your knees, and Angel..."

Her eyes, which had been ogling my dick, snapped to my face and widened.

"If you move those hands from your knees, I'm going to stop. I'm going to put my dick back in my pants, and I'm going to leave this room. You'll have to wait until after dinner before we try this again, hot, bothered, and aroused. Do you understand?"

She gulped so hard I could hear it, but she still didn't speak.

"I asked a question. Do. You. Understand?"

Shit, but I was getting off more than I thought possible being in control. I'd only dabbled in shit like this before, but with her? Those doe-eyes following my every step? It was intoxicating.

She found her voice and breathed out a shaky, "Yes."

"Good girl."

My hand kept moving up and down my cock. I shouldn't stimulate myself, because it felt too damn good. The likelihood of coming prematurely was pretty damn high, but I couldn't help it. I needed something to ease the ache.

The damn coffee table was too fucking close. I had to move it out of the way, sliding it over the carpet. I stepped in front of her, hand proudly on my dick.

All she had to do was lean forward. Her rosebud lips were at the perfect height to suck me dry. I would have to remember that for later tonight.

But this wasn't about me.

"You can have some of this later." I released my cock and folded my large frame until I knelt between her legs. "Damn, but I can smell you and you're so fucking wet."

I slid my hands beneath her thighs and yanked her to the edge of the couch until her ass practically hung off the edge. Pushing my shoulders between her legs, I forced her to open wide for me.

Without waiting another second, I buried my face between her legs and tasted heaven. Having my mouth on her body for the first time drove me insane, and the smoothness of her skin was nirvana.

A low groan escaped me as I devoured her like a wild animal. I couldn't get enough. I was in such a frenzy, I had to force myself to slow down.

I worked my tongue, tasting, licking, and teasing while I learned what drove her crazy.

Angel let out a long shriek as I licked her slit and bit down on her clit. I told her this would be torture, and I intended to make her suffer for every erection I'd endured since laying eyes on her that very first time.

The scruff of my beard rubbed her inner thighs, but she

didn't seem to care. I didn't either and the thought of her suffering a burn from my beard for the next day, or two, fucking sounded delightful.

She would remember me for days.

I settled into a comfortable position with a groan and used my tongue to bring her to the edge of orgasm. Then I stopped and gave a low chuckle when she screamed.

"Fuck Logan! I was almost there."

"Do you want more?"

"Yes!"

"Beg for it."

"Why you fucking little prick."

"Fucking comes next and you've seen my cock. There's nothing little about it, but if you want to come, you have to beg."

"Bastard."

"It's called payback."

While we chatted, I took the opportunity to slide a finger into her pussy. It took half a second to find the little rough patch that was her g-spot. I gave it a little rub and laughed as her eyes rolled back and her hips jerked forward.

She lifted her hand.

"Uh-uh. Put that back. You know what happens if you move your hands."

"I fucking hate you." Her hand went back to her knee.

"I love that you hate me right now." I inserted another finger and slid my fingers in and out. Each time, I pressed on her g-spot, loving the way her breathy moans sounded. "You taste like sin. Now beg."

I growled over her clit and blew softly on the sensitive nub until her cries turned breathy. Then I circled my tongue around it. I buried my whole face between her legs, intent on giving her the best oral sex, and most intense, orgasm of her life.

"Oh my God, I hate you, but please don't stop."

I used my hands to grip her ass and hold her against my face as I slipped my tongue inside of her.

It was all she needed.

She came fast, but it lasted forever, and I didn't let up until she stopped shaking and her body went limp. Her hands had fallen off her knees, but it didn't really matter anymore.

"I need to be in you." But where the fuck were my condoms? "Shit, hang on."

A quick inspection of one of the bedrooms revealed my bag. I dug until I found a condom. By the time I returned to Angel, I had the foil ripped and my cock sheathed.

I stopped before her and her lids fluttered open.

"That was..." She sounded drunk on sex.

"That was nothing."

I knelt before her again. My cock and her pussy were at the perfect height for a little vigorous fucking. Her gaze strayed down to my cock and her hand reached out.

"Can I touch it?"

"It's going to be inside of you in a second. I think it's okay to touch it."

Her delicate fingers wrapped around me and I let out a low groan. She gave a slow pump, jerking me off.

I removed her hand and suddenly lifted her ass up until her pussy was aligned with my cock.

"I've waited forever for this."

Her soft laugh caught me unaware. "It's only been two days."

"The longest two days ever." I looked down so that I could watch the moment I sank into her wet heat. But I would go slow. The thick flare of my cock stretched her entrance and I paused to make sure she was okay.

"That feels so good."

Encouraged, I moved quicker than I wanted, slamming into her with a sudden, and uncontrollable, thrust of my hips.

"Fuuuuck, that feels so good." Her hips moved up to meet that thrust and her tiny gasp encouraged me to move.

I fucked her.

Nothing slow.

Nothing easy.

I gripped her hips with enough force she would likely be bruised, but I didn't care. And she didn't seem to mind as my hips moved like a piston and I fucked her with every-thing I had.

No longer able to piece together a coherent thought,

words failed me. I fucked her hard and her cries pierced the air.

"You're so fucking beautiful, Angel." I leaned forward to capture her lips and her hands wrapped around my neck.

"Harder, Logan. Harder. Don't you dare take it easy on me. I won't break."

I hadn't realized I'd been holding back. It didn't feel like I was.

"You're so gorgeous with my cock inside of you. I wish you could see this." My hips gyrated in a circular motion, as I tried to rub her clit as I fucked her. Balls deep, she fit me like a glove.

"You feel so good," I said. "Fuck, I'm so fucking close."

She wrapped her legs around my hips, letting me in deeper than before. I wanted to place her flat on the floor, cover her with my body and drill into her, but she shook her head when I tried moving us.

"Just. A. Little…ahhhhh." Her muscles clenched around my cock, tightening with each spasm as her orgasm overtook her. She spoke with the most seductive, husky voice. "That was intense."

"Squeeze your pussy around me, baby. Swallow me whole."

When her muscles clenched around my cock, I thrust into her with more force. Reason fled and in its place something else took hold. I was a rutting beast staking claim to what was mine.

Her hair was a hot mess. Her eyes smoldered. She never

looked hotter to me with her naked body wrapped around mine. The slick sounds of our combined arousal, and the slapping of our skin, filled the air.

"You're going to feel me between your legs in the morning."

"I hope so. Harder, Logan. Please. Fuck me."

I moved my hips, getting rougher with her as I let the beast within free. My thrusts sped up and I kissed her roughly on the mouth with none of the finesse from before.

Ramming into her, I savored the addictive taste of her and abandoned her mouth for the creamy expanse of her breasts. I found a nipple, licked it, then bit down hard until she cried out.

That cry drew my balls tight and I finally let go of the hold I had placed on my release. My orgasm crashed down on me. My guttural noises echoed around the room as my body convulsed around hers. I kept moving in and out as my orgasm faded.

"You're so fucking...so fucking wonderful," I said. "Fuck, I want to do that again."

"I do too, but next time you get the couch and I get to swallow you whole."

"Fucking music to my ears." My Angel might be more adventurous than I hoped. "I can't wait to feel your lips wrapped around my cock, but I need a moment to recharge."

"And I'm still wanting that nap. How about some non-aggressive cuddling? Will you hold me while I sleep?"

"Do you mind if my dick pokes you in the ass?"

"Not at all."

I picked her up and carried her to one of the beds. We had two separate rooms, but I had a feeling we would only be sleeping in one. I planned on using every surface in this suite, both horizontal and vertical, to fuck her, but for now we would sleep.

17

ANGEL

LOGAN'S POWERFUL FRAME CURVED AROUND MINE. OUR bodies fit together like two pieces of an unusual puzzle. His arms wrapped around me and I snuggled into his embrace, feeling satiated and incredibly happy.

Other thoughts would come, but I pushed them off to deal with them later.

As I drifted off to sleep, his long length hardened and pushed against the crack of my ass. I should have turned over and helped him relieve that ache, but exhaustion pulled at me.

Sometime around four pm, I woke. Logan was still asleep and I took a moment to admire the gentle lines of his face. Strong and powerful, there was a breathtaking vulnerability in his slumber.

I wandered into the main living area. The remnants of

our lovemaking was scattered around the room. I grabbed his tee-shirt, bringing it close to flood my senses with his unique scent, then decided to pull it over my head. I loved having the scent of him all around me.

In the small kitchenette, I poured myself a glass of water, then went to the majestic floor to ceiling windows to admire the view outside.

Late afternoon, the beach wasn't crowded and I realized it may not be best to stand in front of the windows in nothing other than a tee-shirt which barely covered my ass.

As I stared out the window and quenched my parched throat, chills suddenly ran down my spine. I turned around and found Logan leaning against the doorjamb of the bedroom with his heavy blue eyes taking me in.

"You're fucking gorgeous. You know that?"

Now that we weren't in the throes of passion and heavy sex, an awkwardness overcame me. With the way his hungry gaze raked my body, all my nerves came alive. They sang with desire and my need for him. Rather than my thirst for him being quenched by our previous lovemaking, it was now ten times worse.

He wore nothing, perfectly comfortable with his nudity while I looked for something to cover up. Which didn't make any sense, because I wanted to strip bare and have him fuck me again.

A needy ache settled between my legs.

"Take it off." His low command came barely above a whisper, but it set my heart racing.

"But the window."

"Don't make me ask again."

"But…"

"Don't fucking care. Take it off and come here." He uncrossed his arms and waited for me, as if I would do exactly as he commanded.

And I did.

I walked over to him as I pulled his tee-shirt over my head. He grabbed the shirt from my hands and tossed it to the floor.

"I can't stand seeing anything cover your body. Not when we have only a few hours together."

His cock, fully rigid, stood straight up between his legs. I closed my eyes and took a moment to enjoy his heated gaze as it licked over my skin. I wanted his lips on me, but I would take his sultry gaze for now.

"Are you on the pill?"

"Huh?"

"Are you?"

"Yes."

"We're going to fuck. Several more times. It's going to happen, and I'll go downstairs to buy a box of condoms if I need to. I used up my only one. I'm clean. If you're on the pill, and it's okay, I'd rather not get dressed and go downstairs."

"Okay."

"Turn around and face the wall." The way he took charge during sex seemed to be my kryptonite, because I was immediately wet for him.

He leaned against me, letting his cock rub against my ass as he ground his hips. With a kiss to the back of my neck, he took my wrists in his hands and gently lifted my arms over my head. Placing them against the wall he growled into my ear.

"Don't move." His command came with a chuckle, because he knew this turned me on. "I need to be inside of you, and it's going to be dirty and rough."

He reached between my legs, fingers searching for my slit.

"So fucking wet. You're incredible." He slipped two fingers inside my pussy, then lined up his hips. The hot tip of his penis pressed against my folds. "You like it rough don't you?"

"Yes."

"And hard?"

"Very hard." My legs shook as I admitted my desire.

Without warning, he entered me in one powerful thrust, causing me to gasp against the sudden pain as his cock stretched my walls. He thrust roughly into me, causing me to cry out as he chased his pleasure.

There was nothing gentle about what came next, and there was something insanely erotic about the way he used my body to satisfy his needs. Not that mine didn't respond.

Pressed up against the wall, as he took me from behind, I climaxed fast. As my orgasm ripped through me, he gripped my hair and yanked my head back as his mouth crashed down over mine. He slammed into me, grunting as he came, milking the end of his release.

We stood there breathless and spent.

When he stopped moving, he lifted his mouth from mine and gazed deep into my eyes. "Fucking mine. You're mine now. I'm addicted to you. Do you know that?"

I didn't know what to say, so I remained silent. Thoughts swirled in my head, festering, negative things, because I couldn't shake a bad feeling.

I knew Logan Reid.

The man fucked.

He didn't date.

I never wanted this to end, but it would.

Sometime soon.

Probably at the end of this job.

He would leave. I didn't know how I would survive the desertion, the abandonment, and the loss. But I would.

And I would do it with a smile on my face.

I was so fucking screwed; literally and figuratively.

He pulled out and gave a light tap to my ass. "Come, let's take a shower. We have to get ready for dinner."

I leaned against the wall, not wanting to move from where he'd fucked me. There'd been something primal and insanely sexy about him taking what he wanted, but I did move. I wrapped my arms around myself and admired his firm ass and muscular back as he headed into the bedroom.

"You don't want to eat in?" I asked.

"I want to never leave and fuck you all night long." He

flashed a wink. "I'm an addict and you're my drug, but I've got something amazing planned."

He used his mouth and fingers to make me come one more time in the shower. I took his dick in my hand and slowly stroked until he spurted cum all over my belly and tits.

"You look good with my cum on you." He spread it around my skin, massaging it into my breasts, then helped me wash all of it off. "You know this makes you mine, right?"

I gave a soft nod. "Yeah." I wanted to add, *for the time being*, but I didn't. *Knock it off with these negative thoughts.*

But I couldn't, and as I dressed, they swirled in my head, gaining strength and momentum.

I pulled the black dress over my head and Logan came up to me. He pulled me against his body and leaned down for a kiss.

"If I told you not to wear your bra and panties, what are the chances you'd obey? Do you like it when I tell you what to do?"

Did I? From the sudden throbbing between my legs, I think I did.

I took his lower lip between my teeth and gave a little nibble. "Looks like I read your mind. I'm not wearing any."

"Well, shit. Now I want to fuck you again."

"We'll be late for our six o'clock date."

"I know. Trust me, I'm weighing the options."

"We could stay here. Order in…"

"You make it quite tempting, but I don't want to miss out."

"Miss out on what?"

He stubbornly refused to tell me what his plans were. Only that I was his from six until midnight.

"You'll see. Now, slip on your shoes and let's get out of here before I bend you over that counter and take you from behind."

That sounded like a lot of fun.

"You sure you don't want to stay?"

He smacked my ass. Harder than before, it lifted me on my toes.

"Hey, that hurt."

"Wasn't supposed to tickle. My self-control is slipping. It's time to go. Trust me, you don't want to miss this."

"Fine, you win."

I grabbed my fanny pack. It didn't go with the tiny black dress, but I packed light and only had the fanny pack. As I exited the suite, he grabbed my ass and gave a squeeze.

"So fucking sexy. I'm already hard."

I could've said something. Anything would have sufficed to get him to turn around and spend the rest of the evening inside that suite. It may be a little selfish of me, but we only had this one night left in the Caymans. I wanted to spend all of it wrapped up in each other.

Tomorrow evening, we would take the Truitt's home and leave paradise behind. I could feel the minutes ticking by as we ran out of time.

Down the elevator, through the lobby, I expected us to head to the valet where we would hop in a cab and go to some fancy restaurant. What I didn't expect was for Logan to take me to the beach.

The hotel staff had beached a catamaran. Not one of the big monsters which took tourists on snorkel and sunset cruises, but something smaller. Logan took me directly to it.

"What's this?"

"Sunset dinner cruise and a game of twenty-questions. Or did you forget?"

"I remember the questions, but this is incredible. Is it just us?"

"Yeah, I wanted something intimate and a venue where you were kind of stuck with me. You know, with no escape. Like a captive...how does that sound?"

Sexy as fuck.

"It's time to learn your secrets, my sweet angel."

"And yours."

"True."

"It's not really an intimate dinner. Not on a boat that size when you add in the crew."

He snickered. "Sweetie, it's just going to be you and me."

"But..."

"Call me Captain Reid, aviator and sea-faring captain at your disposal."

"Wow, I'm already learning something new."

"I learned to sail as a kid, and made arrangements with the hotel to let me take this out. That's what I was doing most of the afternoon. They had to check me out on the boat and make sure my boasts weren't just that. We have it until midnight."

"So, truly an *intimate* sunset cruise?"

"Very intimate. I see where your dirty little mind is headed."

"Hmm, full disclosure."

"Yes?"

"I planned on ordering raw oysters for dessert and teasing you as I slurped them down."

"You teased me enough at breakfast, but I like where your mind is headed. I should punish you though, for such wicked thoughts."

If his punishments were anything like earlier, I would misbehave all the time.

He separated from me to talk with the staff who were holding the boat for us. The seas were calm and the boat rocked in the tiny waves lapping the shoreline. A light breeze blew off the water and the sun dipped toward the horizon. We still had an hour or two of light before the sun set.

After I climbed on board, Logan helped to push us off the beach. He jumped on board and we were adrift. The motor engaged and he backed us away from the beach until we passed the outer reef where the swells increased to gently flowing rollers.

The engine disengaged and Logan moved about the boat, putting away the sails.

"Can I help?"

"I got it. You relax and enjoy the ride."

"I'd like that. I haven't ridden the stallion yet."

He froze and turned to me. "We're far too close to the beach for sexy-fun-times. But you'll definitely get a chance. I can't wait to watch your tits bounce as you ride me, but I'm in a quandary."

"A quandary? That's a big word."

"While I love the idea of you fucking me, I kind of have an urge to stick my dick in your mouth and find out if your lips feel as good as I think they will wrapped around me. Do you see the dilemma?"

"I do." I leaned back and soaked up the sun, then I peeked up at him. "I suppose I'm at your mercy, Captain. Your wish is my command."

"Fuck, Angel, you're killing me."

"So, what's it going to be, Captain? Suck your dick or ride that stallion?"

He glanced out over the waters, then stomped over to me. One hand went down to unfasten his pants while the other gripped me by the hair. A quick tug, and I was on my knees, eyes level with his raging erection.

"Open."

I wanted him in my mouth. I wanted to taste him and maybe live out a little bit of a fantasy. Would he take control, or would he allow me to drive him crazy?

Settling on my knees, I looked up and took in his dark scowl.

"You're fucking beautiful on your knees, luv, but you'll be absolutely stunning with my cock in your mouth. Now, open."

His breathing, already labored, became harsh and ragged as I wrapped my hand around the base of his cock. Precum glistened at the tip and I leaned forward and licked it off.

His hand tightened in my hair, and I knew I wouldn't be in control for much longer. Logan moaned as I licked his tip. When I looked up at him, the sun was behind him, heading toward the horizon. His features were cast in shadow but I imagined his eyes rolling back as he tugged on my hair.

"Don't fucking make me wait. Take me in."

He guided my head toward his cock and I opened. With him in control, he shoved his cock all the way down my throat. I sucked and licked as I stroked the silky skin of his thick shaft and traced the lines of the engorged vessels.

"Yes, that's perfect. Suck it, baby. Take me whole. I've wanted this since the moment I saw you. You have no idea how this feels."

He clenched his ass cheeks and his abs rippled as he tightened them. I sucked harder and moved my hand at the base of his shaft in tandem with my mouth.

But it soon became clear that he lost control. I braced my hands on his thighs as he controlled my head, thrusting his hips forward and back, sliding in and out of my mouth. I kept my lips wrapped around his shaft and licked as I could.

Then his body began to shake. "I'm coming."

He started to pull out, which I appreciated, but for some reason I wanted him not to have to short his pleasure. I gripped his thighs and leaned forward, tightening my hold on him with my lips.

"Fuck, Angel, you're going to let me...unngh...I'm fucking going to explode."

I gave a tap of my finger, telling him I was okay. With a final thrust, he buried himself deep into the back of my throat and convulsed with his release. Hot cum shot down the back of my throat and I swallowed all of it.

He was the first man I let come in my mouth. Standing over me, Logan caught his breath, panting with the strength of his release.

When I looked up, it was to see him staring down at me. He looked gloriously disheveled, an Adonis on the water, with his woman on her knees before him.

"You don't want to know what I was thinking through that, babe. God, you give damn good head. Was it okay that I..."

I gave a nod. "I like when you take over like that. It's raw and powerful and..."

"Does it turn you on?" His tone turned serious. "Are you wet for me?"

"Very wet."

"Duly noted, and for the record, I'm finding it a huge turn on too. We should explore that more."

"Whatever you say."

"Fuck, I love it when you say that. Come here."

He bent down and pulled me to my feet and into his arms.

"We're going to fuck like rabbits you and I, because I can't seem to get enough of you. But now, it's your turn."

"We don't have to go tit for tat. It's okay if you just need to…"

"We'll get around to fucking your tits later. I still have so much I want to explore. And as for going tit for tat, lemme see those tits. You're officially deprived of clothing for the rest of the evening."

"But what if someone sees?"

"They'll need a fucking telescope to see you. Look around, there's not a boat in sight. You're all mine, to do with as I please, and right now, I want you naked on your back with your legs wrapped around my head."

"Won't we drift off?"

"We're in the middle of the fucking ocean. We have room to drift. Now, on your back."

I didn't argue, and it took him very little time to make me scream. Knowing nobody was around, I didn't hold back and let my scream erupt from my lungs.

We settled down after that. Me naked before the setting sun and him with his shirt off. The heat of the day lingered, so I was plenty warm, although as the sun set being naked wouldn't be nearly as much fun.

"You ready to get to know each other a little better?"

He pulled out a cooler and settled across from me.

"What do you have in mind?"

"Twenty questions. You have to tell the truth. No matter what."

"What if I don't want to answer the question, or can't?"

"You can pass on five questions, but only five. If you use them up early in the game, you have to answer all remaining questions. Use them wisely."

"Does the same apply to you?"

"Of course."

"I know I'm going to regret this, but let's play."

"All right, first question—"

"You get to go first? What happened to ladies first?"

"In this game, you'll want to be last. The last question is the most damning, but I'll let you go first if you want?"

"Um, no. That's okay. Ask away."

18

LOGAN

You'd think after all the sex, my balls would be empty. They weren't. My body couldn't get enough of Angelique Mars.

My angel.

But I felt like we needed to take a breather. There was so much I wanted to know about her, her life, and her dreams. I wanted to get to know the woman I was falling for, rather than waste all the precious time we had together fucking.

Not that fucking wasn't fun, but who was Angelique Mars? And why was I insanely attracted to her? This woman who got under my skin, what were her secrets?

"First question…" I began the interrogation.

"I'm ready." She sat in front of me and crossed her legs.

The boat rocked on the gentle swells and the water lapped along the hull. Crystal clear, we were in forty feet of water, but could clearly see the coral reef on the bottom. I wanted to be down there with Angel, diving among the fish and exploring a brave new world.

With her.

By my side.

"Dominant sex. Love it or hate it?"

That was probably the most pressing question I had. If I pushed things too far, I could ruin what we had before we figured out what it was that we actually had.

I loved sex and I wasn't afraid to have a bit of fun with it. Shit like that didn't define me. I wasn't a die-hard sexual dominant, although I did like some control when it came to sex. If it came down to it, I could take it or leave it. The most important thing was that we both had fun.

"Hmm, love it."

Yes! Score one for the team.

"Your turn." I encouraged her to play my little game. Twenty questions didn't seem like a lot, but it could get serious fast.

"Longest relationship?"

Shit. If I answered with the truth, what kind of doubt would that set in her mind? But the goal was to be honest. I was honorable enough to hold to my word.

"A month, maybe less, but we were more fuck buddies than dating. I don't think I've ever wanted to be with someone like that until now."

That should do it, but from the way her lips twisted, I wasn't so sure.

"Now?" Her curious tone encouraged me, but we were going to play this game by the rules.

"My turn for a question."

Her eyes narrowed, not liking the deflection.

"Do you love or hate anal?"

"Don't know. Never tried it."

Most girls I dated had tried pretty much everything. It seemed Angel wasn't as experimental as I thought. I'd keep that in mind and not push things too hard. My goal wasn't to scare her away but rather tie her to me.

"Does that mean it's on the table or not?" I was curious.

"Now you're jumping ahead with the questions." She teased me for doing exactly what I'd chastised her for doing. Smart girl.

"Fine, go ahead."

"Do you ever see yourself having kids?"

Shit, she wasn't wasting time feeling me out, but I had this.

"Not now, but I've always seen myself as being a dad someday."

"I suppose that's fair."

"What about you?"

"I've always put my career first. I guess I never found someone I could see myself with like that. I'm not getting any younger. If it's in my future, it's a closer future than I may be ready for."

"I get that. For me, it feels like an eventuality. Family is big with me, but career first for me too."

We were loosening up with each other, sharing more than our questions demanded. But it was like that with her. Opening up came as naturally as breathing.

"My turn," I said. "What was your first thought when you saw me?"

She ducked her head and hid a grin. "I thought you were a cocky bastard and I was pissed that you were late. Why were you? Late that is? It seemed a bit unprofessional."

Considering I'd just had my dick shoved down her throat and fucked her a few times in the same number of hours, I did not want to answer that one.

"I'll take my first pass."

"Really? A pass? That wasn't a hard question. I figured it took you awhile to untangle yourself from some leggy blonde."

"Not answering that, and it's my turn to ask a question."

"Fine."

"How many steady relationships have you been in?"

Her mouth twisted. For a moment, I thought she was going to take a pass, but she finally answered.

"Not that many. Two really. One was serious and the other I thought was going somewhere, but neither worked out."

"I'd say I was sorry, but I'm happy they didn't work out."

She shifted positions and put her legs out in front of her. "Favorite sexual position?"

"Going for something easy?"

"Doing research."

"Well, my favorite sexual position isn't going to be what you expect, but you'll love it."

"Is that so?"

I leaned forward and whispered into her ear. "My favorite position is being in charge."

Her cheeks flushed, turning bright pink to match the glow in the sky.

"Do you have a big family?" I realized I knew next to nothing about her family.

"No."

"Care to elaborate?"

"It's my turn to ask a question. Do you ever wish you were an only child?"

"Never. Despite the age gap, my brothers and I are tight. We're really the best of friends, and the girls are getting more and more tolerable."

"More tolerable? That's an interesting way to put it."

"They were just so much younger than me. I never really understood them. My turn. You don't have a big family, so any siblings?"

"No, but I think I already told you that. How old were you when you lost your virginity?"

"Ah, we're back to that?"

"Yeah, I'm thinking you were an early bloomer. Thirteen? Fourteen?"

"Actually, I was a late bloomer. The first time I had sex was the night of graduation."

"You're kidding?"

"Is that a question?"

"No. It's just I envisioned you as a king of the school kind of guy."

"I was actually quite conservative. It wasn't until I went to flight school that everything changed. For some reason, chicks dig pilots. They were falling all over me."

"Wow. That is a surprise." Her sarcastic tone was not lost on me.

"How about you? When did you lose your virginity?"

"Classic prom night scenario. We both got drunk and figured why not. It was kind of a dare. He came fast and I didn't. Not the most exciting memory."

"Ah, I was always nervous about performing well. Like I said, I was rather conservative. All my friends in high school were hooking up and they all assumed I was too. The more I kept quiet about it the bigger the stories grew. I was really afraid to have sex with any of the girls because I needed it to be spectacular. I may have been overly concerned about my reputation."

"You put a lot of pressure on yourself. No one is that good in high school. Everyone is fumbling about."

"Not me. I didn't have sex until I knew I would blow the girl's mind, and I researched the hell out of it."

"You did?"

"Shit yeah I did. Everything I could learn about fingering a girl, how to find the g-spot, and cunnilingus. I studied everything."

"Well, I can say from personal experience that you're pretty damn good."

"Only good? I'd like to think I rocked your world. As I remember, you were begging."

"Only because you were being a prick about it."

"Yeah, that was kind of fun. Whose turn is it?"

"Mine."

"Go for it."

"How many women have you slept with?"

"I honestly don't know." I leaned forward and took her hands in mine. "Look, I've played the field. We both know this, and I've fucked more than my fair share of women, but please don't hold my past against me. It's one of the few things I'll ask of you. Right now, you're the only one in my life. And I never fuck around. Despite playing the field, I'm a one woman at a time kind of guy."

Shit, that sounded really bad. From the way her shoulders curled inward, I wished I could take that last little bit back.

"For how long?" There was her insecurity, brought right to the surface because I was an asshole who couldn't help but boast about the very past I didn't want her holding against me.

"I can't make you any promises, except to say I've never felt this way about anyone before. I'm not ready for it to end. That's the best I can give you. And for the record, that's two questions."

"You don't have to worry about me." She shifted away, placing distance between us.

"What do you mean?"

"I'm not overly clingy and I'm not trying to get you to commit or anything. We're just two people having fun, right? No strings."

I heard her words, but I didn't believe them. More concerning, however, was they kind of pissed me off.

There was nothing casual about the way I felt. And yes, we fucked. We fucked a lot, but I wasn't using her and I damn well knew she wasn't using me.

"This isn't a fling." It was something more, but I wasn't ready to say that out loud.

For some reason, she was trying to give me an out. Didn't she know?

"I've lost track of whose turn it is for questions." She rubbed at her arms as the wind blew over the water. With the sun going down, the air temperature started to drop.

My mood soured. "Is that what you think of me?"

"Is that one of your questions?"

"Fuck the questions. Is that what you think of me?"

"I'm not sure what you're referring to?"

"Do you think we're just fucking around? That this means nothing?"

"Isn't that exactly what we're doing? Look, you said it yourself. You don't date. You never have. And I'm cool with that." She picked at her arm and refused to meet my gaze.

Her body language said she was anything but cool with

that. I might have been the guy who fucked anything in a skirt, but not Angel. She fucked with the entirety of her heart and she was baring her soul to me.

She shared her worst fear, and the problem was that I was that guy. Or had been.

"This is different." I leaned toward her, but she pulled away.

"Is it?"

"You don't feel it? The way the air crackles between us? The way our bodies slide together like they were made for each other?"

"We have intense chemistry, so yeah, I do feel it. And the sex has been amazing. But…"

"No fucking but about it. I said you were mine and I mean it. If I have to prove it to you every day for the rest of my life, I will."

My voice rose and I had to forcibly keep myself from shouting. It was hard, because anger burned in my blood.

Didn't she know? Didn't she feel it? Did she not trust me to never break her heart?

One look into her eyes told me that answer.

"Fuck."

"What?" The long fringe of her lashes swept across her cheekbones as she gave a slow blink.

"Nothing."

"That wasn't nothing."

She was right about that. I just realized I had fallen in love.

My entire world shifted and it felt as if someone had punched me in the gut.

If she left me, out of fear over whether I would break her heart or not, it would be something I never recovered from.

"Let's take a break, hun. I'm going to put out dinner and grab the champagne."

"Champagne? Interesting choice."

"Well, sunset dinner cruise." I gestured out over the water and to the fiery canvas over our heads. "It seemed like a champagne kind of thing at the time, considering I was planning on seducing you into my bed and all."

"Oh," she ducked her head. "I guess we jumped the gun with that. Sorry. I ruined your great seduction."

At least her humor had returned. Banter was our strength, but so was our physical connection. I would cleave her to me and I had the perfect idea how to do that.

"I wouldn't give up the past few hours for anything, and I don't mind if you want to jump my gun. In fact, you can jump it anytime you want."

I did mind it. Her belief I was going to abandon her twisted at my insides. Hell, my balls drew high and tight when I realized what kind of headspace she was in.

"I thought you wanted me to ride your stallion?" A mischievous glint flashed in her eye.

"Yeah, I want that too." We were going to have sex again. The air sizzled with the promise of it. But we would have it on my terms.

I couldn't ignore our physical attraction, or my need to be inside of her again. Whatever it took, I would show her this meant more to me than a tropical fling of convenience.

And I was acutely aware of her nakedness.

I pointed to the deck. "Lay down on your back."

"Excuse me?"

"You heard me. Right there…" I pointed to the canvas stretched out between the twin hulls of the catamaran. This was going to take a while and I wanted to make sure she was comfortable.

"You want me on my back?"

"That's what I said."

"But I thought we were having dinner."

"We are."

Her brows drew together. "It's kind of hard to eat if I'm lying on my back."

"I guess you have a choice. You can do as I say and see what happens, or you don't and are left to wonder what I had in mind." I allowed my tone to deepen, using the lower registers of my vocal range, to turn my words into a command. "What's it going to be, Angel? Are you going to obey or do I need to put you over my knee?"

Her eyes widened and reflected the ruby glow of the sky. With a squeak, she scooted out onto the canvas and stretched out for me.

I was hard again.

For now, we would play adult games.

19

LOGAN

I RETRIEVED THE COOLER THE HOTEL STAFF PACKED FOR OUR night out. Sitting beside Angel, I stared into her onyx eyes and felt something shift within me.

"Why am I lying on my back?" She gave a slow, languid blink.

"Because your tits are fucking gorgeous. Your belly is flat as a springboard, and your pussy is divine."

"Um, okay?"

"Let me put it another way." I pulled out the appetizer, shrimp cocktail, and showed it to her. Rather than put it in my mouth, or feed her, I placed it on her breast.

"Logan..."

"Shush, you're my dinner. We begin with shrimp cocktail featuring your creamy breasts." I took three shrimp and place them around her tits, then poured the cocktail sauce over her nipples.

She squirmed.

"I'm your dinner?"

"Something like that. Now, shush."

I took out the container with the Alfredo. This was going to get messy, but that would make it that much more fun.

"Alfredo is the main course and it features your delicious belly." A quick pop of the lid and I arranged the noodles along the expanse of her stomach. The sauce was thick enough, it didn't pour off her body, but it did drip deliciously down her sides. I was going to have fun licking it off her skin.

"This is crazy."

"It's perfect." I reached in and took out the chocolate cake. "And this is dessert."

"Where does that go?" Her thighs pressed together and I bet a million dollars she was fucking wet.

I placed the cake in the triangle between her legs.

"Dinner looks delicious."

"And how am I supposed to eat?"

"I'll feed you."

"You sure you won't be distracted by your feast?"

"I make no promises. Now, shush, the table isn't supposed to talk."

"You're taking away my voice?"

"I'm controlling the situation. Are you okay with that?"

"What do I do with my hands?"

"You can do whatever you want with them, as long as you lie still."

She reached out and placed her hand on my jutting erection. I jumped, because I wasn't expecting it.

"You could remove those," she said.

"I could, but if I do that, neither of us will eat because I'd just climb on top of you and fuck your brains out. Now, are you going to let me enjoy my meal in silence, or are you going to be a Chatty Kathy?"

She bit at her lower lip, then pressed her lips together. Her hand remained on my dick, teasing me over the fabric of my shorts. I placed my hand over hers.

"I love the feel of your hand on my dick. Let's make this fun, shall we?"

She gave a slight nod.

"You play with me while I eat dinner, but my shorts stay on. If I come before you do, you have carte blanche to do anything you want with me for the rest of our time here. If I get you to come first, then that privilege falls to me. What do you say? Up for a little game?"

A game which was rigged. There was no way she would win.

She gave another, more cautious, nod but then her fingertips swirled over the tip of my cock. Feather-light, her delicate touch was more of a tickle than what I really wanted. A groan escaped me as I hardened beneath her. This was going to be a challenge if she kept that up.

"Game on." With that, I leaned forward and licked along her tits, slowly making my way to the first shrimp. I sucked it in, then went for the cocktail sauce with my tongue.

Her back arched as I flicked her nipple. Then she screamed when I bit down hard. I held her down with one hand pressed against her hipbone and the other on her shoulder while she squirmed. Needing more cocktail sauce, I licked and sucked while she shuddered beneath me.

I flashed her a wicked grin. "This is going to be so much fun."

She responded by digging her nails into my cock and my hips jerked forward, pressing my dick into her palm. She snickered beneath me, but that was okay. Two could play at this game.

I fed her a shrimp, taking my time to drag it against the creamy expanse of her breast. It was necessary, I told myself, to make sure it was fully coated in cocktail sauce. Then I put the tail in my mouth and leaned over until our eyes locked.

Her pert little lips parted for me and I fed her mouth-to-mouth. Our lips brushed against one another as she sucked the shrimp out of my mouth.

"Mmm." She licked her lips and smiled.

"Definitely the most delicious meal I've ever had. Time for the other breast...I mean shrimp."

Her eyes flared for a second, because we both knew exactly what I was going to do.

A lick.

A suck.

A flick of my tongue.

I tortured her until she squirmed and her breathy moans filled the air. Then I reached between her legs, dipping my fingers into her slit, then dragged them through the icing of the cake.

Her body bowed beneath me as I gave a low, throaty chuckle.

"I was never good at saving desert for last." I made a show of licking my fingers, loving the way her pupils dilated and her body trembled. But the Alfredo was getting cold.

"You hungry?"

"Yes, please."

I fed her one noodle at a time, loving how she sucked the noodle into her mouth. It reminded me of how wonderful her lips had felt wrapped around my cock, but I think that was her point. My girl was playing it up and her skillful fingers hadn't let up on my cock.

I usually needed a firm hand, but this light as a feather thing was doing it just fine.

We finished off the Alfredo and I enjoyed several long minutes licking her breasts and belly clean. Which left only one last thing. My pants were tight, but my release some distance off. Angel, on the other hand, fought hers.

I found it exciting how sensitive her nipples were and how reactive she was to my touch.

"I'm sorry, but I don't think I can share dessert with you. I'm going to be selfish and *eat* it all by myself."

I did exactly that. I went to town and it didn't take long before her orgasm ripped through her. I wanted to fuck her right then, but I held off.

As her cries softly quieted, and her breathing settled, I kissed her slow and gentle, enjoying the way our lips glided against each other and how her fingers twined in the hair at my nape.

"We need to get you cleaned off."

"That was amazing. Definitely a first."

"Can you swim?"

"Huh?"

I scooped her into my arms and asked again. "Can you swim?"

"Of course I can."

"Good." I promptly walked to the side of the boat.

"Oh, no you don't." Her arms locked around my neck.

I'd deployed a swim ladder earlier, anticipating an evening swim. My thought was to toss her overboard and have a little fun, but with the way she clung to my neck, that wasn't going to happen the way I envisioned.

"I most definitely am."

"Logan!"

I tried to toss her in, but she wrapped her body around

mine. So, I did the next best thing. I walked to the rear of the boat.

"Oh, no you don't."

I reached down and grabbed hold of a drift line. It would allow us to be in the water and still stay attached to the boat.

The rest of whatever she was going to say was lost as I jumped in the water. We plunged beneath the waves, her spitting and hissing and me with the biggest fucking smile on my face. Breaching the surface at the same time, she splashed water in my face.

"You bastard!"

"Hey, it was the easiest way to clean up after dinner."

She considered what I said for a moment and her lips pressed together, but she didn't say anything else.

"Can you believe the colors of that sky?" She tipped her head and floated on her back.

I moved to be beside her and held her hand while we floated on our backs and stared at the sky.

Deep reds, fiery oranges, and wispy yellows painted the living canvas. Pushing across the heavens, a blanket of purples, blues and blacks brought the night.

"It's breathtaking," she said.

"I can't believe we get to do this. I wish all our clients were like the Truitt's."

"I know. It's going to be hard to beat this."

"When we get back," I said, "can we talk about what comes next?"

"I suppose."

"That doesn't sound very committed."

Angel rolled off her back to tread water beside me.

"I'm trying not to think beyond this moment."

"Why not?"

"Because once this ends…"

"I have no intention of this ending."

"You don't have to say that. I know what this is."

"And what exactly do you think we're doing? You think this is just fucking for fun?"

"Isn't it?"

"It's a whole hell of a lot more for me. Shit, Angel, I'm committed to more."

"More? What does that mean? You want me as a fuck-buddy?"

"That hurts."

"Why? Isn't that what you do? I've been burned before, and I went into this with my eyes wide open. I know you don't date."

"No, you're right. I don't. I fuck women I don't care about, using them to scratch an itch. Is that what you think I'm doing with you?"

"I just don't want to make this complicated. We're having fun, and it's great, but…"

"But what? Are you trying to let me off the hook here?"

"I didn't want to make things awkward."

"Feels pretty damn awkward to me. Maybe you need to pull the wool out of your ears, because you obviously weren't listening to me when I said you were mine. I don't know what this is between us, but it's more than casual sex. I like to fuck. I like the rawness that brings, but that doesn't mean I'm going to fuck you and leave you."

"I just thought…"

"Wrong. You thought all kinds of wrong. You and I, we're going to fuck tonight, tomorrow, and every day after that, because I'm never letting you go. I don't know what I'm feeling except I've never felt this way before. How's that for complicated?"

"It's pretty complicated."

"Why?" I didn't understand where my anger came from. I should want easy, uncomplicated, and no strings attached.

"Because we can't fly together."

"Why not? Because we're sleeping together?"

"Because we're doing more than just sleeping together."

"Well, at least you decided to get your head out of your ass. You and I? We're a thing. A crazy, insane, never want to be without you, kind of thing."

"This is complicated and intense."

"Don't let that scare you."

"I barely know you, and I don't think lust is a good foundation to build a relationship on. That's what this is. I agree with you. It's insane and our chemistry is crazy intense, but what do we really know about each other? Not to mention, before I met you, I had a deep-seated hatred of all fighter pilots."

"You what?"

"You heard me. Rivalries aside, cocky jet jocks are some of my least favorite people on the planet. They're arrogant assholes and prideful pricks."

"Prideful pricks?" I laughed. "Props for the alliteration. But I hope I've changed your mind about *all* fighter jocks. I may be arrogant and a prick at times, but in general I'm not an asshole and I'd like to think I buried my pride a long time ago. I'm in awe of you and what you've accomplished with your career. My job was to maintain a certain image, a part of the Navy advertising machine. You did the real work, and your flight history speaks for itself. As far as that goes, I bow to your skills every single time."

"Thank you, although you didn't have to say all of that. I wasn't looking for validation, but I wanted you to know how I felt. Two days ago, I hated you for what you were."

"And now that you know me?"

"It's different."

"So, it's settled."

"What's settled?"

"You and I are officially a couple. If you want, we'll arrange so that we don't fly together; keep professional and personal separate."

"I think that's for the best, don't you? No need for messy emotions in the cockpit."

"You said cock." I gave her a wink. "You ready to get back on the boat?"

We climbed on board and fucked. We looked for constellations and fucked. We chased shooting stars, and then we fucked some more.

Eventually, however, everything ends.

Our evening ended at midnight as we beached the catamaran and headed upstairs to our suite where we collapsed with exhaustion in bed.

20

ANGEL

Logan and I woke in a tangle of limbs and we stayed in bed as long as we could. Our flight wasn't until early evening, but we had to check out and make sure the jet was prepped for our return flight home.

"You ready?" Logan did a final sweep of the room, making sure we hadn't left anything behind.

"Ready." I zipped up my suitcase and set it on the floor.

It felt weird, maybe a little surreal, knowing our few days in paradise were coming to an end.

What about the other thing?

I didn't want to think about what would happen once we returned to our real lives. These past few days felt like we'd had existed in a strange bubble, separate from the real world.

When we returned, would I become another conquest in

a long string of one night stands? Or were Logan's words from last night true?

We finished our game of twenty questions as shooting stars flashed across the night sky and I learned a little more about his family, his career, and his hopes for the future.

My answers were more evasive, although I never once told a lie.

We ate lunch on the way to the airport and traded an easy silence as we pushed the food around on our plates. It seemed neither of us were very interested in getting on with the day.

A little after noon, we were back at the airport doing an exterior check on the jet. While Logan completed his walk around, I went over the mechanic's logs.

"How's everything look?" Logan peeked over my shoulder and wrapped a hand around my waist to pull me close.

"Everything's perfect. We're good to go. The fuel truck is on its way and I just got a text from Bianca. They should be here an hour ahead of schedule. Mr. Truitt is eager to get home before Georgina's bedtime."

With fuel onboard, Logan and I lounged in the main cabin while waiting for our clients to arrive. Bianca kept me updated with a string of texts.

My phone beeped and I looked down. "They just arrived."

It would take a few minutes for them to clear security, but Logan and I exited the jet to wait on them.

"I'm going to go help with the luggage." Logan wiped his hands on his pants. He seemed a bit distant, but then I wasn't bright and bubbly either.

The double doors of the passenger terminal opened and Georgina gave an ear-piercing squeal when she saw Logan. Twisting free of her father's grip, she ran with her arms outstretched right into Logan's arms.

"Well, hello there." Logan picked Georgina up and spun her in a circle. The man really was great with kids.

"Mr. Logan, we did it! We did it!" Her happy shrieks brought a smile to my face.

"What did you do, sweetie?"

He may have been talking to Georgina, but his low rumbly voice sent shivers racing down my spine. I was well aware of how many hours we would be sitting shoulder to shoulder in a cramped cockpit unable to touch each other.

"We swam with dolphins," Georgina said. "Mommy and daddy were pushed by the dolphins and I got to ride one too."

"That sounds amazing."

"Hi, Georgina." I gave Georgina a pat to her back. "Did you really swim with them?"

"I did and it was so much fun."

"Can I tell you a secret?" I asked her.

Her voice dropped to a whisper. "Yes!"

"We swam with them too."

Her expression lit up. "Did they push you through the water like mommy and daddy?"

"Yes, it was so much fun. I'm so glad you got to do that."

"I did, and we played with turtles and spent all day on the beach. Daddy made this huge sand castle while mommy slept."

"You ready for takeoff, little girl?" Logan cradled Georgina in his arms, then suddenly flipped her over, belly down, arms spread over her head, and began running her around as he made jet engine noises.

Georgina laughed and told him to run faster.

I went to Bianca and pulled her into a hug. "How was your weekend?"

"It was great. Georgina had the best time. She's informed us she wants a dolphin for Christmas."

Bandit heeled to Bianca's side and sniffed the air with distrust. A smart dog, he knew we were about ready to force him to endure the indignity of flying again.

"Hey boy." I squatted down and scratched between his ears. Then I looked up at Bianca. "A dolphin? Like a real one or a stuffed animal?"

"The real thing."

"Oh, dear." I covered my mouth and tried to hide my laughter.

"Yes, my daughter has decided we will also build a beach for her pet turtles."

Mr. Truitt had his arms full of Hello Kittie gear, plus a few new additions; one stuffed dolphin and a stuffed turtle.

"I wonder where she gets that from?" His gaze shifted to Bianca and her cheeks flushed under his stare.

Is that what I looked like when Logan turned his attention on me?

"Well, it looks like you acquired a couple stand-ins before you have to get the real things," I said. "Hello Kittie has a couple new friends I see."

"Yes, and evidently, I'm their nanny." He gave a soft laugh.

I took the dolphin and turtle from his arms, relieving him of some of his burden. There was no need to help with the bags. Staff from the private terminal took care of that.

"Let's get you two settled while Logan and Georgina play jet pilot."

With Logan distracted, I lowered my voice to a whisper. "Mr. Truitt, do you want to get Logan back for suggesting the dolphin experience?"

"Please, call me Dex, and heck yeah."

I leaned in close. "Of course, *Mr. Truitt*, I have it on good authority that Logan is a recent *Frozen* convert. He can sing most of the songs. Once we get to cruising altitude you could suggest he join you and watch it with Georgina."

"Oh, that's evil." Mr. Truitt glanced at Logan who still carried Georgina in his arms. They were doing dips and rolls as he made jet noises. "I love it."

"Just don't tell him I suggested it."

Everyone got on board and Logan and I went to work.

The sterile cockpit rule did what it was designed to do. I focused one-hundred percent on the task of flying and ignored the sizzling chemistry between us.

Okay, I may not have been one-hundred percent focused on the job at hand, but the strict protocols helped to ignore Logan's intoxicating scent.

When we got to cruising altitude, I announced it to our guests. A few minutes later, there was a light tap on the door.

Mr. Truitt poked his head inside. "Hey Logan…"

Logan twisted in his seat. "Yeah?"

"Can you come back here for a second, Georgina has been asking for you." Mr. Truitt winked at me and Logan's eyes narrowed suspiciously.

"Sure thing." Logan unbuckled and leaned down to whisper in my ear. "Is this your doing?"

I gave a shrug. "I have no idea what you're talking about."

"Hmm, we'll see about that."

As he left the cockpit, Georgina's tiny voice rang through the cabin. "Yay! Is he going to watch with me?"

"You have to ask nicely, Georgina Bina." Bianca's soft tone encouraged her daughter and reminded her of her manners.

"Mr. Logan, will you pleeeeeease watch *Frozen* with me."

I hid a laugh when Logan took a step back and pointed at me. "You are going to pay for this."

"Why, what do you mean, Captain Reid?"

"Payback can be a bitch." He turned back around and answered the little girl. "Of course. I'd love to, but I may not be able to watch the whole thing. I have to help Angel fly the plane."

"Oh, goody!" Georgina patted the chair beside her.

Logan took a seat while she pulled up her favorite movie on the main cabin screen. A chuckle escaped me as Bianca and Mr. Truitt exchanged a look then placed earbuds in their ears.

I turned around and enjoyed the open cockpit, breathing easier for the first time since we took off. Logan's presence simply filled everything, and every breath reminded me how intimately he'd acquainted himself with my body.

A low ache pulsed between my legs. That's what thoughts of him did to me. He turned me into a horny teenager who couldn't get enough.

For the next two hours, I enjoyed the cockpit Logan-free, then I realized it had been much longer than what it took for *Frozen* to play.

We were cruising at thirty-five thousand feet and the autopilot had the helm. Blue water spread from horizon to horizon beneath us and only a few clouds filled the air. In another hour, we'd leave the ocean behind and begin flying overland. Then a few more hours until we arrived in New York.

That's where our journey ended.

It felt like an end and I braced for it by shielding my heart. I told myself lies.

It was just a fling.

A harmless work romance.

It was that and much more.

I unbuckled and opened the door to the cabin. *Frozen* was playing. Georgina sat in Logan's lap and she hugged her new sea turtle friend tight to her chest.

Logan glanced up and gave me a look which said I would most definitely be paying for this.

Georgina saw me and gave a little flap of her hand, but she was engrossed in the movie and quickly ignored me. Bianca and Mr. Truitt sat in their loungers with ear buds in place.

Bianca looked up from her book. "They're on round two. I think I'm going to hire him as a nanny. He knows all the lines."

Logan cleared his throat and gave Bianca a dirty look. Georgina was oblivious, so engrossed in her movies she ignored the adults.

I kept my voice low. "I see."

"Dex keeps cracking up when the songs come on," Bianca said. "He's glad he doesn't have to sing them all."

"Well, I was just checking up on everyone. Is there anything you need?"

"We're good. Thanks, Angel."

I winked at Logan and returned to the cockpit. A few seconds later, a presence loomed behind me.

"Logan? I thought you were watching your encore?"

"I told Georgina you needed me up here."

"I did not say that."

"You sure? Because I most definitely heard you say my presence was required in the cockpit." He came inside, closed the door, then made a point of thrusting his hips in my face as he navigated the small space and climbed into the captain's chair.

"You ditched an adorable girl to squeeze into that seat? I think that makes you a monster." I kept my tone light, ignoring the seductive threat that pulsed between us with each of his breaths.

"She's cool with it, although she did ask her mom if we could have a playdate next Saturday to watch it again."

I practically snorted. "A playdate?"

"Yeah, but I told her I already had a playdate planned."

"You do?"

My stomach churned with that thought. He couldn't already have a date with someone else. Was his social calendar that full? Or were there simply that many women eager to hop in his bed?

"I did say you were going to suffer."

I breathed out a sigh, then got angry at the insecurities I carried. He'd given me no reason to think he was interested in being with other women.

"Is that so?" I tried teasing back, but it fell flat. "What if I'm busy on Saturday?"

"You cancel it."

"What if I can't?" I had nothing planned.

"You tell whatever asshole thinks he's taking you on a date that you belong to me now."

"There's no one else, Logan." It seemed I wasn't the only one with those kinds of thoughts. "I was just teasing."

"Good to know, but since we're talking about it, I want to make things clear. I'm not seeing anyone except you, and I hope you feel the same about me."

"Are you asking if I want to be exclusive?"

He paused for a long moment. "If you want to call it that. I don't like it when things aren't crystal clear. You're mine and I don't share. So, if you don't have an asshole picking you up on Saturday, your time belongs to me."

"Possessive much?"

"Call it determined."

"What if I have plans that don't include other men?"

"Ha, I'd be jealous of anyone who takes you from me. And for the record, I've done the threesome thing before. I'm not interested in sharing you with another man, or another woman. I'm finding I'm growing more and more possessive by the minute. I hope that's not going to be a problem."

"No."

Yes! Maybe? Hell, if I know.

My voice shook, because I had expected him to distance himself the closer we got to the end of this trip, but he seemed to be doing exactly the opposite.

"Oh, and I've been thinking about something," he said with a snicker.

"What's that?"

"It a little fantasy of mine."

"A fantasy?"

"Yeah, it involves you, me, and this cockpit."

"We agreed to keep things professional."

"True, but I'm only talking about a fantasy, not suggesting we act it out, although…"

"Although?"

"Since this is the last time we'll be flying together, and may be the only opportunity to live out my fantasy, I think we'll do just that. But, you'll have to wait until we land."

"And what exactly is your fantasy?"

He pointed to his crotch. "Your tits bouncing in my face while you ride me in this seat. I've always wanted to have sex in the cockpit."

"We can't do that."

"Oh, we're going to do it. Once we land, we'll close up the jet for a mission debrief and…" He gestured to his groin again.

"You're incorrigible."

"I'm also hard." He shifted in his seat. "Growing by the second with that image of you in my head."

"Tough luck, flyboy. Because you're going to have to suffer on your own."

"Hmm, or…" His eyes gleamed and his gaze shifted to the cockpit door. "Luv, do you mind locking that door?"

"We will not do anything like that while flying the plane." I tried to be firm, but couldn't resist the urge to see what he had in mind.

"I never said *we* were going to do anything. But while *you* fly, I'm going to relieve some of this pressure. We still have several hours left."

I bit my lower lip. This was a bad idea. And while it didn't technically cross my *no funny business* rule, it skated very close to the line.

"Hun...the door?" He unbuckled his pants and unzipped the fly.

21

ANGEL

I SHOULDN'T AGREE TO THIS, BUT THE THOUGHT OF SITTING right beside him while he pleasured himself had me wet and more excited than I should be.

Logan enjoyed sex and he wasn't ashamed of his needs, or mine. He normalized everything about it, while I always felt like I couldn't really be free to express myself. He was teaching me to let go, but old habits die hard.

He drew his cock out from behind his briefs. A low moan escaped him. For a moment, I thought I should tell Bianca and Mr. Truitt we were locking the door, make up some bullshit excuse, but I didn't. With a *snick*, I engaged the lock and returned to my seat.

Logan fisted his cock and drew his hand up and down the velvety shaft. "Looks like my little Peeping Tom has graduated. Your eyes, my dear, are as big as saucers. You like this, don't you?"

"I like everything about you."

He gave a low groan as his hand twisted up the shaft. "Do you know what I'm fantasizing about?" His hips thrust upward as he slammed his hand down.

"Tell me." I licked my lips and watched him pleasure himself.

"I'm thinking I just came home from a flight. I text you and tell you when I'm coming home. I'm opening the front door, and stop, shocked, because you're standing there, waiting for me. You're naked. Gloriously naked."

The pace of his strokes quickened.

"I come inside and shut the door while you walk up to me. Your hands go to the buckle of my pants. My mouth is dry because I'm panting. You pull me out. Then you look up at me as you go to your knees. It's something you do when I come home, something just for me. It's like our little ritual."

He leaned back and the chords of his muscles stood out as he pumped harder.

"I say nothing as you wrap your lips around my cock." His breathing deepened and I squirmed in my seat, hot and incredibly aroused.

"My hand wraps in your hair, and I let you tease and lick me, but then I take over. You're on your knees plea-suring me and I know you like it when I get rough."

The slapping of his hand filled the cabin. He thrust hard with his hips into his palm. I watched him acting out his fantasy, taking over the timid blowjob and claiming his release.

"You gag on my cock. I shove it deep down your throat. I make you swallow every inch of me. Holy fuuuuck..." He came all over his hand and it was easily the most erotic sight I had ever seen. Logan leaned back, panting. "Fuck, that was pretty damn intense."

I grabbed a napkin from a stash I kept beside me and handed it over to him to clean up.

He looked at me. "I simply can't get enough of you."

My mouth was dry. I had mouth-breathed through that whole thing.

"You scare me," I finally said.

"Why?" His brows pinched. "Because I want you?"

"No. Because I'm terrified this is going to end."

"It's not going to end."

"Everything ends."

He reached out and placed his hand over mine. "Not this."

I wished I could believe him. Why didn't I?

Because you're scared.

"I've never known a man who will touch himself like that in front of me."

"Really?"

"Yeah, I never knew how hot it could be." Or how intimate. It wasn't just the sex, but a glimpse into something private. He shared that with me.

"It gets the job done, but is a poor cousin to the real

thing. I can't wait to be inside of you again. I look at you and I don't know what I did to get this lucky."

I said nothing and focused on the controls. With the autopilot on, there was literally nothing for me to do, but I checked all the readouts. Anything to distract me from my fears.

He seemed to sense my distress and left me to my silence. I pulled out a book and he did the same. We didn't watch a movie together like we had the last flight.

After some time, he filled the silence with his low, rumbly voice which dripped with the promise of sex. "Hey, what color do you prefer?"

"Huh?"

"What color?"

"It depends on what you're using it for."

"I'm looking up blindfolds." He tapped his screen and turned it to me. He was on a sex toy website and an entire screen of blindfolds greeted me.

"Umm…"

"Does that scare you or excite you?"

"I plead the fifth?"

"No. You don't get to do that." He expanded a picture and showed me the black silk blindfold. "I prefer black. I'm thinking since you won't be able to see, maybe it doesn't matter which color you prefer."

"I think your enthusiasm for blindfolds is worrisome."

"Oh, don't worry about those. That's just a little simple fun. You don't want to see the rest of my browsing history."

I coughed with that, because I knew exactly what he'd been browsing. He'd made a list of supplies from what he fondly dubbed his *research book* and left the post-it note on his controls.

There was nothing subtle about Logan Reid.

"I don't think it's in my best interest to encourage you."

"Everything I do, I do for you." He gave me a devilish look and went back to shopping while I monitored the approach of our next course change.

I spoke to air traffic control as we exited one airspace and moved into the next.

The rest of the flight passed quickly. Soon, we were on approach. Logan took over the controls as we entered one of the busiest airspaces on the planet.

Before I knew it, our wheels touched down and Logan had us taxiing to our designated parking spot.

"I'll check on our passengers." Unbuckling, I edged out of my seat.

"Remember, Angel, we have a mission debrief before you leave. I've got a few points I want to slide into place. You know, work things back and forth. See if things are a good fit."

"You're incorrigible."

"And hard. Standing up and needing attention."

I unlocked the cockpit door, realizing we hadn't left the small space since Logan returned from his *Frozen* adventure.

"How's everyone doing?" I asked our passengers.

Bianca put a finger to her mouth. "Georgina just went to sleep."

"Oh," I lowered my voice. "We'll be opening the door in a second. What can I help you with?"

Georgina cuddled with her new dolphin and turtle friends. Poor Hello Kittie had been tossed to the floor.

Mr. Truitt started picking up stuffed animals. "I wish I could sleep like that. Great flight, it was really enjoyable."

Bandit yawned and stretched. He cocked his head, looking at the door he knew would soon be his path to freedom.

"Anytime, Mr. Truitt. Always my pleasure to take you where you need to go."

"Is that so? Because I may just have an opportunity for you."

"Really?"

"But only if you call me Dex from here on out."

"Umm, that depends on the opportunity."

"I want you to fly for me, or rather my company. We have a need for a pilot with your skills."

"Um, I'm not really looking, but thank you."

"Oh, I'm sorry, but Logan said you might be."

"Is that so?" I spun around and crossed my arms over my chest as I glared at Logan. "Is that what you told him?"

Logan mirrored my pose. "Not that it's my place to say, but it comes with a substantial raise and promotion to captain. You deserve it and since we can't fly together anymore, why not?" He gave a shrug.

"Why can't you two fly together?" Bianca gathered her things.

Dex Truitt placed a hand on his wife's arm and whispered into her ear. Bianca's eyes widened and a smile bloomed on her face.

Not wanting to burn bridges, and what could be a great opportunity with a major promotion, I didn't allow my anger to surface.

But what the ever-loving fuck?

Logan had no right saying anything about our fledgling relationship to anyone. But, I couldn't in good conscience refuse the offer outright.

"That's incredibly generous. I would like to have some time to think about it."

"Absolutely, and I'll have a formal offer sent over that spells everything out. But, I'm serious. You'd be a great asset to Montague Enterprises."

"Thank you, that's incredible praise coming from you."

"Any time." He bent down and somehow managed to gather Georgina in his arms without waking the little girl.

Bianca and I corralled the remaining stuffed animals and Bandit danced around our feet while Logan opened the outer door.

Once we got the Truitt's settled in their car, and the bags loaded, Logan said goodbye to a very sleepy Georgina. She waved to Logan and made him promise to come over for a tea party. I was invited by association after Bianca explained how it was proper manners to do so.

Logan took my hand in his. "Hey, about that mission debrief…"

"How about you telling Dexter Truitt that you and I are sleeping together? That was completely unacceptable. Things are different for me. I wish they weren't, but I can't let it get around that I sleep with my coworkers. I really wish you hadn't done that." My voice rose in pitch with each word.

My anger surprised Logan, but what the ever-loving fuck had he been thinking?

"I'm sorry?" He sounded confused, not sorry.

"You crossed a line."

"We were just talking and I pitched it to him. I didn't go into the details."

"He's an incredibly intuitive man. I'm sure it wasn't hard to put two and two together. I really wish you hadn't done that."

An ugly surge of anger boiled up inside of me. My cheeks heated. Logan didn't understand. He'd never had to fight against the stereotypes I faced my entire career.

No longer interested in a quick fuck, I yanked my hand out of his grip. "I think I'm going to get my things." I went to pull my bag out of the baggage compartment.

"Hey, it's no big deal. And you'll get a raise and a promotion. I'd think you'd be thanking me, not storming off in a huff."

"But it *is* a big deal." Heat pricked behind my lids.

I hated how my emotions spilled out into the world. I

wish I could be more like a man, stoic and closed off from the devastating effects of emotions. But I wasn't. I was weak, emotional, and doing exactly what Logan said.

Rather than explaining why it bothered me, or talking about it like a rational adult, I yanked my bag out of the plane and stormed off...in a huff.

He called after me, but I ignored him. And he couldn't come after me. The jet had to be locked down. I was acting like a child, but I couldn't stop myself.

And I knew it was wrong. I knew it was irrational. I also kept walking through the terminal to the curb where I caught a cab and headed home.

Alone.

22

LOGAN

WELL, ANGEL HAD A BUG UP HER BUTT.

What exactly did I do wrong?

She's the one who said we couldn't work together, except we could. We could see each other and work together. I could keep things professional. She could too.

Not agreeing with her didn't mean I didn't respect her thoughts.

So, I asked Dex if his company was hiring.

Why was that such a big deal?

He didn't know the details about Montague Enterprises air fleet division, but the man in charge didn't need to know details. All it took was him thinking it was a good idea.

Dex liked Angel. He respected her.

It was a perfect fit.

Combined with a promotion and raise, it solved all our problems.

So, what the fuck?

I was still scratching my head later that night, and now she wasn't returning my phone calls, or responding to my texts.

There may have been more than a few texts.

Confused, and ego-bruised, I opened up the family chat to let mom and everyone else know I was back in the states. Our mother was weird about that. Whenever any of us traveled, she wanted to know when we left, when we arrived, and when we made it home safe and sound.

Me: Home safe and sound.

Mom: Hope you had a good time.

Me: I did. I had the best time.

Gabriel: The best? Thought you said it was complicated?

Mom: Is something wrong?

Fucking Gabriel stirring up shit.

Me: No. It was great. No problems.

What I wanted to say was that I'd found the perfect woman then somehow managed to piss her off in the span of three days. It wouldn't be the quickest relationship I'd ever been in and out of, but it was the only relationship I didn't want to end. Like ever. And that scared the shit out of me.

I chatted with my mother for a while, catching up on what she was doing with her girlfriends at the country club.

She said nothing about Lizzy or the engagement, which

meant the siblings had been able to keep it a secret for the time being.

Mom: When are you coming home?

Me: I don't know. Work is pretty intense.

Mom: Ah, well we're sending Lizzy off to college soon. It would be great if you could come.

The sibling chat popped open.

Angie: Ace, you gotta come home. Lizzy is going to announce it. She wants everyone there.

Me: Everyone? Mom will figure something's up.

Angie: She'll think one of us is having a baby.

Me: Is anyone else having a baby?

Our eldest brother Gabriel was having his fourth, but our mother already knew about that.

Angie: Nobody is pregnant.

Me: What about Lizzy?

Lizzy: I'm NOT preggers!

Me: Hey stalker. Didn't know you were here.

Lizzy: I just got out of the shower, and I'm not pregnant.

Me: You sure? Because…

Angie: Don't be an ass. Can you come or not?

Me: Send me the deets. I'll see if I can make it work.

It had been some time since I'd been home and if everyone was going to be there it would be a blast.

As the years went by, our busy family grew and everyone tried their best to make it home, but it didn't always work out.

I wanted something like that in my life. All my siblings

were moving on with their lives, getting married, settling down, and having kids. Well, Gabriel and the girls were.

Colt, Ryder, Dylan and I remained unattached. But of the four of us, I was the only one who couldn't seem to stay in a relationship.

I seemed to be the only one stuck standing still.

Something had shifted over the past few days, a feeling I could have the same kind of thing. I knew exactly who I wanted it with, only she wasn't speaking to me.

Phone in hand, I dialed her number again. Nearly midnight, I didn't expect her to pick up, but I did leave another message?

"Hey Angel, I'm sorry. Call me."

It was always best to lead with an apology. Relationships weren't my thing. If they ever showed signs of becoming complicated, I headed out the door. I was there for companionship to stave off boredom and to enjoy vigorous sex.

I'd never been interested in getting to know the woman I was with beyond the basics.

That may say more about me than I wanted to admit, but it didn't matter. I never lied about my intentions and I never led a woman on. All my relationships, if that's what we're calling them, ended amicably.

I continued blathering on, leaving a message to Angel about how sorry I was, how I crossed a line—whatever line that was—and how I wanted to make it up to her. Preferably in person and hopefully in a way that eased the painful ache in my balls.

But I had to finally face the truth she wasn't going to pick up, call me back, or respond to my texts.

Honestly, it was a little annoying.

Not that it phased me one bit. A quick search of the employee call roster and I had everything I needed.

This was one woman who was not going to slip away.

Only one question remained.

How?

How upset was she really?

How was I going to break the ice?

How was I going to knock some sense into her without literally knocking sense into her?

I had a feeling Angel could be obstinate. She'd been hurt before, leaving me to wonder if I'd inadvertently triggered something from her past.

She was overly sensitive about her career. We'd danced around some of those issues. Maybe, I'd done all that and more.

She hated me before she met me because I was a fighter jock. My mind stirred up all the stereotypes and I cringed. If I'd been her, I probably would've hated me too.

That wasn't the issue though. I crossed a line, but how?

Figure that out and I'd be golden. I was certain she told me.

Angel wasn't the kind of chick to beat around the bush, but no matter how many times I replayed our conversation, I couldn't understand why she wasn't over-the-moon excited about the opportunity Dex offered. As far as dream jobs went, it was the golden ticket.

A private text popped up from Gabriel.

Gabriel: Tell me what happened.

He wasn't using the Bro' box and I gulped. He was my oldest brother, ten years my senior, but had always been much more, especially after our father died.

Gabriel was more like an uncle to me than a brother, a grownup who I could confide in, who gave me advice, and called me out on all my shit.

Me: Nothing happened.

I wasn't ready to get into shit about Angel.

Gabriel: Lying bastard. Tell me. What did you do?

Me: If I knew that, things wouldn't be complicated.

Gabriel: How about start at the beginning?

Me: I don't want to.

Gabriel: Don't be a little shit. Obviously, you found a girl, fucked her, and messed things up. Considering that's your M.O., why is it complicated?

He never beat around the bush, and he wasn't going to let me off the hook. I spent the next half hour telling him all about Angel, our days in paradise, mushy feeling crap, and how she stormed off.

Gabriel: Well you fucked that up.

Me: Obviously.

Gabriel: What are you going to do?

Me: If I knew what I did, I'd fix it.

Gabriel: You can't be that dense. She told you exactly what you did.

Me: She did not.

Gabriel: You just told me what she said. Even I can figure it out.

Me: Because I got her a dream job?

Gabriel: No shithead, because you blabbed about the two of you fucking to a client and potential boss. You really are a dumbass. You violated her trust. You better get on your belly and crawl back to her and beg forgiveness.

Me: It's no big deal.

Gabriel: And this is why you're single. Do you understand women at all, or just use them while they're willing to spread their legs for you? It's time to grow up.

Me: Fuck you.

Gabriel: Not interested. Go fix your mess, lil' bro.

Fix my mess? I was trying to fix my mess, but she wasn't answering my texts.

Frustrated, I crawled into bed, jerked off to thoughts about fucking Angel in every imaginable position, then drifted into a troubled sleep.

I woke with sunlight streaming through my windows, thoughts of Angel spinning through my head, and another erection.

I took care of my morning wood in the shower where I also conceived my plan of attack.

An hour later, I stood outside her front door with my fist raised to knock and sweat beading my brow. I wasn't good at this kind of shit.

But I knocked and waited.

It took a moment, but then the soft tread of bare feet sounded from the other side of the door.

"Who is it?"

I imagined Angel on her tiptoes, looking through the peephole. Wrong thing to think about, because that made me remember her Peeping Tom activities and all that followed from that.

Putting on my biggest smile, I locked my wrists behind my back and rocked back on my heels.

When she didn't open the door, I took a step forward and pressed my palm against the warm wood. I leaned against the door, placing my cheek where I imagined her face would be.

"Can we talk?"

"I'm not dressed."

What an odd thing to say considering I'd eaten off her naked body.

You did a hell of a lot more than that.

Shit, didn't I know.

"Please." Begging was not beneath me, not when it determined whether I would see her or not.

"Hang on, let me get dressed."

"Angel, you don't have to—" But I didn't bother finishing.

Her light steps disappeared and I was left to wait on her front porch. Several long minutes later, when I thought maybe she wasn't coming out, I settled onto her porch swing determined to wait as long as it took. I slowly rocked back and forth thinking about what I needed to say.

When the door opened, I jumped to my feet.

"Angel."

She squeezed through the narrow opening. Rather than inviting me inside, she joined me on the porch.

"You're *not* inviting me in?"

"My place is a mess."

"Is it really, or is this your way of giving me the brush off?"

"Logan..."

"No, I mean it. What the fuck, Angel?" I paced the length of her porch and spun around, trying to keep my rising anger under control. "You don't answer my texts. You don't answer your phone. Do you not want to see me? Is that what you want? Because I'm pretty sure something incredible is happening between us."

"I didn't answer my phone, or your texts, because I was angry. I didn't want to say something I'd regret."

"That sounds like past-tense, like you're not angry with me anymore?" Hope stirred in my gut. "Will you please invite me in?"

She nibbled at her lower lip. "I don't think that's such a good idea."

"Why's that?"

She didn't answer, but she didn't need to. The flush in her cheeks told me everything I needed to know.

"Okay, will you at least let me take you to breakfast? Someplace safe?"

"Safe?"

"Yeah, someplace where I can't jump your bones, because I have to tell you, being around you stirs up all kinds of reactions."

"Let me get my purse."

She retreated inside, leaving me to stew on the porch. She was angry with me.

Correction, she had been angry. Which meant she'd probably spent the night thinking about me.

I considered that a win.

23

LOGAN

MY BROTHER SAID I NEEDED TO FIX THIS MESS AND THERE was only one way I knew how to do that.

It involved vigorous fucking, but I had a feeling I'd have to use words instead.

I wasn't very good with those.

When Angel returned, it took every ounce of self-control I had not to touch her. I knew what happened when we touched. We were combustible and already I could feel the static electricity building between us.

I let her open her own door to the car and waited for her to buckle in before I strapped myself in.

If our hands inadvertently touched, I wouldn't survive what came next.

"I hope you're hungry." I put the car in gear and backed out of her driveway.

It had been far easier to get her to agree to go with me than I thought. Although, I'd honestly thought I'd be in her house, probably fucking her by now, but I'd take this.

"I am. Where are we going?"

"Someplace quiet where we can talk."

"I really don't want to talk."

And yet, she got dressed and joined me in my car. If she didn't want to talk, what the hell was she doing with me?

"You mean about us?"

I didn't like the slight bob of her head.

It took a little less than half an hour before we pulled up to my favorite diner.

A throwback from the fifties, Mel's served fluffy pancakes, waffles you could drown in, burgers which melted in your mouth, and of course milkshakes which gave the best brain freeze in the industry.

We were lucky. The back corner booth sat empty and I led her over to the round booth. I slid in one side of the booth while she slid in the other.

If I kept scooting around, I'd be able to touch her, but I stayed where I was.

We stared at each other across the table while the waitress took our drink orders and handed over the menus.

I didn't need to look at the menu. I'd been coming here for years, but I sat quietly while Angel perused the options.

"The waffles are incredible. Deep pockets for butter and syrup. The pancakes are the fluffiest in town. And the eggs are pretty good too."

"I was looking at the burgers." She peered intently at the menu.

"We're having breakfast."

"Nothing wrong with a burger for breakfast."

"I guess not."

The waitress returned and I ordered Belgium waffles, extra butter, no syrup while Angel ordered a bacon cheeseburger with fries and a shake.

It was funny, because I was used to the women I dated ordering salads and other rabbit food. I guess they thought I cared what they ate. I didn't. I didn't give one fuck about what they ate.

But I loved the freedom with which Angel embraced life. She didn't worry about what I may or may not think. She simply ordered what she wanted and didn't give a shit.

We weren't talking.

I stared at Angel while she looked away. An awkwardness settled over us until I had no choice but to break through it.

"You walked away from me."

"I did."

At least we weren't going to debate what happened.

"You had every right to do so. You're right, I crossed a line. I shared something that was private with the one person I should have never said anything to. I apologize, and if I could take it back I would."

"Thank you."

"Shit, that was a fucking lie."

"What?"

"I'm sorry, but I won't take it back. Look JetAire is crazy for not promoting you. You have way more experience than me." I ticked off each point, my voice growing louder. "More hours. More takeoffs and landings. More years behind the stick. You flew tankers which are far closer to commercial jets than a fighter. You're far more qualified than me, and yet they hired me in as a captain and you as a first officer."

"And?" Her left brow lifted.

"Do I think your sex factored into that?"

"No. Jet jocks get preferential treatment. My sex didn't matter."

"Look, Dex is willing to bring you on as a captain with a significant pay increase. I'm not sorry you have that opportunity. And I'm not sorry spilling the beans about us was poor form. I won't apologize for getting you that opportunity. Whether you choose to piss it away because you're mad at me is on your shoulders not mine."

"That's one hell of a shitty apology."

Our waitress returned with our food, sliding a plate full of steaming waffles in front of me with butter already melting. I eyed Angel's hamburger. It looked pretty amazing as well.

She took a knife and sliced her burger in half. I didn't understand why she would bother until I realized her tiny hands were too small to fit around the massive burger.

That had me thinking about her hands sliding up and down my cock. I shifted in my seat and held back a groan.

We each took a bite. I glared at her while she ignored me.

"Mmm…this is really good." Ketchup dripped down her chin and she laughed as she licked it off her lip.

"You missed a spot." I pointed to the ketchup still on her chin.

Angel was mad at me and yet this felt completely normal. Natural.

We simply fit together. Whether fucking or sharing a meal, we were meant to be together.

I wanted to kiss her lips, lick her chin, spread my butter over her creamy skin and simply devour her whole, but the staff at Mel's might take offense if I stretched Angel out on the table and went to town.

Then I realized what I really wanted.

"What are you doing next Saturday?"

"Next Saturday?"

"There you go again, answering everything with a question. Are you going to start repeating yourself again?"

Her brows pinched together with her little frown and I pointed again to the ketchup on her chin.

"Either take care of that, or I will."

"You'll do what?"

"Another question, I see, but you know exactly what I'm thinking. Trust me when I say you don't want to test me on this, because I'll start licking at your chin and finish much further down." The angle of my gaze slanted down, letting her know exactly what I was thinking.

She squirmed and her cheeks flushed.

"Your mind is perpetually in the gutter."

"Agree. I've already fantasied about laying you out on this table, and watching you squirm as I pour that ice-cold milkshake on your tits."

"I don't think we should..." Her voice trailed off, and I jumped in to fill the gap.

"I want to know if that's something you still want." My voice deepened, demanding a response.

She glanced around the diner, a look of arousal buried beneath alarm. "I don't think that's appropriate right now."

"It's highly inappropriate, but answer the damn question. Is that something you'd like to do with me?"

Is it something you still want to do with me?

Her shoulders curled inward and her voice dropped to a whisper. "I honestly don't know. I don't know if I can trust you."

"You can trust me." What the fuck?

She shook her head. "We moved too fast. I moved too fast. I know your relationships are like that, fast and furious with little thought about the consequences, but it's not like that for me. Doing what you did, saying what you did to Mr. Truitt... it was a violation of my trust. I realized how very little we know about each other. We had a fling and I confused lust for something else. I don't want to be with someone who doesn't take into consideration how their actions affect me, my livelihood, and my life. It kind of just came to a head and I realized how big of a mistake it had all been."

I ground my teeth together.

Everything she said was spot on. I did all of that and more. This thing between us, it didn't make sense.

But it didn't need to.

I couldn't control it and neither could she. We were a force of nature, a tempest which couldn't be controlled, and if we were going to make this work it would require a little faith.

"Point taken," I said, "but it's not about trust. It's about what you want."

"What I want? That's a dangerous question. Are you sure you want an answer?"

She regarded me with an expression so serious my balls drew up and my voice tried rising an octave.

I cleared my throat and forced my voice to its usual register. "It's an honest question and yes, I want your honest answer."

"Fine. I want someone who won't betray my trust. I don't give it easily and I gave it to you without thinking about what I was giving away. It didn't take a day before you betrayed me."

"I did it for you. I did it for us."

"But you don't get to decide what's best for me."

"You said it wasn't safe for us to work together, so I found a solution that would work for both of us, and more."

"Without consulting me." Her voice rose and people sitting a few tables over turned to look.

"I didn't think it was necessary."

"Exactly, you didn't think. You assumed."

"And what's wrong with that?"

"Because it's my life. My choice. My move to make. If I wanted to look for a different job, I would have done so. You didn't offer to give up your position to work for Montague Enterprises. Instead, you decided I would be the one to change jobs."

"It makes the most sense and from a career perspective is a good move."

"There's more to it than that, and you didn't even think to include me in the conversation before taking it upon yourself to determine the course of my career."

"Why not?"

"This is so typical."

"What is?" She was really confusing me.

"Just because I like something in my personal life doesn't mean I let that bleed over into my professional life. You had no right to make any decision for me. It never occurred to you to talk to me first, and I don't know if I can get past that."

"What do you mean you can't get past it? I made a small inquiry. Look, I may not have come to you first, but it was a spur of the moment thing. An idea struck me and I went with it."

"By telling the CEO of Montague Enterprises I was a cheap slut who slept around?" She crossed her arms over her chest.

"That's not what I told him."

"What exactly did you say?"

Well, shit, I didn't want to answer that.

"Logan?" Her gaze pinned me in place. "What did you say?"

"I plead the fifth."

"That's not good enough."

"Look, I fucked up, but that doesn't mean we just end this. You don't get to walk away."

"I can do whatever I think is best."

"And is that what's best for you? Ignoring my texts? Refusing my calls? You're not doing what's best for you."

"I don't think you get to decide that."

"I'm calling you out on your bullshit."

"What?"

"You're playing things safe and cutting yourself off from something you know is amazing."

"You?" She shook her head. "Because you're such a great catch? Or is it because no woman has ever said no to you? I think this is more about you than it is me. Your ego is bruised."

"Bullshit. You're scared and you're looking for any reason to justify running way. Truth? You're right, I've never had a woman say no to me, but that's not what this is about. It's not about me at all. And it's not even about you."

"Then what is it about?"

"It's about us." Didn't she understand? "It's about you being scared as shit about what happened in the Caymans. You stepped out of your comfort zone and, it terrified you."

"No, it didn't."

"It did, and you confused it for something else. You keep such a tight grip on your professional life, the goals you seek, striving to always be the best, and given the respect you rightfully earned that you've never considered someone might want the same for you."

From the way her mouth twisted, and her brows pinched together, she clearly didn't understand.

"Just because we explored certain things with sex doesn't mean any of that spills over into the rest of our lives." Was she capable of understanding that giving me control during sex didn't mean that's what I wanted all the time? "Do you think about us lying together naked?"

"Huh?"

"I do. I think about it all the time. And I'm not willing to give that up."

"Logan…"

I held up my hand and she pressed her lips together. I needed to get this off my chest. She needed to understand.

"What I did wasn't malicious or deceitful. I wasn't trying to control your life, or your career. And despite what you think, I wasn't bragging about sleeping with you. All I told him was we were seeing each other and we didn't think it would be best to work together. I mentioned how promotion opportunities were limited at JetAire. Honestly, I saw an opportunity that would give you everything you needed. You're right, I didn't ask your permission. I'm sorry for that. I never meant to offend you. But there was nothing that I did that was meant to harm you."

"I wasn't offended." She twisted her fingers and refused to look at me.

"I wanted to do something for you, something amazing, and you know what? I've never wanted to do that for anyone else in my life before. All I can think about is you. How to make you happy. How to help you succeed. How to make all your dreams come true. And if you can't see that for what it is, then we don't have what I thought we did."

"What do we have?"

"Ah Angel, don't you see?" I wanted to reach across the table and collect her in my arms, but my hands only grasped empty air. "We have a chance at forever."

24

ANGEL

FOREVER?

My heart pounded faster. My breaths became a little more ragged.

Ragged?

Hell, I was practically panting. This man talked about forever as if it were a foregone conclusion.

All we'd done was fuck.

That was it.

But why did my heart feel a little lighter thinking about a chance at forever? Maybe I wasn't that upset with Logan Reid.

"Logan...this is too much."

It was far more than too much. It was off the charts, out of bounds, not even in this solar system kind of too far.

"I don't think so." A smug expression settled on his face.

I wanted to slap it right off his face. I wanted to kick him in the nuts and show him who was boss.

He's the boss.

I wanted to curl up against him as his delicious voice told me everything would be okay. I wanted something impossible.

"We made a mistake." If I said the words with confidence, that meant they would stick.

Right?

Wasn't that how it was supposed to work?

"I don't believe we're a mistake, luv, and I'm going to prove it."

"How?" I didn't believe him, but he certainly seemed convinced. What did he have up his sleeve?

"By slowing down."

"Slowing down?"

That made no sense.

"Hell, if that's what it takes, I'll slow this way the hell down." His voice rumbled across the table and licked along my skin.

A shiver worked its way down my spine as goosebumps lifted on my skin.

There was no slowing this down. We were a tinder box primed to ignite. We had two speeds; smoldering and explosive. There was nothing else.

"I don't understand what you mean." I rubbed at my arms, trying to lay down the fine hairs which lifted with each rumble of his voice.

How could we slow anything down after what happened in the Caymans? I'd been in his bed in less than a day and never left it. My body still ached from the way this man had fucked me.

He put his entire body and soul into it, until I no longer knew where I stopped and he began. The control he wielded during sex brought out a side of me I'd never seen before.

As a woman driven to succeed in a man's world, I never caved before the power of a man. I fought it. I rose above it. I did whatever it took to prove I was, if not just as good, better.

With Logan Reid, a switch flipped within me. I became compliant, delicate, and highly suggestive of his commands. I hated to use the word submissive, because that wasn't what it was, but something within me yielded when I was with him.

In that surrender, I rediscovered what it meant to be feminine.

And I loved it.

"You said we moved too fast." His sinful voice licked along my skin, making me shiver. "I might agree, but honestly that's the only speed I know. I see something I want and I go for it."

"I'm not a thing."

"I know that, but when we started this you were just another chick. I wanted you. I had you, but then you changed the game."

"I knew it was wrong to be with you, because I knew I'd get hurt, but I didn't care. I wanted a *fling,* and you wanted one too. We should simply stop while we're ahead."

I tried rationalizing what had happened in the Caymans, but it sounded false.

"Funny how we both got so much more. I can't explain what happened. I don't know why you're different. All I can say is that I feel it in here." He placed his palm over his heart. "And I know it up here." He tapped his temple. "I also know you feel it as well. You can use all the words to deny it, but I'm not listening to what you say. I'm watching what your body does, and Angel, it's telling me everything."

"My body isn't saying anything." I sat back with alarm.

He saw through me too easily. Was I that transparent?

That terrified me if it was true. From the hungry look in his eyes, I had no doubt he saw every thought in my head, every beat of my heart, and every pulsating throb between my legs.

Combustible? Yeah, we were an explosive combination.

But was that it?

Sex didn't sustain two people through forever and there was still much we didn't know about the other.

Do you want him scouring through the pieces of your life?

"I want to suggest something." He pressed the pads of his fingers on the table and leaned forward. His face twisted into a mask of disapproval. Not at me, but rather at the thoughts inside his head.

Maybe he was becoming a little transparent to me as

well? Whatever he was about to offer wasn't something he thought was a good idea. But he would say it.

This was something I needed to hear. Whatever it was that threw him off his game might be something I could use to my advantage.

"I have a deal. Are you willing to hear me out?"

"I'm waiting, flyboy."

The corner of his mouth curved up. He leaned back and his long fingers drew back along the table.

My mouth dried up thinking about the talent in those fingers.

He glanced down to his hands and gave a low chuckle.

"This is not something I propose lightly, because it's doomed from the start. But I'm willing to try it if it's something you think might help."

"Help with what?"

"Getting to know each other outside of sex. What would you say to a no-sex rule?"

In the middle of drinking water, I coughed as it went down the wrong pipe. "Excuse me?"

"Let's take sex off the table and spend some time getting to know each other."

"You want to take sex off the table?" Was he capable of such a thing?

"I'd rather have sex on *this* table, but there are a few laws and felony charges which make that impossible."

"I don't think you're capable of being with a woman and not having a physical relationship."

"I never said anything about not being physical. I just said no sex."

"You'll have to define what no sex means."

He glanced around the diner and leaned in, lowering his voice. "No fucking, obviously. No oral sex and no hands, or digits, on my private parts or in yours."

"Kissing?"

"Absolutely."

"Hugging?"

"Of course."

"Handholding?"

"Wouldn't have it another way."

I leaned back and laughed. "You had me going there for a minute, flyboy. That's really funny. There's no way that's happening."

He wouldn't be able to keep his hands off me and I didn't think I'd be able to keep mine off him. After the erotic dreams which had tormented me through the night, I didn't think I'd be capable of not having sex with him.

"I mean it, but I have one condition."

"A condition?"

"I want you to talk to Dexter Truitt, and if not him, then at least the head of his aviation department. It's a great opportunity. If things don't work out for us, you'll have something you definitely deserve."

"We're back to that, are we?"

"Hun, we never left it. I came over here to apologize and to get you to stop ignoring my texts." He lifted his index finger into the air. "We'll have to make a few rules. First one will be no more ignoring me. If you're mad at me, if I've pissed you off, we talk about it. We discuss it like grown ass adults. I won't have you running off and hiding your feelings from me. And I want you to make the call. You don't deserve to pass up this opportunity because of misplaced pride, or because I embarrassed you. You're a kick ass woman. Go out there and kick ass."

"What if that ass is yours?"

"Then kick my ass, but don't run from me. Don't hide your feelings from me."

"Since we're trading conditions, I have one of my own."

"Lay it on me."

"Don't do that shit again. I work hard for what I have and I'm very private. My professional life is mine. I don't want you interfering in it again."

He held up two fingers. "Scout's Honor, I'll never stick my nose where it doesn't belong."

"Please tell me you weren't an Eagle Scout?"

"Why? What's wrong with that?"

"Because it makes you perfect."

"A perfect scoundrel."

"A cocky bastard."

"A man who can't get enough of his angel." He thrust out his hand. "Do we have a deal? Will you forgive me?"

"I will."

"Will you follow up with Dex?"

"Will you stay out of my business?"

"Hell no. I plan to be balls deep in your business."

"I thought we said no sex."

"We said it, but we both know it's not going to last."

I couldn't help but laugh. "You're incorrigible."

"And forgiven?" He looked at me with hope in his eyes.

"Forgiven, but stay away from my career. I need you to promise me that."

"I swore on my honor, and I really am sorry I overstepped. It won't happen again."

"Thank you."

"Great." He dug into his pants pocket and placed cash on the table to cover our bill. "How about we get out of here and begin with date number one."

"Date number one?"

"Yes, ten dates to get to know each other. After that, the ban on sex is lifted."

"I thought you said we'd never make it."

"We're going to make it, luv. I have no doubt about that, but we need to get to know each other. So, I propose ten dates. I'll pick first, then we'll alternate. Let's try to keep them to public places. It'll force us to behave."

"This is crazy. I can't believe I'm agreeing to any of this."

"Hey, I'm the guy who agreed not to fuck your brains out, although if you want to watch the peepshow, it'll be open every night."

It did not escape my notice that watching him pleasure himself was not on the list of forbidden things.

"Wouldn't this technically be our first date then?" I pushed away my plate and propped my elbows on the table. Cradling my chin in my hands, I took a moment to admire the man sitting across from me.

He came to grovel, to beg forgiveness, but there was nothing about him except an absolute assurance things would go his way.

I didn't know if that made me weak, or said I was too infatuated to care. All I really cared about was that the man sitting across from me wanted a forever with me.

"I don't think we'll count this one as date number one. I want to take you home, have you put on something a little more comfortable than those tight-assed shorts, and you'll need something comfortable to walk in."

"Really? Where are you taking me?"

"It's a surprise."

25

LOGAN

I LITERALLY HAD NO IDEA WHAT THE HELL I WAS DOING.

Winging it?

That was probably the best description of what this was.

No sex?

What the fuck possessed me to offer that up? Insanity? Desperation?

That static charge which always filled the space between Angel and I was no less potent now than it had been the first day we met.

The lightness of her scent, floral and fresh, filled the air inside my car. Every time my arm brushed hers the hairs stood on end. My pulse thrummed in my veins and headed straight to my cock.

My entire body ached to claim her.

But I put a stop to it all.

That made me certifiable.

"Are you going to tell me where we're going?" She unbuckled as I drove up to her home.

"No, but put on shoes you can walk in."

"What about the tight-assed shorts?"

"I changed my mind. You can keep them." I was going to spend my day staring at the way her ass cheeks peek out of the bottom of those shorts. It was going to be agony.

"Do you want to come in?"

"You're inviting me?"

"Just to come in. You can sit on the couch instead of out here. It's hot."

It wasn't that hot. It was the time of year when summer blended into fall. The days were getting shorter, but the heat of lazy summer days and long summer nights still lingered.

What the hell are you going to do with her?

I had no idea. By the time she returned, I hoped I figured it out. Although an idea was beginning to form in my head. I should have told her to bring boots. I sent a quick text to Colt.

Me: I'm headed to your property today. You there?

Colt: No, I'm in the city today.

Me: I'm taking out the ATV.

Colt: Have at it.

The dots on my screen bounced. They kept going. Was he writing a damn novel?

Colt: This wouldn't have anything to do with a certain complicated someone, would it? Because I don't think bringing a chick out there is really on the list of top ten places to apologize. Unless you're thinking of getting her out in the woods and doing shit that would make me blush.

There was very little that made Colt blush.

Me: Angel's not like other women.

Colt: Ah, we finally have a name. Is that a real name or a pet name?

Me: Real.

Colt: And dragging her around on an ATV is her idea of a romantic date?

No, but he didn't need to know that.

Colt: For the record, not that you need my advice, but fucking in the woods is a lot like fucking on the beach. It sounds hot, but when ants are biting her on the ass, or spiders are crawling in her pants, it turns into something else. Beware poison ivy too, because getting that on tender bits is never good.

Me: Speaking from personal experience?

Colt: Yeah. That's an ER visit I never want to repeat.

Me: I'm just taking her for a ride.

Colt: Just a ride?

Me: Fuck you.

Yes, I wanted to take Angel for a ride. I wanted to bury myself so deep inside of her I lost track of where I ended and she began. I was completely, and utterly, fascinated with my co-pilot and she wanted to walk away from what we could become.

No way in hell would I let that happen, and if I had to

keep my hands off her long enough to convince her of that fact, then I would suffer and deal with it.

Angel returned and I shoved my phone in my pocket.

"You changed?"

She had removed the short shorts and put on those weird capris length pants women seemed to like so much.

"I didn't know what we were doing. If we're going to be inside, my legs tend to get cold."

My gaze angled down to her feet and the well-used running shoes. They weren't boots, but would do for the trails.

"Actually, we're spending the day outside."

"Really? Doing what?"

"You can't stand not knowing, can you?"

"I've never been good at surprises."

"Well, I'm not going to tell you."

"What part of me not liking surprises do you not understand?"

"The part where it drives you bat shit crazy makes it all the more fun. While you sit there and squirm because you're dying to know where I'm taking you, I'm sitting here with a hard-on and blue balls. I think that's a fair exchange."

"That's not fair and it's a poor comparison."

"But it's still fun to tease you."

"What if I don't like where you're taking me for our first date?"

She reminded me this was the first of our string of ten official dates.

I reached across the seat and did something I shouldn't have. I took her hand in mine.

Her entire body stiffened, and I quickly released her hand.

"Sorry."

"No." She reached for my hand, taking it out of my lap. "I want to hold your hand."

Electricity shot up my arm and a warmth spread to my chest. Her touch did that to me. It flipped a switch within me which simply felt right.

"I don't want things to be awkward between us."

"They're not awkward."

I gave her a sideline glance. "Seriously?"

There should be no reason for any awkwardness between us. We should be in her house, on her bed, twisting the sheets into fucking knots with our naked bodies, but this was where we were, smack dab in the middle of awkward.

"Okay, they're all kinds of awkward, but not something I want to shy away from."

"So, am I forgiven for interfering?"

"I actually got a text this morning."

"You did?"

"Yeah."

When she didn't immediately answer, I tightened my grip. "Care to share?"

"And spoil the surprise?"

"Surprise? What surprise? Did you take the job?"

While it had been my idea—me putting my huge-assed

foot in my mouth—I wasn't as thrilled about her leaving JetAire as I thought I would be. That was our connection. The thing which brought us together.

I could lose her if I fucked this up.

"So where are you taking me?"

"We're going ATVing on my brother's property."

"That doesn't sound very public."

"It's not." It was the opposite of public. Colt had several hundred acres in the country. "But it's a couple hours drive. Plenty of time to get to know each other better, and since I'm driving you're safe."

"Safe?"

"From me."

"I don't feel unsafe around you."

"I know, and that's not what I meant. I meant more that it doesn't have to be all about sex between us." I wanted to fuck her right now. "I really enjoyed the day we spent in the Caymans with the turtles, the dolphins, soaring over the reefs, and walking on the beach. You're right, we need more of that."

We needed more skin on skin and sliding in and out. I repressed a groan and shifted to ease the tightness of my pants.

Angel appeared oblivious to my discomfort.

"That really was fun. Probably one of my top ten best days ever."

"Only top ten?"

"For now. Let's see how the rest of this day goes."

"I like that."

The rest of our ride remained agonizingly chaste. I asked about her childhood and after a little hesitation, she opened up about her family. Or lack thereof.

"I'm an only child, but you already knew that."

"Tell me about your parents."

"My mother was amazing. She worked hard to raise me, did whatever it took, and managed to scrape by, but we struggled. We were too rich for government handouts, but too poor to really make ends meet. I grew up on peanut butter and freeze-dried noodles."

"That had to have been tough."

"It was, but it's also where I got my strength. I had to work for anything I wanted and I learned early that education was my ticket out. I did well in school. We didn't have a television or computer at home, which meant I studied a lot and read a bunch. My grades, helped me get a college scholarship. I did the work. I got the grades. And I'd like to think it paid off. I didn't have many friends, we moved around every three to six months."

"What? Every three months? How is that possible?"

"My mother was a travel nurse. We went where the jobs were. She tried to put me in regular school, but it was too hard to make friends, and then I stopped trying. It was what it was."

"That had to have been incredibly hard growing up."

"It was all I knew. I've always been focused. I did well with homeschool and look at me now."

I was looking, and I saw an angel.

"Where was your father?" It felt like an intimate question, but that was the point. We'd been physically intimate. It was time to break down all the walls.

She glanced out the window. "He died when I was very young. My mother tried to stay in our house, but we couldn't. He got sick and died from cancer and their insurance wasn't that good. Thankfully, mom was a nurse. She had a career to fall back on, but she stopped working when I was born and had to reenter the workforce. She basically started from the bottom again."

"Where is your mother now?"

Angel pursed her lips together. "She passed a few years ago."

"I'm so sorry. That had to have been incredibly hard."

My angel had no family. I couldn't comprehend that kind of pain.

"We never really got around to talking about my family."

"Yeah," I gave a snort. "Just fucking."

She laughed, which lightened the mood. "You're my first, by the way."

"First what?"

"First one night stand."

"Um, technically, we didn't have a one night stand and I did work for it. We had a three day fling, and it was fucking amazing."

I turned down a gravel lane and pulled up outside my brother's country home.

"Are you ready to get dirty?"

Her brows lifted. "You say the filthiest things."

"Well, I want to do filthy things to you, but I also want to give us a chance."

"So, you don't want sex?"

"I always want sex? Are you offering?"

"Are you taking?"

"As much as I'd love to do just that, no."

"No?"

"I'm a man of my word, and you had me swear on my scout's honor. I can't go back on that."

"We're really not going to have sex until our ten dates are done?"

"If that's okay with you?"

"You are full of surprises."

"I can keep my junk in my jeans."

"And your prick in your pants."

"And the stallion in the stable."

She held her sides, laughing, and swiped at her cheeks. "I think that's what I love most about you."

"My colorful language?"

"That too, but your freedom with your sexuality. Even when you're talking about not having sex, every word is exactly about having sex."

"All I heard was there was something you loved about me. I'm calling that a win."

Putting the car into park, I exited the vehicle, eager to spend a day with Angel riding on my brother's land.

"It's incredibly beautiful here."

"I come here whenever I can. Colt let's everyone use his place. There's a lake to swim in, a stream for fishing. He's got a pistol and rifle range."

"Sounds like he's an outdoorsy kind of guy."

"We all are. We hunt in the winter, fish in the spring and summer. Gabriel and Veronica bring their kids out to swim and play in the stream. It's perfect."

"And what are we going to do?"

"We're going to ride ATVs. It's up to you if you want to take two out or ride double."

"If we ride double, who drives?"

I gave a low chuckle. "Well, you know how I love being in control."

"So, you want me to be your ATV bitch? Ride behind you with my arms wrapped around your waist?"

"Yeah." I shrugged, but I really wanted that.

I wanted her tight body clinging to me. Her tits brushing against my back. Her arms curving around my waist. Her thighs wrapping around my hips. And most importantly, her hot pussy pressed tight against the crack of my ass.

"But if you want to ride your own, Colt has plenty."

Angel did a poor job of hiding her emotions. Old pain creased her lovely brow and turned the corners of her full lips down, but when she looked at me all of that disappeared. Her eyes showed her soul and that's where I found her growing love for me.

All the beauty of the universe couldn't hope to compete for her passion in life. It didn't erase her pain, but it eased some of it. An adventurous spirit, she went out into the world to make it a better place. She clung to that with passion, a passion so profound it made her beautiful inside and out.

She made my heart ache, because I wanted to be worthy of a love like hers.

Please don't ride alone. I wanted to feel her against me.

Her pert little mouth twisted. "No. I'll sit behind you."

Yes!

"You sure?"

"Yeah, it's the best way to tease the shit out of you."

26

ANGEL

COMPETITIVE BY NATURE, LOGAN AND I HAD FUN WITH OUR dates. He took me out on Colt's property, showing me all the places he and his brothers hung out, telling me so much about them that by the end of the day I felt like I knew them well.

He had a tight bond with his brothers and a close, loving bond with his sisters. To my surprise, despite stopping and hiking to a secluded waterfall and swimming hole, he kept his hands to himself.

From the depths of his eyes to the gentle expressions he graced me with, his voice touched me the most.

Deep and rumbly, raspy and hot, I loved the way his voice quickened when he spoke to me. The gentle sweep of his hand against my skin made my body tremble and I lost myself in the moment.

That's where I gave him my heart and kept his safe.

He brought me home late that night and we set up our next date. I had a week to think of something as amazing as our day riding on the ATV.

And it had to knock his socks off.

When he picked me up, I didn't tell him where we were headed. When we drove up to a quarry where a handful of cars were parked he lifted his brow.

"What are we doing here?" His voice sparked with interest.

"You're going to love it."

"Are we swimming?"

There was a swimming area at the bottom of the quarry, but that wasn't our destination.

I walked over to Bill, our guide. I'd met him at the local outdoor sports store where I first noticed the advertisement for spelunking.

Logan and I spent our date underground, with another couple and three eager college kids. It was public—aka no sex allowed—and pretty damn cool.

He upped the stakes on date number three, taking me to one of those indoor skydiving places.

As military pilots, we'd had basic instruction in parachuting as part of our training. I'd jumped out of a plane before, but this was fun and easily one of my favorite things. I brought him back to the same place for date number four.

We always scheduled an activity with a meal afterwards.

In those moments, we learned everything there was to know about the other.

I mentioned my love of thrill rides. He took me to play miniature golf and forced me to ride on the kiddy rollercoaster and spinning tea cups.

We laughed through that entire date, and yes, I won all three rounds of miniature golf.

He told me he loved rock music and hated musicals. I took him to a musical for date number six.

For date number seven, he took me to a five-star restaurant, white tablecloth service, and then to a nightclub where we spent the rest of the evening grinding against one another on the dance floor until we were desperately horny and broke the no sex clause in a bathroom stall.

We weren't perfect, but we certainly had fun.

After I tortured him with the musical, I surprised him with tickets to see Disturbed in concert for date number eight. He flipped his lid and was still talking about it.

Today was date number nine and he refused to tell me where we were headed next.

My instructions were to dress comfortably and that we would be inside and outside for the day.

I had less than an hour left to get ready and for whatever reason I obsessed over what to wear, how much makeup to apply, and what the hell to do with my long, wavy hair.

Up or down?

I tried several styles, but eventually got frustrated enough to simply leave it flowing down my back. Logan loved running his fingers through my hair and pulling on it during sex.

Down it was.

As for what to wear, I opted for a light sundress with a plunging neckline. For shoes, I put on a pair of sneakers. I might be wearing a dress, but I would be comfortable.

A knock sounded at my door and I rushed to greet Logan.

When I opened it, his eyes widened and dropped to the low neckline and abundant cleavage I displayed just for him.

"Fuck, but you look amazing."

I did a little twirl, letting him get the full effect of my outfit.

"Do you like it?"

"I do. I want to rip it off of you." He swallowed a curse. "Fuck, if we weren't running late I would." He stepped to the side. "Come on, let's go before I lose my mind."

I grabbed my purse and joined him outside. "So, date number nine?"

"Yup."

"Where are we headed?"

It had been a couple months since our dating game began. Even in slowing things down, we still raced forward at breakneck speed.

Our dates spanned hours and when we weren't with each other, we texted nonstop. Late night, we spent on the phone with him teaching me how to talk dirty and the joys of phone sex.

In between our dates, we flew. Never together.

"I'm not telling you." He took my hand in his and kissed the backs of my knuckles. His knee bounced and he kept tightening his grip on the wheel.

"Are you nervous about something?" I knew him well enough to begin picking out his moods.

He was excited and yet very nervous at the same time.

"Maybe."

"Care to share?"

"If I do that it'll spoil the surprise." He rubbed his palm on his pants and tapped the steering wheel.

He was definitely nervous. I figured out why when we pulled up to a sprawling house just outside of town.

Cars filled the driveway, at least twelve, and three little kids played on the front lawn while adults watched from the porch.

"You brought me to your home? Is this a meet the family kind of date? You could've warned me. Shit, I would've put on makeup, tied my hair up…"

I would've worn something much more conservative than a summer dress with a plunging neckline. A glance down revealed more cleavage than I was willing to parade around his brothers and sisters.

"Is this your mother's house?"

"It is. We're having a get-together. Lizzy is heading to college for the fall and we're giving her a sendoff."

"And you brought me? Don't you think this should be a family thing, not a bring your girlfriend kind of thing?"

"It feels exactly like a *bring your girlfriend* kind of thing." He huffed a laugh. "Don't you want to meet my family?"

"Eventually, but not today. Not all at once. This really isn't something you spring on a girl." I twisted my fingers and tried to figure out an exit strategy. Since Logan drove, I was stuck.

Suck it up buttercup!

"You can handle it."

"Are you sure about that?"

"Of course, you're fucking badass. Don't tell me you're scared of my family."

I wasn't scared of his family. What terrified me was what this might mean. How serious was Logan? How serious did I want him to be?

We pulled up to the drive and parked with the other cars.

I took in a deep breath as Logan practically vaulted out of the car and raced around to open my door. Another glance down and I gave an exasperated sigh. My assets were going to be on display with more cleavage than was wise.

He opened my door and extended his hand. Not that I needed his help getting out of the car, but I certainly needed the connection his touch brought.

I was meeting his family.

Deep breath. You've got this!

My mini-pick-me-up didn't work.

"Come on. I want to introduce you to the girls."

Five women looked on from the porch. Their eyes

widened at first, then gentle smiles filled their faces. One of them elbowed another in the ribs and they put their heads together. There was no doubt what—or rather who—they were talking about.

Logan pulled me toward the porch, grin plastered on his face and with a stride far more determined than mine. At the foot of the stairs, he released my hand and took the steps two at a time leaving me to stand alone.

"Angie." He pulled a pretty brunette into his arms and kissed her on the cheek, then turned to a woman with the most amazing auburn hair. "Hey Veronica, how are the munchkins?"

She folded into Logan's hug with a soft laugh. "Terrorizing the place, but haven't broken any of Linda's things yet. I'm calling it a win."

"Hey Logan, how's it going?" A brilliant cascade of dark blonde ringlets flowed down a third woman's back. Her crystalline blue eyes matched Logan's exact shade.

"Wonderful, Christina." He pulled her into a hug after releasing Veronica.

"You brought someone…" Christina's attention shifted to me and her eyes softened with a welcome I felt deep in my bones.

Logan took the remaining two women in a double hug. One had her hair cut in a short bob and the other's mahogany waves hung down to her waist.

"It's so good to see you." Logan gave each of them a kiss on the cheek, then turned and raced back down the steps to collect me. With a tug on my arm, I had no choice but to join him.

"Angel, I'd like you to meet my sisters. Angie, Christina, Delia, and the baby of the family, Lizzy. And this is Veronica, Gabriel's better half. There are miniature versions of them running around. Watch out or they'll run you over."

Before I could react, Angie had me buried in a hug. They passed me around, greeting me with affectionate hugs as they repeated their names.

Angie was the oldest of the girls, but six years younger than Logan. Christina, with her auburn ringlets hugged and then kissed me on the cheek.

"It's a pleasure to finally meet you," Angie said with a soft smile.

Finally?

Delia, the one with the cute bob, hugged me then took both my hands in hers, squeezing them gently. "Logan said he was bringing an angel to meet us, but I had no idea. You're gorgeous and that dress is to die for. You have to tell me where you got it."

Lizzy, ten years younger than Logan, with the long wavy hair, pulled me tight and didn't let go. She whispered into my ear. "It's about time he brought someone home. I'm so happy to meet you."

"Um, thanks." I looked to the girls and bit at my lower lip. "I'm horrible with names, so apologies in advance when I forget."

They laughed with me and just like that all the tension

in my body eased. There was nothing scary about these women. It amazed me how readily they welcomed me as one of their own.

"Where's mom?" Logan asked. "And have you spilled the beans? Are we too late?"

There had been a delay on the freeway. I'd thought nothing of it, but looking back I realized that's when some of Logan's nervousness began.

"You're just in time," Angie said. "The guys are out back figuring out how to man the grill and mom is inside fussing at everyone to stay out of her kitchen. We've been waiting for you, but you're far from late. Lizzy's fiancé is out back with the guys."

"Great." Logan turned to me. "Wanna meet my mom?"

When I hesitated, Christina gave a soft laugh. "I have a feeling our brother sprung this event on poor Angel. Is that true?"

I gave a nod. "It's date number nine. I wasn't expecting something like this."

"Date number nine?" Lizzy cocked her head. "That's it?"

"Well, yes and no." How was I going to explain our series of ten dates?

Logan bounced on his heels beside me, rubbernecking as he tried to peek inside the house.

"Ace!" Angie snapped her fingers to get his attention. "Go out back and say hi to everyone. We'll take care of Angel."

"You think I'll trust the five of you alone with my girl?" He gave a swift shake of his head, then looked at me. "You stick by my side, luv. My siblings are not to be trusted. They'll have you spilling all our secrets in less time than you can count to ten."

His sisters snickered, none of them denying what he said. I found myself once again dragged forward, through the front entrance and to the back of the house.

"If you girls don't get out of my kitchen, I'm going to—"

"Mom, it's me and I brought a guest."

Logan pulled me around a corner and tugged me tight to his side. He wrapped an arm around my waist and beamed with pride, possession, and something much more concerning.

It was as if he claimed every bit of me as his alone.

"This is Angel."

Logan's mother held a long wooden spoon and wore a crisp white apron over a floral dress. Her long auburn hair, streaked with gray, was done up in a bun. She took me in with a set of piercing blue eyes. A smile tugged at the corners of her eyes as she took me in.

She put down the spoon and wiped her hands on a kitchen towel. "When Logan told me he was bringing a girl home, I didn't believe him."

"You promised, mom," Logan said in a warning growl.

"Oh hush!" She turned to me and clasped her hands over her breasts.

"It's nice to meet you, Mrs. Reid."

"Please, call me Linda and it's very nice to meet you." Her astute gaze took me in with a sweep from my head to my toes and back up again. "Logan tells me you're a pilot and something of a legend?"

"Yes, ma'am. Well, at least I'm a pilot. Not so sure about the legend bit."

"A girl with manners. Now isn't that nice." Instead of pulling me into a hug like her daughters had done, she took my hands in her strong grip and took another long look at me.

I felt weighed and measured and didn't know how I came out on the other end.

"Logan, your brothers are trying to break my grill. Why don't you go outside and help them out?"

"Sure." He didn't look convinced but reached for my hand.

"Leave Angel with me." His mother's tone brooked no nonsense.

The look on Logan's face made me laugh.

Hell, I felt my balls withering under that tone and I didn't have any balls to shrivel.

Logan did and he snapped at the command in his mother's tone.

27

ANGEL

I swallowed thickly, not sure if I wanted to stay with Logan's mother or head out to meet his brothers.

His sisters were easy.

They were younger than me and female. That made them kindred spirits.

His brothers? They intimidated me.

Logan's eyes shifted to me, wary and unsure, but I gave him a wink. I had this. To see him squirm, and after catching mischief in his mother's eyes, I knew I had nothing to fear.

"Go on." His mother released me, but only to shoo him out the back door.

Logan gave one last glance over his shoulder as the door practically hit him in the ass.

"Now," his mother said with a clap of her hands, "you

and I can chat. From the look in your eyes, I'm guessing my son did not tell you he was bringing you here."

"Does it show that much?"

"Your doe-in-the-headlights stare gave you away, but please, make yourself at home. Can I get you something to drink?"

"Yes please. Water would be great."

"I can pour you a glass of water, or I can give you some lemonade and add whiskey. For this crowd, meeting everyone at once, I'm thinking you need something a little stronger than water."

"I like your style, Mrs. Reid."

"Uh-uh, call me Linda."

"Thank you, Linda."

"That's more like it." She bustled over to a cabinet and pulled out a tall glass. A trip to the fridge and she filled the glass halfway with lemonade. "Now don't tell the kids, but I keep a special stash of whiskey here." She opened the corner cupboard. "You ask me for a glass of lemonade and I get you fixed up." She topped the lemonade with a generous portion of whiskey then handed it to me. Her hands went to her hips and she waited until I took a sip.

"Mm, that's perfect."

"So, if he didn't tell you he was bringing you here, where did you think you were going?"

"Well, we're kind of playing a dating game."

"Really?"

"Yes, ten dates. We're alternating and today is his day." I

lowered my voice to a conspiratorial whisper. Something told me I could trust Logan's mom. "We've kind of been trying to one up the other. You know, do things that make the other uncomfortable. I took him spelunking, indoor skydiving, to a musical, and a Disturbed concert. He brought me here. I think it's payback for the musical."

Her eyes glittered and she covered her mouth as lilting laughter escaped her mouth. "I'm thinking he wins this round, hun. Bringing a girl to a family cookout, and not just any family. We can be intimidating to the uninitiated."

I couldn't help but laugh with her. "He definitely upped the stakes, but date number ten is mine, and payback is a bitch."

"I like your spunk." She glanced over her shoulder at the closed door leading out back. "Need any help?"

"You'd help me get one over on your son?"

"Heck yeah. It'd be my pleasure to show that cocksure brat a thing or two, mother's prerogative, honey." She winked at me. "Tell me about the other dates."

Linda put me to work in the kitchen while I relayed our string of dates. A smile twitched at the corners of her lips but that was the extent of the emotion she displayed.

I swear she gave a snicker here and there.

"Hm, you're going to have to work to get him back. There's very little that ruffles his feathers." She put an array of bowls in front of me. "Help me make the salad, please?"

With no way to say no, I went to the sink and washed my hands. "I'm not really sure where to go after this."

"We'll figure it out."

I couldn't believe Logan's mother was going to help me with the last date. Our little game of ten dates seemed a bit moot after we broke the no sex clause in the bathroom at the nightclub.

That was the only time we'd had sex since our dating game began and I could feel Logan's restlessness growing. It built within me too; an aching desperation to feel him inside of me.

I took a deep breath and tried to focus on the task at hand.

"I have an idea." Linda stood right beside me. "Do you want to make my son squirm? I see how he loves watching you blush. Ever want to turn the tables?"

I hadn't realized I had blushed. It seemed status quo anymore whenever I was around him.

"Absolutely."

She leaned close and whispered in my ear, laying out her idea.

"You're kidding!"

"It's perfect, isn't it?" Her impish grin told me much about this woman. She loved her children dearly, but she also enjoyed putting them on the spot. I realized where Logan got his humor from.

"Perfect." With a plan in place, I helped Linda prep the salad and set out the rest of the food.

For some reason, all her children were banned from her kitchen, but she welcomed me with open arms. And I learned what it took to feed a virtual army of nine siblings. We had enough food to feed an army.

We settled into easy conversation. There was something about Linda which allowed me to open up. Innocuous conversation floated around us and choking laughter filled the in-between times when she told me embarrassing moments about Logan's childhood.

We covered safe topics, firing questions back and forth in a kind of friendly interrogation until all the food had been prepped.

Logan knocked softly on the back door, opening it a crack to peek his head in.

"When do I get Angelique back?" His rumbly voice wrapped around my name and I loved the way his lips moved around the syllables. It was as if he savored them, devoured them, and made them solely his.

My pulse pounded in my throat and I placed a hand over my heart. Surely it couldn't beat that fast?

A palpable energy electrified the air, humming in the space between us. It danced down my arms, lifting the fine hairs, and skittered along my nerve endings. Heat rose in my cheeks and Linda looked between the two of us and arched her brow.

"Here dear," she shoved a bowl of fruit salad in my hands. "Logan will show you where that goes. You…" She pointed to her son. "You can take this."

Logan stepped inside, looking like he didn't belong, but

wrapped his powerful arms around a massive bowl of ambrosia.

"Come." He whispered out of the corner of his mouth. "I'll rescue you."

"No need for rescue, son." His mother scolded him. "Angel and I had a great time getting to know each other. Didn't we dear?"

I laughed. "We absolutely did."

Linda made it incredibly easy to like her. Not what I was expecting from the mother of my boyfriend, and now she was my coconspirator. I loved it.

Logan held the door with his foot while I squeezed through the narrow opening.

"What did the two of you talk about?"

His whisper fluttered over my skin and made my heart race. That husky tone did it to me every time, making my body hyper alert and compliant to his demands.

"Nothing." Denying him caused a physical ache to lodge itself in my gut.

"Liar!"

I laughed and took the steps down to the back deck, then I came to an abrupt standstill when I came face to face with his brothers.

Five incredibly handsome men turned as one to stare at me. Then I remembered why we were here. The youngest man, the one with the baby face, had to be Lizzy's unofficial fiancé.

I nearly dropped the salad I was carrying and would have if one of them hadn't taken it from me.

"Here, let me help you." The stranger had the kind of face that stopped you in its tracks. Rugged and handsome, he was an older version of Logan.

All the Reid men were incredibly handsome. I guessed this one was used to that sudden pause when a stranger looked at him for the first time. He flashed me a nonchalant gaze and a tender smile.

Linda called out from the back door. "Don't all of you stand there like idiots. Put down the beer and help bring the food out. Gabe, after you help Angel, go find your gorgeous wife and corral those hellions of yours."

Gabriel gave me a wink. "Nice to meet you."

"Likewise."

He gave me a long hard assessment. "Did he tell you that you were the first?"

"Excuse me?"

"Logan's never brought a girl home before. You're special."

"Gabriel, get away from my girl." Logan's low growl rumbled in the air. "And stop with the special shit."

"Or what?"

"I'll take you out."

"I'd like to see you try." But Gabe, or Gabriel, didn't stick around to throw down with Logan. He disappeared into the house, leaving me standing with my arms empty and three other men staring at me.

Lizzy's boyfriend—er…unofficial fiancé—had already leapt up the stairs and headed inside. He came out a second later with the platter of raw hamburger meat patties Linda and I had shaped.

Logan waved at each of his brothers "Angel, meet Colt, Ryder, and Dylan. Guys, this is Angel. Behave."

Colt shoved out his hand first. "Pleasure." Eyes of crystalline blue with shaggy brown hair to his shoulders, he too had been gifted with the Reid genes for stopping a girl's heart with one devastating look.

Ryder was second. "Nice to meet you. We've heard almost nothing about you." Molten, sizzling green, the shade of his eyes was his most unique feature. A girl didn't stand a chance against that mesmerizing intensity.

I glanced at Logan and arched my brow. He came and put an arm around my waist. "I told you to behave."

"Colt! Ryder! Dylan! Get up here now!" Linda's voice cracked through the air and her sons snapped to obey.

Dylan thrust out his hand. "Nice to meet you, Angel. Can't wait to get to know you." Hair cut short, neat, not a hair out of place, he greeted me with a solid grip to my hand. He shared the same arresting gaze as all the brothers, but with a tawny, nearly gold hazel instead of green or blue.

Logan slugged Dylan in the arm. "Mom is calling."

"You can help too, you know." Dylan teased back.

Logan tightened his grip and tugged me tighter to his side. "I have a guest. Therefore, I'm excused."

While his brothers disappeared inside to help carry out

the food to the rows of picnic tables, Logan pulled me aside. "Okay, spill."

"Spill what?"

"What did she say to you?"

"What are you worried about?"

"You don't know my mother. She can be something fierce. She's been known to take people we bring home, chew them up, and spit them out."

"But you've never brought anyone home before."

"Doesn't matter. That woman is not to be trusted."

I pressed my finger to the tip of his nose. "You have nothing to be worried about."

I was going to be in so much trouble when date number ten came around.

The air crackled around us. His brow lifted as he glanced down at me.

"What have you been up to, my naughty little angel? Do I need to take you to the woodshed for a little punishment?"

I gulped and squeezed my legs together against the instant rush of excitement. That was something I would very much enjoy, but not at a family picnic.

"Nothing much." I practically squeaked the words as he yanked me hard against him.

And he was hard.

The length of his erection pressed against the thin cotton of my dress. He barely touched me and yet my body responded. It was on high alert and ready for whatever came next.

Hopefully, the presence of his brothers, sisters, and very interesting mother, would keep him well behaved. One look into his penetrating gaze and I knew that was not going to be the case.

"Come." He took my wrist and pulled me away from the house.

"What are you doing?"

I tried to fight him, to resist, but my heart really wasn't in it. My body ached with the same hunger as his. There was only one way to ease our pain. That began, and ended, with skin on skin, the slapping of flesh on flesh, and him buried deep inside of me.

We went to the woodshed and fucked.

I'm pretty certain everyone knew exactly what we did because when we emerged the entire family was seated at the picnic tables.

No one said a word about our tardiness. Or the direction we returned from.

Colt tried to give Logan a fist bump, but Logan clocked his older brother in the ear. The girls said nothing, but I endured their stares.

The only one who didn't react was Linda.

She gave me a long, appraising look followed by a solitary nod. Then she clapped her hands and told everyone they'd better eat or there would be no pie.

It wasn't the introduction I would have wanted for Logan's family, but it seemed to be perfect otherwise.

We stayed all day and into the night. As the sun went

down, the men built a bonfire and the women brought out pie, ice-cream, marshmallows, chocolate bars, and graham crackers.

A boisterous lot, they shouted over one another, but their love for one another seeped deep into my bones.

That was especially true when a hush suddenly fell over the family. Lizzy surreptitiously slipped a ring on her left ring finger and walked over to Linda.

With a huge smile, she revealed the rock on her finger.

Linda hopped up with a scream and hugged her youngest daughter to her breast, then she gestured for Lizzy's fiancé to join in on the hug. The siblings gave a shout and the party raged from there.

I never knew this kind of familial bond. There had only ever been my mother and me, and never enough money to make ends meet. I envied Logan and I wanted what he had.

It was bittersweet leaving.

My head spun from a little too much alcohol and my heart ached for something I would never have. Logan eased the pain. He climbed into bed with me and wrapped his arms around my shoulders.

Together, we fell asleep and I felt loved.

28

LOGAN

A WEEK PASSED AND I EAGERLY AWAITED MY LAST DATE WITH Angel. It would be an ending, and I'd spent most of the week in the Bro' box talking to my brothers.

Forever stretched out before Angel and I, and I ached to cleave her to me.

Colt thought it was funny as shit how Angel had gotten under my skin. Gabriel said relatively little. I think he understood. My other brothers were single. They didn't know. Ryder and Dylan had their fun with me, but eventually shut up enough to offer a little helpful advice.

Odd how a few short weeks ago, I never would have conceived of such a thing.

Maybe it was the happiness Gabriel displayed with his fourth kid on the way which kicked my ass in gear.

Or maybe, it had to do with Lizzy and her engagement.

She and her fiancé were far too young to get hitched, but the joy in her eyes as she announced her engagement to our mother was something I felt deep in my bones whenever I held Angel in my arms.

This felt right.

One date left.

I pulled up outside Angel's home and practically flew up the steps to knock on her door, but there was no need.

She opened it before I got there with a smile on her face and a book tucked under her arm.

"What's that?" I plucked the book out of her grip and my jaw dropped. "You're bringing this on our date?"

The book which redefined romance and opened up a new world to millions had a well-worn cover and numerous dog-eared pages.

"I am."

I glanced at the book, thumbing it open to one of the dog-ears. "You do know this is unacceptable."

"What is?"

I flipped the dog ear straight and frowned at the crease left behind in the paper. "It's sacrilege to dog-ear pages. Are you a heathen?"

She yanked the book out of my hand. "My book, my rules. There's nothing wrong with dog-earing the parts I like."

A quick tug and the book was back in my hands. I opened to another favored passage and my eyes widened. "You like the sex scenes, you dirty girl."

"Everyone likes the sex scenes." She crossed her arms over her chest and my eyes followed the movement.

"You know this is our tenth date, right?"

"Yes, flyboy, I can count."

"My package arrived yesterday."

"What package?"

"The one I was ordering the last time we flew together."

Angel had yet to accept the job from Dex Truitt and still flew with JetAire. So far, we'd been successful in keeping our work schedules separate, but I missed sharing the cockpit with her. None of my other co-pilots were half as interesting as Angel. Not to mention they were all male.

We talked sports and politics, shot the shit, and I endured the monotonous conversation.

Angel refused to bend on her rule about the two of us not flying together. I thought it was a bit ridiculous, but respected her enough not to force the issue. Besides, I had it on good authority she would soon be handing in a resignation.

I may, or may not, have been in touch with my good friend Dex Truitt. Sometimes it helped when you knew the man in charge.

"So, why are you bringing this book on our date? And where exactly are we going?"

"You'll know soon enough. I'm more concerned about what's in that package."

"You know exactly what's in it. I showed you." I glanced at the book. "You know, there may be a scene in here that we could act out. What do you say to that? After this date, all restrictions are tossed out the window."

"I'd say all restrictions were tossed out the window when you fucked me in the bathroom stall of that club."

I glanced down as the bulge behind my zipper grew. "How about we nix date ten and head inside?"

She pressed a hand to my chest and scooted by me. "Oh no. We're doing this."

"I want to do you."

"I have no doubt, but you may want to get control of that stallion."

I didn't understand her snicker.

Thirty minutes later, I side-eyed her wondering what the hell she had up her sleeve.

"What the fuck are we doing here?"

She had me drive to the country club where my mother was a member. She worked out with her girlfriends on Saturdays, then went to the mall where they walked as a group and gathered for coffee to exchange gossip.

"We're meeting some lovely ladies." Her snicker returned.

"And what are we doing with said lovely ladies? Water aerobics?"

"We can do water aerobics if you want, but that's not the plan."

"What exactly is the plan?" The fine hairs on the back of my neck lifted. I didn't trust the goofy grin plastered all over Angel's face.

"I'd tell you, but seeing how you love to keep me in suspense, I think I'm going to see how long it takes you to figure it out." She unbuckled and opened her door. "Come on flyboy, everyone's waiting."

"What do you mean everyone's waiting?"

She grabbed her copy of Fifty Shades and shut the door. Without waiting for me, Angel headed toward the double glass doors of the community center. Her steps were far too light and there'd been a glimmer in her eye.

Something was up and I had a feeling I was at the butt end of a joke I didn't want to be within a hundred yards of.

I caught up to her at the door, held it open for her, and ran the flat of my palm over her ass which made her jump.

Inside, I tugged her close. "Tell me what we're doing here."

Spending the afternoon at my mother's country club did not sound like an exciting time.

Angel rewarded me with a twinkle in her eyes and said nothing. She glanced at the announcements, seemed to find whatever she was looking for, and flounced down the hall leading to the smaller conference rooms.

I glanced at the announcement board wondering what she had up her sleeve.

There were times posted for water aerobics, a tennis pro coaching class, the Purple Hat club—whatever that was— and a putting workshop.

Nothing stood out.

I followed Angel down the long hall, winding through

the building until she stopped at a door. Propped outside, a sign designated this as the monthly Purple Hat get together.

"What is this?"

Angel pushed on the door. About forty women turned around and stared at us.

They all wore ridiculous purple hats done up in every conceivable way. Perched in the front row, my mother flashed me one of her signature *gotcha* smiles.

Before I could back the hell out of there, Angel pulled me inside. The door slammed shut with some fucking strong hinges. Someone was going to lose a finger or two.

It slammed with a note of finality, sealing me inside with a group of women decades older than me.

"You made it." My mother clapped and popped to her feet. "I didn't think you'd get him to come."

"I didn't tell him where we were going." Angel released my hand. "Payback's a bitch, flyboy."

"Ah, so he doesn't know?" There was an evil glint in my mother's eyes.

"What don't I know?" I looked warily between my mother and Angel, then glanced down the rows of women who all twisted to gape at our exchange.

Angel pulled me down the aisle as all the older women checked me out. It didn't escape my notice there was one chair at the very front, facing the gathering.

I'd been expertly corralled.

Another glance around revealed one notable feature. Every woman clutched a book. The same damn book.

"Angel...what the fuck is happening?" I kept my voice low, but it was deep and resonated through the entire room. Some of the women gave twittering laughs.

Angel tugged me to the front of the room while my mother faced the gathering.

"Ladies, this is my youngest son, Logan Reid, and he's graciously agreed to join us today."

"I agreed to nothing." My comment made some of the women laugh.

"Ah, but this is going to be so much fun." She couldn't keep her laughter from spilling out and I turned to Angel.

"You two are in cahoots!"

Angel pressed her lips together, fighting off her own laughter.

I pointed to the both of them. "Just remember payback is a bitch." I smiled at the ladies and their garish purple hats. "Hello everyone. I think it's obvious I don't belong here. I'll just leave you to your—"

"Oh no," Angel took my hand in hers, "you're the star guest today."

I grumbled something unintelligible, then leaned in close to whisper low enough only she would hear. "You're going to pay for whatever this is."

"I hope so. Good thing your package came in." She turned to the women. "Ladies, Logan has graciously agreed to join your book club today." She lifted her paperback with its ragged cover and dog-eared pages. "He even brought his book."

"That is not my book."

Angel gave a snicker. "Logan says this is his favorite. I thought it would be great if he read for you today."

All the blood drained from my face and my balls clenched.

"What?" My voice came out two octaves higher than normal. Yeah, my balls were in my fucking throat and my mouth suddenly went dry. "You want me to do what?"

Angel just smiled, a sublime self-satisfied smile which was going to cost her dearly when we got out of here.

I thrust my finger toward her. "You're going down."

She fluttered her eyelashes at me and snickered. "Really? Considering date number nine, this pales in comparison."

My mother's voice rang out, loud and clear. "Have a seat son. We've been looking forward to this all week."

"We?"

"Yes," my mother said with a nod, "*we* most definitely have."

"And what have *we* been planning?" I propped my hand on my hips as I tried to take in both Angel and my mother.

Despite the surprise, and very unusual venue for a date, I could get into this.

Sit around with a group of thirty some-odd older women and talk about a romance novel?

Sure, I could do that. Did they want a man's perspective about some of the dominant sex this book was famous for? A bit awkward, but I could step up to that plate.

Very little unnerved me.

My mother had a relatively open policy about sex. Not about being promiscuous, but rather she answered every question any of us asked. She made sure we knew sex was normal, nothing to be ashamed of, and something of value between two people who cared deeply about each other.

I didn't think there was a single one of her children who grew up a prude, but that didn't mean I wanted to discuss this book with her in this room.

Given a chance, I would read the book cover to cover with Angel just to try out all the sexy scenes. If I could do that and figure out all the delicious things which turned her on, I'd spend my days doing nothing but that.

A room full of older women whom I didn't know?

This was going to be a challenge.

I rolled up my sleeves, determined to get through this. "Okay, what do we do? Sit in a circle and talk about our favorite parts?"

My mother and Angel exchanged a look while the women shifted in their chairs.

"Not exactly." Angel thumbed open her copy and glanced at the page. "Ladies, please open your books to page 489. Logan is going to read to us."

"What? You're serious?" My voice did that squeaky thing again, rising in pitch as my balls drew up inside my body.

Angel handed me the open book. "You can start here."

She flashed me a wink and I about smacked her ass in

front of all the lovely ladies. Who wears purple hats as a thing anyway? Was this a secret smut club where they read all the steamy novels?

My Adam's Apple bobbed when I read the first few lines. Angel was going to pay for this. Then my gaze shot to my mother and the smirk on her face. Knowing the two of them planned this together had me squirming, but there was no way in hell I was going to let them win.

They wanted me to read this smut to a group of forty women in freaky purple hats?

I was going to read the hell out of it. If that made my mother squirm, then so be it. I was a grown assed man with a healthy sexual appetite. Now Angel, on the other hand, would pay dearly for this later on.

I cleared my throat and began. "Page 489. Is this the place?"

Angel gave a nod and I took in a deep breath. Was it possible to get through this without a raging erection? A brief scan of the text said no. One look at my mother and I felt like I'd been doused in ice water.

Yeah, I had this locked down.

"Okay ladies, have you ever had a man read to you before?"

I was going to have a shit ton of fun with this and fuck the chair.

Angel thought she put me in a tight spot by putting me in front of everyone. Well, I was going to strut my stuff and knock the socks off these women.

A lady with silver-white hair, and a hat with what looked to be a stuffed squirrel holding two nuts, bobbed her head. I pointed to her.

"What's your name, dear?"

"Lucy." She was easily twice my age with a soft, tremulous voice, twinkling eyes and bright red lipstick.

"Well Lucy, is this what you want to hear? Starting from page 489?"

"Yes…it's hot." Lucy's entire face turned beet red, as did the faces of her friends sitting beside her. They tucked their heads together twittering with laughter.

"And you like the hot scenes?"

Her head bobbed.

"Yes." Her fragile voice wavered around the solitary syllable.

"Ah, then let's get to this." I stood and held the book, placing my fingers in just the right way to stop all the hearts in the room.

I knew the effect I had on women and I was going to rock their world. I cleared my throat again, then began, dropping my voice by an octave until it rumbled through the room.

I went to Lucy and stood in the aisle next to her. My mother sat in the first row and I couldn't see her as my filthy mouth began to read aloud.

Low and raspy, I pitched my voice to be as sexy as possible. "I tease each of her nipples…"

Lucy's eyes widened and her hands folded in her lap.

Her cheeks flushed and she couldn't look me in the eye. Nearly two-thirds of the women were unable to meet my gaze. I continued with a grin.

"She writhes as much as the restraints allow…"

The scene was one where our eccentric billionaire teased Ana's nipples while he has her restrained. It went on to show how he licked along her belly, worshiping her, as he moved down to eat her pussy. It was explicit. It was hot.

And it was everything I wanted to do to Angel.

I was on a roll, getting into teasing the women, and my voice brimmed with masculine power. I had the entire room entranced. They hung on my every word.

Several gasps peppered the air and I moved to the next row and the next woman with her silly purple hat.

She lifted her eyes to meet my gaze. I gave a little smile to the woman who had to have been in her nineties.

I spoke directly to her, pretending she was the only woman in the room. She probably had grandchildren older than me. I began with a wink, because this was far more fun than I thought possible.

The next few lines made her catch her breath because they used explicit words like *pubic hair* and *clitoris*.

I continued and turned my attention to Angel who stood at the front of the room.

"I feel her tremble…" Our billionaire friend scolded his captive beauty in this scene, teasing her and refusing an orgasm. "Oh no. Not yet…Angel."

I altered the name used in the book. Angel's wide-eyed stare was my reward.

She gripped the back of the chair, knuckles turning white and knees pressed close together. I turned back to my new ninety-year-old friend and read the next line about our horny billionaire freeing his erection.

29

ANGEL

SEX ON A STICK EASILY DEFINED LOGAN ON AN ORDINARY day. Him reading smut to a room full of sex-starved women? I didn't think I was going to survive.

He read the entire scene, not once breaking down. Instead, he owned the words and made them entirely his.

Wandering around the room, he played with his audience, teasing them with titillating passages.

When he got done with one explicit scene, he asked for the next, and the women went crazy calling out their favorites.

My thought had been to make him squirm. He'd certainly done that to me.

Although, I had fun at his mother's house. Over the past week, while Linda and I planned this event, I found myself growing to really like his mother.

But still. This was not what I envisioned.

Logan walked around the room, narrating all the best sex scenes with his sexy voice. I kept my legs pressed together, trying to ease the terrible ache, and failing miserably. My panties grew wet and I was mortified knowing he could smell my arousal.

Each time one of the scenes had something to do with a blindfold, he turned to me and spoke the dirty lines. I prayed his mother missed the intensity he levied on me, but I would never know. I couldn't look at her and keep a straight face.

This was backfiring in the worst way and I would pay for it later. I both eagerly anticipated that and warily wished it would never come.

Over the next hour, I squirmed while Logan talked about cocks, erections, blindfolds, pussy, and blowjobs. His mother's attention shifted between the two of us, cautious and knowing.

"Well ladies," Logan finally closed the book. "I'm afraid that's all my poor voice can handle."

His announcement was met with a low rumbling of discontent, but he turned to me. "Don't worry, maybe next time Angel and I can co-read for you."

Hell to the no! I had to get him out of here before that suggestion turned into a promise.

Jumping to my feet, I made some excuse. Honestly, I was in such a rush to leave, I have no idea what came out of my mouth.

I had his hand in mine, tugging him toward the exit, while his mother called the meeting to order to discuss club business.

Once I was out in the hall, Logan spun me around until my back slammed into a wall.

"That was fucking torture." His lips crashed down on mine and he wrapped a hand around the back of my neck.

A moan escaped me. After the last hour, listening to him read nothing but sex, I was horny as hell and ready to fuck.

He devoured my lips, flicking his tongue around the inside of my mouth with a desperation I met and matched.

The way he kissed me, like he was trying to hold back, should have been my cue to hold back. Only I was desperate for him. Another low moan escaped me and he lost the battle with his restraint. I loved watching him come unglued. I enjoyed being the force behind that even more.

He wrapped his palms around my cheeks and deepened our kiss. I met him lash for lash of his tongue, desperate to let out all the sexual frustration that had built up within me over the past hour while he read the most sinful words.

I moaned into his mouth. I clutched at his crisp, collared shirt, I practically climbed up his muscular physique with the intent of dry humping him right there.

Every bit of me was kissing Logan. His dick was hard as a rock. It pressed against my belly as he ground his hips against me. It looked like I wasn't the only one willing to dry hump in the hallway.

His taste coated my tongue, a delicious and dark sensation that was uniquely him. I panted into his mouth as his erection pressed against my abdomen. My breasts pressed against his chest and the tight buds of my nipples ached each time he shifted his feet.

My heart pounded against my ribcage, demanding and insistent. I grasped the back of his neck, needing him closer. Not that there was any space between us. His hand went to my ass, palming it, then lifting my leg to wrap around his waist.

I got the urge to jump up, wrap both legs around his waist, but I was acutely aware of where we stood and the ladies just inside the other room with their cute little purple hats.

"Logan…" I panted between kisses, "we can't…"

"We can and we will." He lowered my leg and drew me down the hall, opening up every door along the way.

Adrenaline rushed through me, mixed with a touch of fear that we'd get caught. I ached for him to fuck me, but I wasn't willing to get caught doing so in his mother's country club.

"Logan, we can't do this here." I suddenly stopped and he turned to me.

His eyes were wide and the pupils were blown black with his lust.

"I'm fucking you." He grabbed my wrist and continued down the hall.

"We should wait." I wanted to express physically all the emotions bottled up inside of me. I was more certain that my heart belonged to him than ever, but someone had to keep a head on their shoulders.

"Logan…" I pulled back. It was becoming harder and harder to look him in the eyes because I wanted what was mirrored in his face.

His expression was hard, resolute, and nonnegotiable. My eyes softened as I cupped his face. My heart reached out to him.

Leaning in he kissed me deeply, and that was all it took. My hips had a mind of their own as they ground against him.

"Yeah, that's what I thought."

We were moving down the hall again. Logan tried every door until one finally opened. A smaller room, all the tables and chairs had been stacked in neat ordered rows along the wall.

His lips curved into a purely masculine smile, hungry and possessive as he shut the door behind us. There was no lock, but he took one of the chairs and wedged it beneath the doorknob.

In one fluid motion, he removed his tee-shirt over his head and tossed it to the floor.

"You'd better keep up with me, luv. This is happening."

Struck dumb by the rippling of his muscles, my mouth dried up as he drew the zipper of his pants down and hooked his thumbs in the waist band.

"Strip!" His order spiked through the air and slammed into my chest. From there it tunneled into my heart. I found myself obeying, moving to the natural rhythm between us.

I grabbed the hem of my shirt and slowly pulled it over my head as he stepped out of his pants. I let my shirt drift down to the floor as I bit my lower lip in awe of the beauty of the man before me.

Full of lethal sexual prowess, I was completely at his mercy. He stood before me in his boxer briefs and raised a brow.

"Do I have to rip those clothes off?"

I shook my head and shimmied out of my pants. I stood before him in a red lace bra and matching panties. In fact, these were the same pair of bra and panties I had worn the day we met.

He stared at me and I could read his thoughts.

"Jesus Christ, Angel, you're breathtaking."

I unhooked my bra and let it fall to my feet. He took a step forward.

"You're stunning." His voice was nothing but a hoarse whisper.

I had to agree with him. Not that I was stunning, but that he was gorgeous and somehow all mine. His intoxicating eyes travelled a path down my body and I felt the heat of that gaze over every inch of my skin.

Closing the distance between us, I touched his chest. He stood there, unmoving as I traced the ridges and dips of the muscles of his chest and stomach. My hands came to a rest at the waistband of his briefs where I curled my fingers over the elastic.

I nudged them over the swell of his erection while leaning forward at the same time to place a kiss over his heart.

"You're pretty damn incredible too, Logan Reid."

I reached down and wrapped my hand around his shaft while his head tipped back and a low grown escaped him. My arousal mirrored his own and my panties grew damp with my need for him.

"I need to be inside of you, luv. I need it now."

But I wasn't finished worshiping him. I kissed over his heart again, then laid a line of kisses down the stacked terrace of muscle leading to the curve of his hip. From there, I traced the groove angling down from there until I found myself on my knees before him.

When I glanced up, he stared down at me with eyes that were no longer blue but black with his lust.

"Put it in your mouth." His throaty command shifted the dynamic between us and my pussy pulsed with the power of his command.

I sucked him in and his hips thrust forward. He gripped the top of my head and dug his fingers into my hair.

"That feels so fucking good."

I sucked him, licking along the vein on the bottom of his cock, while he slowly rocked in and out of my mouth. But he didn't keep me on my knees and slowly pulled out with another of those low, throaty groans which turned my insides to mush.

He pointed to the floor and I laid back. Then he bent to his knees and prowled toward me.

"You know all those passages I read?"

I licked my lips because my mouth was dry. "Yes?"

"I'm going to do every single one of them with you."

My eyes widened because there was a lot more than a blindfold in those scenes. There were crops and spankings and…

He gave a slow nod. "Oh yes, my naughty angel, every fucking scene. I'm going to have so much fun with you, but right now? Right now, I need to be inside of you."

He planted his hand beside my head, then lowered to his elbow. He ran his fingers over the lace of my panties.

"These are in the way."

At his insistence, I lifted my hips as he removed the offending fabric from my body. I laid bare before him, beneath his scrutiny, and tried my hardest not to squirm.

He watched me intently, then nudged his nose against mine. Then his fingers touched my breast and brushed over my nipple, making me gasp. He glided his finger to my other breast and repeated the movement.

I squirmed beneath him and my breaths quickened. I'd always been responsive to his touch.

He took my hand and kissed my palm then stretched it over my head where he held it in place. Covering my body with his, he kissed me on the lips, along my jawline, down my neck, and across my collarbone. He worked his way down as my senses came alive.

I shoved my hands in his hair and breathed as he kissed my belly.

"I will kiss every inch of you until every bit of you is mine. I want to drive you wild and make you beg."

He cupped my pussy in his broad hand, putting steady, gentle pressure on the sensitive area, but nothing that I really wanted.

"Please." I wasn't beyond begging and bit my lower lip. My cheeks were hot, flushed, and my back arched when he pushed a finger against my clit.

He rubbed my wet pussy with just the fingertip, tempting me, but didn't sink inside. That was where I wanted him. Instead, he just glided his finger over the lips and my clit in a teasing, too light of a sensation.

"Is this what you want?"

"Yes, please."

"Hmm, you don't want my cock?"

I wanted it all.

"No."

"I don't understand. Tell me what you want." He kissed his way across my lower belly to my other hip, teasing me while I squirmed beneath him.

He dragged his fingertips up and down my thighs, pushing them apart while I quivered beneath him.

My fingers dug into his scalp. I wanted to push him

down, place his face between my legs, but I was not in control.

"Logan...please." *Please stop torturing me.*

For a man who wanted to fuck, he was sure taking his sweet time.

But from his low, rumbly chuckle, I knew that's exactly his plan.

He moved suddenly and dipped his head down between my legs. Leaning in, he took one long swipe of his tongue from my wet opening all the way to my aching clit. I cried out and practically jackknifed in half, but he pressed me down with one hand splayed on my belly and buried his head between my legs.

As he nuzzled between my legs, teasing that hard nub, a cry escaped me. But I silenced it. I was very aware of where we were, how naked we were, and prayed there weren't any security cameras in this room. If there were, we were giving them one hell of a show.

He slowly fucked me with his finger and kissed his way back up my body, but that wasn't what I wanted. He bit my nipples and kissed up my neck until he was finally back to my lips.

"Please," I begged, "I need you inside of me." I wrapped my arms around his neck and hooked one leg around his hips.

"I thought you'd never ask." His rumbly voice was enough to make me come.

He took himself in his hand and slid the tip through my

slick folds, more teasing, but this time we both moaned. He was as turned on as I was.

"You're killing me." I squirmed beneath him.

"Am I?" His cocksure response was perfect, but I needed him now.

I reached down between us, wrapped my hand around his cock and placed it at my entrance. "Now. Please."

He slid inside in one long, fluid motion. The pleasure was intoxicating and overwhelming. He paused when he was buried balls-deep inside of me and placed his lips over mine.

"Open your eyes, my sweet angel. I want to watch you come. You feel like heaven." His hips rotated and he pulled back in one agonizing glide, then he pushed back inside.

The rhythm he set drove me wild, moving in and out in long strokes as he claimed me. My legs shook and my whole body tensed. I could feel my orgasm racing toward me.

He nibbled at the corner of my lips as my back arched off the floor and my pussy spasmed around his cock. My arms tightened around his neck and I held on through my orgasm. But it wasn't just me. He followed me through the most amazing orgasm of my life.

We came together with ragged breaths in the quiet of the room. He rolled us to our sides and tucked me tight against him.

While cradled against his chest, the doorknob gave a little wiggle. Someone pushed on the door, but the chair propped against it prevented it from opening.

"Shit!" I jumped to my feet and grabbed at my clothes.

Logan gave a snicker and joined me in shoving our clothes back on.

"What do we do?" I glanced at the door and the confused sounds of someone trying to figure out why the door wouldn't open.

He pointed to the back of the room, to a door marked exit. "Make a dash for it?"

"Is it alarmed?"

"Do you care?"

No, I didn't. I'd rather race out the back of this room and set off an emergency exit alarm than face whoever it was trying to get in.

"Let's do it."

He took my hand in his and we ran to the exit. When he pushed on it, I braced, but we didn't set off any alarms.

With huge grins plastered on our faces we sprinted for his car. Like Bonnie and Clyde, our tires spun as we got the hell out of Dodge.

30

LOGAN

NERVES JUMBLED INSIDE OF ME AS I WALKED ANGEL TO HER door. Date number ten was behind us. An uncertain future stretched in front of us.

Everything this woman did brought a smile to my lips. Not that I typically paid attention to shit like that. In my life, as long as a woman was fun in bed and didn't get too attached, I called it a win.

But Angel was different.

The sex was pretty damn hot. She was adventurous. I liked that and couldn't wait to make her squirm. I fully intended on fulfilling my promise.

Every one of those scenes I'd been forced to read aloud to the crazy ladies in purple hats was going to be reenacted between Angel and I.

I wanted to tumble her into bed and mess her up. I

craved it with a hunger I couldn't explain, but I enjoyed her company more. That had never happened with any other woman.

Making Angel smile made my stomach clench and my heart ache. Hearing her gentle laughter set my world to rights. When she slid her hand into mine, I couldn't describe the feeling within me, except to say it simply felt right when our fingers linked.

It was as if our souls joined.

Hers was the easiest touch I'd ever had because it came without expectations. That was a problem, because I wanted her to need me.

Shit, I sounded like a love-sick puppy.

You don't date. You fuck.

Her words whispered in my head and drew me up short. They were true. Or had been. It was her greatest fear and the one thing holding her back from embracing this thing between us.

"What are you doing for the rest of the day?" I suddenly asked.

"I hadn't really planned anything after this."

"I want to take you out." I was going to do much more than that. It finally hit me—what I wanted—and I was a man who went after what I wanted with every intention of making it mine.

The truth was I craved her company. The thought of being without her brought real physical pain. She made parts of me come alive I hadn't realized were even dead inside of me and I couldn't stop the pressing need I felt to have her in every way.

For the first time in my life, having a woman in every way meant something other than sex.

I needed to talk to my brothers, because what I was contemplating was huge.

"I need to do something, but how about I pick you up around six?"

"For dinner?"

For that and more.

"Wear something slinky the kind of something where you can't wear anything beneath it."

I left her sputtering and rushed to my car. A plan formed in my head, but I was going to need help.

I dialed my brother.

"Hey Ace, what's up?" Gabriel's solid tone set me at ease. He had always been my sounding block growing up. The big brother who was my role model and so much more.

"I want her."

"Her as in Angel?"

"Her as in the woman I want to spend the rest of my life with."

"Well shit. I knew she was special. You sure about this?"

"Never been more certain."

"Okay, what do you need?"

Something epic. But what? What would knock her socks off? Then it hit me.

"Let me call my friend. I'll give you a call right back."

I dialed Dex Truitt.

"Hey Logan, what's up?"

"I need you to get Angel to take the job."

"It's been offered. She's still thinking about it."

"Well, this is important."

"How's that?"

"I need you to get her to fly you and Bianca to Vegas."

"Vegas? Why would we go there? It's not really kid friendly."

"How would Bianca feel if you left the kid behind?"

"Georgina would die if we went somewhere with you and she wasn't invited."

"This is kind of a grown-up thing." Although, come to think of it having Georgina there would be kind of epic. "She can come, but she can't ruin the surprise. You can tell her she can wear her princess dress."

"What exactly do you have in mind?"

I explained and his low laughter told me he was totally on board.

Dex was a good friend and I was well aware of what he had done to tie Bianca to him.

This was child's play next to assuming an entire new identity.

Dex had done that, becoming Jay Reed for Bianca. He'd built an entire persona around Jay and jumped through hoops to get Bianca to fall in love with him.

"Sounds pretty epic, but there's no way Georgina can keep a secret. I'll tell you what. I'll call Angel and beg her to work for me. If she does, no problem. If not, then I'll make sure she flies me to Vegas for a very important business meeting. Bianca and Georgina will go separate."

I breathed out a sigh of relief. I didn't trust my surprise to an overly inquisitive child, but it would be perfect to have her there. After all, Georgina had been there when Angel and I met.

I settled all the details with Dex and then called Gabriel back. He would handle things on his end. Everything was perfect.

Now, to get my girl. I started that with our date and the promise of dinner.

Her slinky black dress took my breath away and we had the best evening. It began with dinner and ended with a late breakfast.

The timeline I set for myself was insane, but the whole idea swirling in my head was the definition of insanity. But I knew it was the right thing, the only thing that made sense. In less than a week, Angel would be mine.

Forever.

31

LOGAN

I WALKED TO THE JET WITH NERVES RATTLING AROUND IN MY gut. Angel still hadn't accepted Dex's offer to fly for his fleet of jets. He was able to finagle her into being assigned as my co-pilot for his trip to Vegas.

This time, I was early. With my inspection of the exterior of the jet complete, I sat in the cockpit waiting for Angel to arrive.

Our roles had been reversed, because the first time we'd flown together, she had been waiting on me. This would likely be our last time sharing the cockpit, because if she didn't take the job with Montague Enterprises, I would. Then I would make damn sure JetAire gave her the promotion she deserved.

When I looked up, I couldn't help but jump to my feet. Or as much as I could without banging my head on the low ceiling. I crawled out of my seat and went to meet Angel and Dex at the door.

She wore her baggy flight suit with JetAire's emblem embroidered on her left breast pocket. Dex walked beside her in a dark gray suit carrying a briefcase in his hand.

He glanced up at me and gave a wink.

"Just you today?" I pretended this wasn't all my plan to get Angel to Vegas.

"Just me. Bianca refuses to take Georgina to the City of Sin."

Except I knew Bianca was on a nearly identical flight as we spoke with one of Montague's jets.

"Looks like I've got the A-team today," Dex said. "There seemed to be a rash of co-pilot cancellations. Any idea what that's about." He gestured for Angel to head up the stairs before him.

Fucker. He was dangerously close to crossing a line and spilling the beans. Angel was smart. She'd figure it out if we weren't careful.

"What do you mean?" I asked.

"Larry and Brody were scheduled to fly, but they're sick." Angel answered. "Guess we're flying together."

"That's odd."

"Evidently they went to the same barbecue yesterday? Said it was the potato salad." Angel's soft smile made my heart stop.

"Well, I appreciate you agreeing to fly me today," Dex

said. "I really need to make this meeting and we seem to be having issues with our mechanics."

"You should be thankful for your mechanics. I doubt there's anything wrong, but a good mechanic won't let the boss fly in something they're not one-hundred percent sure of." She responded to Dex's comment as I would, which told me she had no idea what we had planned.

"I appreciate it, nonetheless." Dex picked out his seat and buckled in while Angel gave him the standard safety briefing he'd heard a thousand times and she'd given just as many.

With that task done, she joined me in the cockpit.

"He asked us to stay overnight and fly him back." I hoped that would be okay with her. It wasn't unusual for JetAire to keep a plane out of service if they could avoid it, but for a client like Dex Truitt they usually bent over backwards.

"That's what I heard."

"Is this going to be a problem?"

We'd both been busy with our jobs, but hadn't flown together since the Caymans. Angel was very strict on her no-fly rule.

"Nah, should be fun. I haven't been to Vegas in a while. I think it's changed a ton."

"I have. How about you let me take you around? Do you trust me?"

She laughed. "Do I have a choice?"

"You always have a choice." And I hoped she would choose me.

"Well of course. As long as it doesn't involve strip clubs or sex clubs."

"If you're going to take all the fun out of it…"

"I'm sure you'll figure something out."

I already had.

"Great. You're mine from the moment we touch down."

She squirmed in her seat, then cleared her throat. "Um, maybe we should focus on the job at hand? This is why I don't want to fly with you."

"I didn't mean…"

"I know. That's not the problem. The issue is that it creeps into the work."

Unfortunately, I understood. There was no way we could work together. Not when I wanted to touch her the way I did and I knew my mouth.

Sexual innuendos flew out of it every time I turned around. This would be our last flight together.

"Ready to push off?"

She gave a nod and we entered the realm of the sterile cockpit. Until we passed ten-thousand feet, we were laser-focused on the job at hand and put everything else to the side.

The trip was short enough that neither of us got out of our chairs and Dex didn't bother us. I assumed he really was working on business back there.

We landed, taxied, and deplaned. A car picked up Dex which left Angel and I alone.

We had an hour to kill.

"Let me get a car."

She held up her phone. "Already did. It's should be here in just a few minutes."

We had rooms at a nearby hotel, but I needed to get Angel to our destination and there was no reason to be checking into the crappy hotel JetAire put us up in.

"Cancel it. I've got better plans." We had both packed light and I swung my backpack over my shoulder and grabbed her small rolling suitcase.

"I don't want to drag those all over the place."

She had a point. "Okay, we'll check in but then I'm taking you out."

Checking into a hotel I had no intention of staying at would eat into my timetable, but if I insisted on bringing the luggage, it would look suspicious.

We hopped into a cab and checked into our rooms.

Two rooms.

JetAire didn't know we were sleeping together. I deposited both our bags in one of the rooms, and waited impatiently for her to change out of her baggy flight suit. When she looked at me, I tugged off my polo shirt with the company logo on it and put on a tee-shirt.

What we wore didn't matter. We would soon be changing into something else, hopefully very soon.

I handled the Uber because I didn't want her to see our

destination until the last possible moment. Which was why I had the driver park at the corner of the block.

"Why are we here? I thought we were going to the strip?"

Because the chapels at the strip sucked and I wanted to get married in this one. It had special significance because my parents had eloped and been married here. Somehow it felt right.

There was only one way to do this.

But I hesitated.

"Logan? Is everything okay?"

Okay? It was fucking amazing.

Just pony up, Stallion! Spit it out! Propose to her!

"I'm in love with you." My jaw ticked and my fists clenched.

That sounded like shit. Angry shit.

That wasn't how I meant to tell her I loved her, full of anger and pride.

I was nervous. Unsure of myself. And it showed.

"Excuse me?" Indignation filled her tone, but who could blame her when I spit it out like that?

I swallowed my anger and softened my tone. "I fucking love you."

I took her in my arms, right where she belonged and clutched her to my body with a desperate determination. Breath surged out of me as I rubbed my hands up and down her back.

"I fucking love you."

"Okay, but why say it like that?"

"What do you mean?" Except I knew exactly what she meant.

"Like you hate having to say it."

"I don't hate it, but I've never said it before." It killed me to admit it, but it was the truth. I was the most self-assured person I knew, but I struggled to tell Angel how I felt.

"Do you mean it?" She looked at me like she expected me to tuck tail and run.

I nodded. "More than anything. Look, I'm not good at this. Obviously. I've never done this before, but I am flat out in love with you. So much so that it's terrifying. But I'd rather be scared shitless with you than live the rest of my life without you."

I wasn't able to take a breath. Admitting that I loved her bared my soul. It made me vulnerable and if she didn't say yes, I wouldn't survive the aftermath.

"How do I know that won't change?" She didn't trust me, but that was really my fault.

I was a cocksure fighter pilot who never had to beg for a date. With a snap of my fingers, I could fill my bed with any woman I chose. I'd done that too many times to count, with too many women, many of whom I couldn't remember. Their faces were a blur and their names forgotten.

"Because I feel it in here." I gripped her hand and pressed it against my chest. "I am unequivocally, desperately, in love with you."

"I want to believe you."

"Then believe."

"You don't do love. This isn't real."

"I never knew what love was before you."

Her eyes were glassy from unshed tears. I didn't know if it was because she was sad or incredibly happy like me.

"I thought I was incapable of love until an angel showed me the way." I cupped her cheeks in my palms and pressed my forehead to hers. "Believe me. I can't live another day without you by my side."

"It's too much. We're still getting to know each other."

"So?" I gave a low chuckle. "We spend the rest of our lives together getting to know every dirty secret, every filthy thought. I still have that blindfold and several naughty scenes I need to reenact with you."

Her cheeks flushed, turning her skin the prettiest shade of pink.

"I think you want that too."

She gave a little nod.

Music to my ears, but now to get her to say that while wearing white with my ring sliding over her finger.

"So?" I needed to hear her say it, convince me I wasn't wrong, make me believe we could do this together. But I couldn't force the words. We danced around them many times, but this felt like our beginning. "Will you marry me?"

It wasn't the best proposal in the history of mankind, but it was mine, heartfelt and true.

"Marry you?"

"Yes. I want you to marry me."

"Logan…I…" She sputtered, at a loss for words.

"I want to marry you. Today."

"Today?"

"Right now." I tugged her until we stood in front of what had to be the smallest chapel in Vegas: The Chapel of the Stars was tiny with a parking lot for only two cars.

"You want to get married now?" Her brows practically crawled up her forehead. "Like now? This is a joke, right?"

"Not a joke. I want to do this."

She nibbled at her lower lip.

That wasn't a solid *Oh Hell No!*

Could it be a cautious maybe?

Hell, I was standing on pins and needles here. My entire family was inside that chapel waiting on the bride and groom to make their appearance. Larry and Brody weren't sick, they'd flown my entire family, with Bianca, Georgina, and even poor Bandit to Vegas for this. We were already fifteen minutes late.

"What do you say? Wanna get hitched?"

"This is crazy."

"It's the best way to be."

"You really want to marry me?"

"Only if you say yes. If you don't, I'm going to lick my wounds for a very long time."

I took her hands in mine and rubbed a circle over her ring finger on her left hand. Gabriel had better have the damn rings. I had my best man on the job. Gabriel had just sent the final text.

Everything was ready. Everyone was present. Angel didn't have any family left, but she had me and I had plenty to share. And Bianca would be there. I didn't know any of Angel's friends. There was still so much we didn't know about each other.

A tiny shriek cut through the silence. Angel and I both looked up and I shook my head.

Georgina Bina raced out of the chapel in her Frozen princess dress with Bandit running by her side. Bianca ran out after her daughter, then stopped in her tracks.

"I'm sorry! She peeked out the windows and when she saw you…"

Angel glanced at me and her mouth gaped as Georgina flung herself into my arms. "Look at my dress!"

Oh, I was looking at it all right. And I was looking into Angel's shocked face.

Georgina pointed at Angel. "You can't get married in that. Mommy has your dress waiting for you and you're late."

Angel shook her head and gave a soft laugh. Her hands went to her hips as her attention turned to me. "I'm not even going to ask."

"Well, don't ask, but can you at least give me your answer. I have a lot of people in there."

"Do you now? And what if I had said no?"

"Ah-ha!" I pointed at her and placed Georgina on the ground. "That isn't a no." I cupped my hand over my mouth and shouted. "She said yes!" With my arms held high over my head, I gave a little victory dance.

Bianca rushed up and collected her daughter. "Sorry about that. I really tried to keep her inside." Bandit danced around them as Bianca tried ushering her daughter and dog back inside.

Georgina wasn't having any of that. She scampered over to Angel and took a hold of her hand, tugging her toward the door. "You have to get in your dress."

Angel let the little girl lead her away and glanced over her shoulder at me. "I can't believe you did this."

"Luv, can you please say yes?" I was still dying without that one word.

"Hm, can you say payback? I guess you won't know."

She left me standing there, gaping on the sidewalk, as Georgina and Bianca led her inside. My brothers spilled out a second later, running up to congratulate me.

Dex followed them out and shook my hand before pulling me into a hug. "I can't believe she said yes."

I swallowed my nerves. "Technically, she hasn't yet."

Gabriel, Colt, Ryder, and Dylan surrounded me, patting me on the back and tugging me tight. They eventually pulled me inside the chapel where I drew my mother, with her misty eyes, into my arms.

"Hey there."

"Go!" She pointed to a door off to the side which was labeled *Groom*. "You need to get your suit on."

"Where are the girls?"

"Inside, making everything pretty. Now hurry up. They are pretty strict with their damn schedules."

Dex walked up. "Don't worry about that. I bought them another hour, consider it a poor wedding gift, but it took you two long enough to get here."

Gabriel dragged me into the tiny changing room and helped me get into my suit while my brothers escorted my mother into the chapel.

"You ready for this?" Gabriel smacked my back.

"Yeah."

"Funny. I never thought you'd get married, and you've thrown Lizzy into a tizzy. She thought she was next."

"She will be. All the girls are married, or soon will be. I guess it's up to you and me to get Colt, Ryder and Dylan women who can stand to be with them more than a minute or two."

"I suppose so, little bro. I suppose so."

Gabriel stood beside me as my best man. Bianca stepped up as Angel's Matron of Honor.

The Chapel of the Stars was not big on space and my family filled the two small rows of pews, sitting on both sides of the aisle. I hoped Angel was ready for the crazy family she was marrying into.

Hell, I hoped she was marrying into it. My heart didn't stop pounding until the music began and she appeared at the end of the aisle.

Georgina walked down the aisle first, tossing fake petals

on the floor. My mother collected her at the front of the chapel and had Georgina sit in her lap.

To my surprise, Dex stepped beside Angel and whispered in her ear. He crooked his arm and she settled her hand in his as he led her down the aisle.

Angel had no family, but she had all the family she needed in this room.

When Dex released her, handing her over to me, Angel whispered in my ear. "I love you too, flyboy. Don't ever make me regret it."

"Never."

Words were said that I don't remember.

Gabriel had the rings.

Angel slipped a platinum band over my finger and I put a diamond solitaire on hers. My mother and sisters had picked it out, following my specifications, and it was perfect, glittery, and very large.

There were vows, but all I remembered were the words "You may kiss the bride."

"Do you love me?" I asked.

"I love you very much," she replied.

My eyes closed. I took my angel into my arms and kissed her to the cheers of our family. Her tears wetted my cheeks and I found my version of heaven in the arms of an angel.

———

Two weeks later...

.   .   .

"Now, how about you take that job? Dex is waiting for you to sign on the dotted line."

"How do you know that?" Angel unpacked her suitcase, separating her clothes into what needed to be washed and what had never been worn.

Dex and Bianca sprung a two-week honeymoon on us and sent us to the Caymans. Instead of staying at a hotel, we stayed in a private residence they had set up. Since we were alone, we spent most of our vacation naked and in bed, which explained why most of her clothes had never been worn.

"We talk all the time. Now, are you going to fly for him?"

"Yes. I think so. It's actually a pretty awesome job."

"Great." I was glad that was settled. "Now, let's talk babies."

"Babies?"

"Yes, lots of babies."

I wanted to fill her life with the love which came with a large family. It would be tough with her job. Pregnancy would ground her from flying in the later trimesters, but I had already decided I'd quit my job to take care of the kids after she gave birth...when she gave birth. I didn't know if it was too early to start talking about having a family.

My girl belonged in the skies, soaring like an angel, and I would do whatever it took to make her dreams come true.

She smiled at me. "God, I love you, but how about we take it one at a time?"

"That's not a no." I rubbed my hands together, excited for a future with her and little minions running us ragged.

"It's not, and speaking of..."

"Speaking of what?"

"How do you feel about being a dad sooner rather than later?"

I think my eyes bugged out of my head. "How soon?"

"How about eight months?"

I literally fell on my ass and gazed up at my beautiful, newly pregnant, wife while she laughed at me.

We fucked like rabbits and had not been using protection except for her birth control pills.

It shouldn't be possible, and I wasn't going to ask the obvious question. I knew how babies were made and that not all protection was foolproof.

One look in her eyes and I had no doubt what she said was true. I went to my knees and kissed her belly. "You're amazing."

She ran her fingers through my hair. "I think we're amazing."

I'd never heard truer words.

THE END

———

Want to keep up with all of the new releases in Vi Keeland
and Penelope Ward's Cocky Hero Club world? Check out
the Cocky Hero Club website www.cockyheroclub.com.
Make sure you sign up for the official Cocky Hero Club
newsletter for all the latest on our upcoming books: https://
www.subscribepage.com/CockyHeroClub

Enjoyed Cocky Captain? If so, you'll enjoy reading Aiden,
book 1 of my The One I Want Series. Do you believe in
love at first sight? You can get your copy Click HERE.
Interested in the first chapter? Simply turn the page.

32

THE ONE I WANT SERIES

AIDEN

Powerfully written by co-authors Jet & Ellie, a husband and wife team, Aiden & Ariel's story delivers a suspenseful and dramatic story about love, loss, and life. Be prepared to get blown away.

WITH A CATEGORY FIVE HURRICANE BARRELING DOWN ON the Gulf, medevac helicopter pilot, Ariel Black, is on a mission to evacuate wounded men from an oil rig in the path of the storm. It's the worst possible time to fall in love, but she does. Ariel falls hard and fast…right into the installation manager's arms. Aiden Cole makes her heart race, her pulse pound, and the butterflies in her stomach soar.

Could he be the one?

When it seems like she's going to get her happily-ever-after, disaster strikes. The massive storm arrives ahead of schedule. Ariel's helicopter is grounded. She and her men, along with Aiden and his wounded, must ride out the hurricane on the rig.

With their lives in danger, will she lose the love of a lifetime? Or will true love conquer all?

Ariel

HURRICANE JULIAN WOULD BE the tenth storm of the season. The Category Five monster barreled down on the Gulf with the tenacity of a bull staring down a china shop. Chomping at the bit, Julian dug in, ready to destroy, and Ariel intended to fly directly into the maw of Julian's fury. Metaphors aside, things were about to get ugly, and she loved every minute of it.

It had been far too long since adrenaline spiked in her veins. After leaving the military, she'd taken a job as a medevac pilot, flying her helicopter to any of the many oil rigs peppered throughout the Gulf. Dangerous work, injuries were an unfortunate occurrence, despite rigid safety protocols. Her crew answered the calls, heading out to ferry the sick and injured back to definitive medical care.

It wasn't a kickass job steeped in death and glory, not like the military, but it had its moments. Most of the time it was a thankless job, but it paid the bills, and it kept her flying. She never felt more alive than with a stick in her hands and air beneath her feet.

This promised to be an interesting run because everyone was headed off the oil rigs rather than flying to them. They fled the storm she willingly flew into.

Pre-flight prep took most of her concentration, but she thought back to the last time she had braced for the worst. This was a cake walk compared to that. Her third combat tour in the desert was a shitstorm and ended her career in the Army.

IT HAD BEEN early morning on base when the call came in. A special ops team had injured men on the ground, were pinned down and had requested helicopter evacuation. The area was to be secured by the time her team arrived. After the briefing, she and her co-pilot, Reggie, aka Rocks, went to their helicopter.

They checked the exterior of the helicopter while the four special ops surgical team members loaded the crew area with their gear. Then, she and Rocks climbed on board to complete their pre-flight checks. They were in a hurry but didn't skimp on safety. Rocks dusted off the gauges. The ever-present sand and grit permeated everything. While the team in back secured their gear, she and Rocks went over the flight plan. Once finished, they each squeezed the rabbit's foot they hung in the cockpit for good luck. It began their tour gleaming white but was now a dusty brown from all the sand.

"You ready Angel?" Her call sign had been Battle Angel, or Angel

for short, a play on a famous Manga character because she was small but packed a punch.

"Ready."

Their mission was to pick up two wounded near a forward oper-ating base. A team had gone on patrol, ran into difficulty, and now battled insurgents.

They lifted off and headed into the desert. Perspiration beaded her brow and sweat trickled down her back and between her boobs. Fifty clicks out, she dropped down, using the rocky terrain to hide their radar signature.

As they approached their target, flashes of gunfire burst from the rocky scree. Pings sounded as bullets struck the outer shell of the helicopter.

"Shit!" The area was supposed to have been secured, but it was too hot to land. She piled on speed and began defensive maneuvers as Rocks radioed in a status update.

"They're telling us to leave," he said.

One of the worst parts of the job was aborting a mission and leaving men on the ground, but she couldn't disobey orders. They would return, just as soon as it was safe.

As she angled away, a man stood up from behind a large group of rocks with an RPG propped on his shoulder. The man staggered as he fired. A smoke trail headed directly for her bringing a rocket grenade on a direct intercept.

"Evade! Evade! Evade!" She banked hard left, angling down to pick up speed.

Rocks gripped his seat as the helicopter shuddered under the impact. The rocket grenade exploded, taking out the tail section and putting her into a spin a hundred and fifty feet off the ground. Her entire instrument cluster lit up like a Christmas tree, lights flashing, alarms blaring.

She fought for control as they went down. They were going to crash; her job was to make sure they didn't die on impact. With deafening alarms screeching in her ears and lights flashing on her display, she fought the deadly spiral.

The helicopter slammed into the ground, crunching and groaning as metal twisted and broke apart. The hard landing bounced them on the rocks and flipped the helicopter on its side.

When she came to, her head felt like it'd been split in two. An acrid smell burned the sensitive tissues of her nostrils. Smoke poured down her throat, making her cough. The coppery taint of blood coated her tongue, and she spit out the offensive substance. Blood blurred her vision, but not the macabre scene of Reggie and the shrapnel which speared him through the chest. His eyes stared back at her, filled with the terror of his death. She looked over her shoulder while pulling on the straps securing her to her seat. Two of the SOST team were dead. Two others were injured.

Only after unbuckling did she realize her left leg had been shattered. Smoke filled the air. They were on fire and moments from an explosion. She bit back a scream as she clutched her injured leg and breathed in fumes.

The whole thing was going to blow.

Crawling to the back, she dragged one of the wounded men out of the helicopter, then headed back to rescue the other. The dead could wait. A bullet ricocheted off a nearby rock, but she never once thought to stop. She grabbed the last survivor and dragged him toward safety. Bullets peppered the ground around her head, over her shoulders, and beside her *hips and her feet. She gave hasty thanks for their terrible aim, at least until one of the shots scored a hit in her good leg.*

Gritting her teeth, she dragged the last man behind a sheltering clump of rocks, getting the three of them to safety. Her last thought had been to grab for her sidearm, but blackness overcame her and she passed out.

Two years later, her shattered leg and lack of sufficient rehabilitation to make her combat ready again, found her sitting before a medical evaluation board. They could have kicked her out, but the Army awarded her a medal and a medical retirement instead.

Her military career was over. Her career in aviation hadn't been ruined, but it had been sidelined.

THEY DIDN'T HAVE hurricanes in the desert, but they had hostiles with guns, plenty of ammunition, itchy trigger fingers, and a fanatical will to kill infidels. She had battled sandstorms and survived getting shot down. Now, she was lucky to battle a sudden violent gust or maneuver around a localized storm.

Back then, she'd flown in hot, hand steady on the stick, with a crew of medics hanging on for dear life with clenched hands and puckered assholes. Landing in the midst of gunfire could make the cockiest pilot quake in their boots or shit their pants, but she faced those kinds of missions with steely determination and eerily cool composure.

She did that now.

A distinguished combat veteran, her hand remained

steady as she lifted out of Mobile, Alabama with a critical care transport team strapped in the back of her helicopter.

Hurricane Julian churned a couple hundred miles offshore, flirting with the western coastline of Florida as it barreled directly toward Mobile. Instead of petering out, it looked to be picking up steam. Earlier, it had looked like any other gorgeous day on the Gulf; deep blue skies with barely any clouds and nearly mirror smooth waters. The calm before the storm lied about the hell to come.

There were no blue skies for this flight, however. The sun had set over an hour ago. She flew into the inky blackness and headed out to sea.

"It's bumpy as shit back here," Andrew, the flight nurse, called out through their integrated headsets.

"How's Julian?" Larry, their medic, sounded concerned.

She didn't blame him. It was going to be a rough flight, but they were still far ahead of the storm.

Ariel glanced at her weather radar. "Still on a direct course."

"How much time?" Larry asked.

"Enough." She tried to soothe him but was too busy flying to settle Larry's nerves.

While devastating, hurricanes traveled at a relative snail's pace. However, the winds were already kicking up and tossed the Gulf into a frenzy. Below them, the normally calm waters churned and the waves kicked up. Gusts would make her job harder, but she looked forward to the challenge.

"Lots of air traffic." Andrew's voice crackled through the headset.

A glance left confirmed Andrew's statement, although it wasn't a surprise. Lights from other helicopters dotted the night sky as they ferried crew off all active rigs in Julian's path. Beneath them, tossing about in the waves, a steady stream of boat traffic lit up the dark waters.

Flights would continue until all crew members were evacuated from the fixed platforms. Per protocol, stationary rigs evacuated their entire crews, while drillships off-loaded only nonessential personnel. They would then disconnect from their wells, and steer the drillship away from the storm to wait things out.

Their patients were on the former, a stationary rig with a complete evacuation underway. Last man off would turn out the lights as it were. A glance at the clock and she gave a nod. They would have plenty of time to stabilize the wounded crew and make it back far in advance of the worst of the weather. Unfortunately, their helicopter would block the evacuation of the last crewmen remaining.

Hopefully, all non-essential personnel would be gone by the time her crew arrived. The rig she flew toward was located a little more than a hundred miles offshore. They had a relatively quick flight and would be there in thirty to forty-five minutes, depending on changes in wind speed as Julian approached.

She called the rig and confirmed her ETA and avail-ability of the landing pad, which gave her twenty minutes to obsess over things she couldn't control. It would be nice to have a little more action and pretend the rest of the world didn't exist.

During the flight, the slow drizzle turned to rain and the wind kicked up. Hopefully, the heavy stuff was still some distance off. When they approached the rig, she called in and moved toward a helideck suspended two-hundred feet above a seething sea.

Weather in the Gulf was relatively calm compared to other places around the globe, but she held a healthy respect for it. Summers could be pristine without a breath of wind or turn into full-blown squalls within minutes. In the winter, cold fronts moved fast, bringing dramatic wind shifts and plummeting temperatures. Fog was more common than not, the result of the high humidity, and of course, there were the ever-present thunderstorms which cropped up with the worst timing, bringing high winds. More than one helicopter had been tossed off a helideck and plunged into the Gulf.

Her respect wasn't healthy. It was profound.

She battled gusts with concerned not only about landing, but a takeoff that threatened to pitch her into the water below. It was getting sketchy out here. They wouldn't be able to spend much time on deck, especially with the rain getting heavier. Julian wasn't fooling around and had picked up speed. He came to enact a profound vengeance upon the world and the last thing she wanted was to be anywhere near the full brunt of his fury.

"Hang on," she called to her passengers. "It's going to be bumpy, and don't unbuckle until I tell you."

Understandably, the flight nurse and paramedic were eager to get to their patients, but if they got out before the skids were anchored, it could be the last thing they did. Before touching down, she armed the floats, a precaution in case she didn't stick the landing. If the gusts bucked them off the platform, the floats would deploy giving them a chance of escaping the helicopter. Her motto was to plan for the worst and pray for the best.

Right now, she wished for a break in the sheets of rain pouring down. She couldn't see crap.

Almost there.

A gust blew her off the helideck and she cursed. This was turning into a real goat rope. But she regained altitude and realigned for a second approach. Winds gusted from the southeast, Julian testing the waters. Okay, easy now. There was a flare boom to the right and a crane to the left she needed to avoid. She kicked the tail a little to the right after clearing a stairwell. One more check to make sure the floats were armed.

Holy crap! Where did that antenna come from?

Hands steady, she cleared the antenna and made a note to speak to their Offshore Installation Manager about putting stuff up above the deck level. The skids touched down and she radioed an update back to base. The whine of the engine powered down and the rotors came to a stop. In the back, Andrew and Larry gathered their gear, hefting packs to their backs and readying the stretcher. They waited for her to give the all clear.

Outside, three men waited. Shrouded in rain gear, their bulky yellow shapes flashed in the landing lights. Beneath their hoods, their faces fell into shadow.

Ariel spent eight years in the military. Alpha men were a dime a dozen in the Army, but they all had the same purpose, the same mission. The business of oil drilling attracted a similar breed, rough and rugged men, only these didn't hold to a code she understood. With the military, everyone marched to the same drummer, followed the same orders, and could be trusted implicitly. Drillers? They were a rough lot.

They made her uncomfortable, and she didn't trust them.

Gusts buffeted the helideck and the craft shuddered. As the whine of the engine disappeared another sound replaced it. A deep, thunderous booming, felt more than heard, joined the roar of the wind. Vibrations from waves crashing against the support pillars ripped through the super-structure. Nature's power literally shook the world.

She popped open her door and signaled to the waiting crew it was safe to approach. They rushed forward and secured her skids, bracing the helicopter against the rising winds. They did the same to the rotors overhead.

Once the skids were locked securely to the helideck, she gave the signal for Andrew and Larry. The two men jumped out, packs strapped to their backs, and portable stretcher in tow. This wasn't their first foray to one of the thousands of oil rigs distributed throughout the Gulf. The imposing structures never failed to inspire awe and she felt some of that now pounding in her blood. Or maybe that was adrenaline spiking along her nerves? It didn't matter. Everything about this situation was intense.

Safety protocols had been drilled into her, as it had for her crew. Many of the walkways, stairwells, and ladders spanned vast distances with deadly drops beneath them. One hand on the rail at all times. It was a mantra they lived with. A fall here could be fatal. Drilling remained one of the most dangerous professions for a reason.

A thick arm braced her door as a gust tried to slam it shut on her leg.

"Careful!" a gruff voice shouted.

"Thanks."

"What?" He pulled back, a look of surprise on his face. "You're a chick."

"All day. Every day."

"Huh." He held the door open against the wind. "Come with me."

"I'll stay here, thank you."

"Not happening. Too dangerous." His gruff features brooked no argument as he studied her face. An aura of authority surrounded him, rolled off him, and slammed into her with the absolute assurance she would do as he said.

Her entire career had been spent facing down dominant men and overcoming male and female stereotypes that defined who she could and couldn't be. She earned her right to pilot the helicopter and wouldn't let his overwhelming presence force her into feeling less because she happened to be a chick.

But that authoritative aura?

It did things; spun her thoughts, teased her mind, and drew forth a powerful need to cave to his demands. To dispel the effect he was having on her, she shook her head and gritted her teeth.

"I'm staying with the helicopter."

"No. You're not." He propped open the door, leaned in, and pulled her out of her seat.

GRAB YOUR COPY HERE

PLEASE CONSIDER LEAVING A REVIEW

I HOPE YOU ENJOYED THIS BOOK AS MUCH AS I ENJOYED writing it. If you enjoyed reading this story, please consider leaving a review and please let other people know. A sentence is all it takes. Thank you in advance!

ALSO BY ELLIE MASTERS

Sign up to Ellie's Newsletter and get a free gift. https:// elliemasters.com/FreeBook

YOU CAN FIND ELLIE'S BOOKS HERE:

ELLIEMASTERS.COM/BOOKS

Contemporary Romance

Mistletoe Mischief

Cocky Captain

(VI KEELAND & PENELOPE WARD'S COCKY HERO WORLD)

Firestorm

(KRISTY BROMBERG'S EVERYDAY HEROES WORLD)

Romantic Suspense

EACH BOOK IS A STANDALONE NOVEL.

Twist of Fate

The Starling

Redemption

The One I Want Series

(Small Town, Military Heroes)

By Jet & Ellie Masters

EACH BOOK IN THIS SERIES CAN BE READ AS A STANDALONE AND IS ABOUT A DIFFERENT COUPLE WITH AN HEA.

Aiden

Brent

Caleb

Dax

Light BDSM Romance

The Ties that Bind

EACH BOOK IN THIS SERIES CAN BE READ AS A STANDALONE AND IS ABOUT A DIFFERENT COUPLE WITH AN HEA.

Alexa

Penny

Michelle

Ivy

Rockstar Romance

The Angel Fire Rock Romance Series

EACH BOOK IN THIS SERIES CAN BE READ AS A STANDALONE AND IS

ABOUT A DIFFERENT COUPLE WITH AN HEA. IT IS RECOMMENDED THEY ARE READ IN ORDER.

Ashes to New (prequel)

Heart's Insanity (book 1)

Heart's Desire (book 2)

Heart's Collide (book 3)

Hearts Divided (book 4)

Dark Romance

Captive Hearts Series

EACH BOOK IN THIS SERIES CAN BE READ AS A STANDALONE AND IS ABOUT A DIFFERENT COUPLE WITH AN HEA. IT IS RECOMMENDED THEY ARE READ IN ORDER.

She's MINE

Embracing FATE

Forest's FALL

Romantic Suspense

Changing Roles Series:

THIS SERIES IS ABOUT ONE COUPLE AND MUST BE READ IN ORDER.

Book 1: Command

Book 2: Control

Book 3: Collar

HOT READS

EACH BOOK IS A STANDALONE NOVEL.

Off Duty

Nondisclosure

Down the Rabbit Hole

HOT READS

Becoming His Series

THIS SERIES IS ABOUT ONE COUPLE AND MUST BE READ IN ORDER.

Book 1: The Ballet

Book 2: Learning to Breathe

Book 3: Becoming His

Sweet Contemporary Romance

Finding Peace

~AND~

Science Fiction

Ellie Masters writing as L.A. Warren

Vendel Rising: a Science Fiction Serialized Novel

ABOUT THE AUTHOR

ELLIE MASTERS is a multi-genre and best-selling author, writing the stories she loves to read. These are dark erotic tales. Or maybe, sweet contemporary stories. How about a romantic thriller to whet your appetite? Ellie writes it all. Want to read passionate poems and sensual secrets? She does that, too. Dip into the eclectic mind of Ellie Masters, spend time exploring the sensual realm where she breathes life into her characters and brings them from her mind to the page and into the heart of her readers every day.

Ellie Masters has been exploring the worlds of romance, dark erotica, science fiction, and fantasy by writing the stories she wants to read. When not writing, Ellie can be found outside, where her passion for all things outdoor reigns supreme: off-roading, riding ATVs, scuba diving, hiking, and breathing fresh air are top on her list.

She has lived all over the United States—east, west, north, south and central—but grew up under the Hawaiian sun. She's also been privileged to have lived overseas, experiencing other cultures and making lifelong friends. Now, Ellie is proud to call herself a Southern transplant, learning to say y'all and "bless her heart" with the best of them. She lives with her beloved husband, two children who refuse to flee the nest, and four fur-babies; three cats who rule the household, and a dog who wants nothing other than for the cats to be his best friends. The cats have a different opinion regarding this matter.

Ellie's favorite way to spend an evening is curled up on a couch, laptop in place, watching a fire, drinking a good wine, and bringing forth all the characters from her mind to the page and hopefully into the hearts of her readers.

FOR MORE INFORMATION
WWW.ELLIEMASTERS.COM

g goodreads.com/Ellie_Masters

CONNECT WITH ELLIE MASTERS

Connect with Ellie Masters

Website:

elliemasters.com

Amazon Author Page:

elliemasters.com/amazon

Facebook:

elliemasters.com/Facebook

Goodreads:

elliemasters.com/Goodreads

Instagram:

elliemasters.com/Instagram

FINAL THOUGHTS

I hope you enjoyed COCKY CAPTAIN as much as I enjoyed writing it. If you enjoyed reading this story, please consider leaving a review on Amazon and Goodreads, and please let other people know. A sentence is all it takes. Friend recommendations are the strongest catalyst for readers' purchase decisions! And I'd love to be able to continue bringing the characters and stories from My-Mind-to-the-Page.

Second, call or e-mail a friend and tell them about this book. If you really want them to read it, gift it to them. If you prefer digital friends, please use the "Recommend" feature of Goodreads to spread the word.

Or visit my blog https://elliemasters.com, where you can find out more about my writing process and personal life.

Come visit The EDGE: Dark Discussions where we'll have a chance to talk about my works, their creation, and maybe what the future has in store for my writing.

Facebook Reader Group: The EDGE

Thank you so much for your support!

Love,

Ellie